Wings of Glass

This Large Print Book carries the
Seal of Approval of N.A.V.H.

WINGS OF GLASS

GINA HOLMES

THORNDIKE PRESS
A part of Gale, Cengage Learning

Detroit • New York • San Francisco • New Haven, Conn • Waterville, Maine • London

Thorndike Press, a part of Gale, Cengage Learning.

Wings of Glass is a work of fiction. Where real people, events, establishments, organizations, or locales appear, they are used fictitiously. All other elements of the novel are drawn from the author's imagination.
Thorndike Press® Large Print Christian Fiction.
The text of this Large Print edition is unabridged.
Other aspects of the book may vary from the original edition.
Set in 16 pt. Plantin.

LIBRARY OF CONGRESS CATALOGING-IN-PUBLICATION DATA

Holmes, Gina.
Wings of glass / by Gina Holmes. — Large print edition.
pages ; cm. — (Thorndike Press large print Christian fiction)
ISBN-13: 978-1-4104-6054-7 (hardcover)
ISBN-10: 1-4104-6054-1 (hardcover)
1. Female friendship—Fiction. 2. Abused wives—Fiction. 3. Large type books. I. Title.
PS3608.O494354W56 2013b
813'.6—dc23 2013016233

Published in 2013 by arrangement with Tyndale House Publishers, Inc.

Printed in the United States of America
1 2 3 4 5 6 7 17 16 15 14 13

A person standing alone can be attacked and defeated, but two can stand back-to-back and conquer. Three are even better for a triple-braided cord is not easily broken.

ECCLESIASTES 4:12

What the caterpillar calls the end of the world, the master calls a butterfly.

RICHARD BACH

For Mom and Chrissy

ACKNOWLEDGMENTS

Thank you to:

- God, for giving me wings that will never shatter.
- My husband and children, for their love and support.
- My two critique partners and right-hand girls: Jessica Dotta and Ane Mulligan.
- My amazing editors: Kathryn Olson, Karen Watson, and Stephanie Broene; and the design team (who always give me beautiful covers).
- The rest of the Tyndale team: Ron Beers, Babette Rea, Linda MacKillop, and all the sales, PR, marketing, editorial, administrative folks. You all are amazing!
- Cindy Sproles, Eddie Jones, and Bonnie Calhoun.
- River Laker and Roanoke City Librar-

ies for your support and fabulous book launch parties.

- Chip MacGregor, the best agent an author could hope to have.
- The NovelRocket.com team. You guys are the best.
- Early readers who gave invaluable feedback: Adam, Leah Morgan, Casey Herringshaw, Katy Lewis, Jen Schuch, Alycia Morales, Gina Conroy, and those who I'm sure I forgot but am still grateful to!
- Rachel McRae, for her support and kindness.
- To all those struggling bookstore folks who continue on for the love of words. We authors appreciate you.
- Nora and Fred St. Laurent and all of the wonderful friends who support me.
- Last, but certainly not least — my parents and family.

Prologue

He always said if I left he would kill me, but there are far worse fates than death. Guess I hadn't really known that until I met and married Trent Taylor. I didn't mind the cuts and bruises half as much as the insults and accusations. Whoever said "Sticks and stones may break my bones, but words will never hurt me" has never been on the other end of a tongue that really knows how to cut.

I hope you never know that kind of pain, Son. More than that, I hope you never cause it. How could you? You have such a soft heart. My sweet Emmanuel.

Surely by now I've told you your name means "God with us." Because he was, Manny. He is. Even if you haven't realized it yet, you're lucky to have such a wonderful name. I used to hate mine — Penny — because that's exactly how much I felt I was worth for most of my life. But God used you to change all that.

It's important to tell you before I begin this story that it's not my intention to make you hate your father. He's a man — fallen, like the rest of us. But I know you'll ask about him, and I decided when you were old enough, I would share with you all I know. That day hasn't come yet — you're just beginning to talk! — but I'd best write it down while it's fresh in my mind. Although some of it, I know, will never fade.

Reading this won't be easy, and please don't feel you have to if it's too much. I'm not one to believe all truths need to be spoken, but just in case you want to know, need to know, I'd rather you hear it from me as a whole story than get bits and pieces of the puzzle from others and not be able to make them fit together quite right.

Besides, your grandmother told me long ago the best way not to repeat history is to know it. I think that's probably right.

One

Trent Taylor sauntered into my life wearing faded blue jeans, dusty work boots, and an attitude I couldn't take my eyes off.

We had a bumper crop that summer of '99, so Daddy was able to hire a farmhand to help for a change. We were all so happy to have a little money in our pockets and another set of harvesting hands, we didn't look a gift horse in his mouth. It was just like that story from the Trojan War. We all let him right in without looking first to see what was inside him.

It's surreal to think that if the rains hadn't fallen just right and the price of tobacco hadn't been up due to a blight that seemed to be hitting every farm but ours, we wouldn't have been able to afford to hire Trent. How much pain I could have been spared . . . but then I wouldn't have you, Manny. I'd go through it all a million times just to have you.

Being late August, the air outside was steam and the smell of the roast Daddy insisted Mama cook every Thursday carried past me on what little breeze there was. As usual, our cat, Seymour, kept busy chasing the chickens around the yard. He loved to terrorize those poor birds. I yelled at him like I always did, but he never paid me — or anyone besides Daddy — any mind.

Until that afternoon, I'd never seen those chickens do anything but run from mean old Seymour, but that day the smallest one turned around and pecked him right between the eyes. I still laugh when I think of that cat howling in surprise and jumping back ten feet in the air, tail first, as if God himself had snatched him, only to drop him.

After Seymour tore off and the chickens returned to scratching dirt, I bent over my laundry basket and got back to work, humming something or other through the splintered clothespins tucked between my lips.

Even though we owned a dryer, your grandpappy hardly ever let Mama or me use it. He couldn't see the sense in wasting money on electricity when the sun and wind would do the job for free. I would have offered to pay the measly expense myself, but in my father's household, women were meant to be seen working, not heard complaining.

I bent down to pin up my daddy's undershorts, doing my best not to touch anything but the outermost corner of the waistband, when I felt hot breath on the back of my ear and a rough hand cover my own. Paralyzed, I just stood there staring straight ahead at the dirt road leading from our driveway. I could feel my pulse pounding my temples as I held my breath.

Trent must have taken my lack of protest as encouragement because his other hand wrapped tight around my waist and he yanked me back against him. He whispered in my ear with a voice somehow both rough as sandpaper and smooth as whipped cream, "This better be the last time I ever see my woman touching another man's underwear."

I could barely breathe. At seventeen, I'd never been touched by a man except to have my tail whipped for disobeying. I'd never even held a boy's hand, and here was a man, a grown man, staking claim to me. Just then, the screen door squealed open and your grandpappy's heavy footsteps pounded across the porch.

When Trent stepped back, I finally got the courage to turn around and look him in the eye. He'd been around for a couple of weeks by then and I'd seen him dozens of times, but until that moment, I hadn't noticed the crinkles around his eyes that made him look like he was always squinting against the sun, or the small scar cutting into the fullness of his bottom lip. His longish hair was a shade darker than my dirty blonde, and there was something about the way his nose flared just so that brought to mind a fighter plane. People might have said a lot of things about your father back then, but no one could suggest he wasn't beautiful.

"What are you doing over there?" My father stood on the porch, leaning his hip against the column and holding a glass of water that was sweating as much as he was.

I yanked up my laundry basket, still half full, intending to bound inside, but didn't make it a step before I felt that rough hand of Trent's wrap tight around my wrist again.

"Just taking a break," he said to my father, though he never took his eyes off me. He stared right through me, wearing a smirk. I would get to know that Cheshire grin real well in the years that followed. It was the look he wore when he knew he had won, or was about to. I wonder just what it was he had seen that gave me away.

"You best get on back to work." Daddy's voice was loud as thunder, and it shook me.

Trent's grin only widened. "Now, don't

be that way to your future son-in-law." His eyes wandered over the front of me like he was eyeing a ham steak he was getting ready to cut into.

Those roving eyes of his sent unfamiliar jolts through me.

Daddy slammed down his glass on the porch ledge. "Are you listening, boy? I ain't going to tell you again."

Trent put his hands up like he was under arrest. "Take it easy, man. I'm just talking to her."

My heart felt like a butterfly caught in a mason jar. No one spoke to my father that way.

What an idiot I was to think Trent's bravado was because he was so taken with me. In my mind I was the princess, Daddy was the dragon, and Trent, of course, was the knight who'd come to rescue me from the tower.

With my father's eyes on us, Trent whispered I was the prettiest thing he ever laid eyes on. I twisted my mouth like he was crazy, but inside, I was done for. I'd never had a man tell me I was pretty.

I took the bait. With one pathetic cast of his line, I was snagged, swallowing his words happily as that hook dug deep into my flesh.

When Daddy's face took on a shade of

sunburn and he started down the stairs, Trent pretended to tip the hat he wasn't wearing and leaned over to whisper that he would be waiting for me at the well at midnight and his woman had best be there. *Woman,* I repeated in my mind, liking the sound of it. He reeled me in that night, and before week's end I'd agreed to elope.

At Trent's direction, I left a note for my parents telling them they shouldn't come looking for me.

Despite my fears, though — and eventually, my hopes — my parents never did come knocking to reclaim me. No one did.

Two

I never wanted anything as badly as I wanted you, Manny. Of course, I didn't know you'd be you. You could have been a little girl, a set of twins, or an elf with two heads for all I cared. I just wanted someone who would love me whether or not I burned the biscuits or made the bed. I just wanted to be enough.

I used to think your father couldn't give me the unconditional love I craved because I was flawed somehow, but now I know the problem was him. Love keeps no record of wrongs, but Trent was a master scorekeeper. If I was late getting supper on the table, he made sure I suffered for it. I was convinced he hated me for not giving him a child, and if only I could, our lives would be so much better. You don't need to tell me how faulty my thinking was.

One day it dawned on me we'd been trying to have a baby for more than a decade.

That realization hit me so hard, I doubled over, crying until I couldn't cry anymore. After I ran out of tears, I curled up right there on the floor, begging God to put me out of my misery.

"Get up off the ground, Penny. The neighbors are going to think I'm murdering you in here with you carrying on like that."

The ceramic tiles were cold against my cheek, and a crack in one of them pressed into my skin. I sat and gazed up at him. He wasn't that much bigger than me when we stood nose to nose, but every year, he seemed a little taller. I felt like Thumbelina right then.

He grunted. "If you would put half the time you worry about having a crying poop maker into being a good wife, I wouldn't be embarrassed to bring my friends into this dump."

His words cut deep. Maybe because they were true. Our little tar-papered house *had* gotten to be a bit of a mess lately. I didn't know it back then, but it's clear as crystal now that I was dealing with serious depression. I kept the shades down and the fresh air out. I stopped cutting flowers and bringing them inside. I stopped doing most anything except the bare minimum of cooking dinner and washing clothes and dishes.

"I'm sorry, Trent." My voice crackled.

He scrunched his face. *"I-I-I'm sorry, Trent,"* he repeated, mocking me. *"I just want a baby so bad. That way I can spend even more time neglecting you."* He flicked the cigarette he had been smoking at me. The orange tip bit my forearm, and I jumped.

I looked down at my arm. A small half moon of red formed right below a yellowing bruise. I licked my middle finger and ran the spit over the sting to cool it. "You used to want a son too." His father had neglected him to the point of pitifulness, and in our younger, better days, Trent shared his overwhelming desire to get a do-over and show his father what it meant to be a real dad.

"If wishes were pennies, I'd have more lazy women than I could feed."

I hated him using my name as a pun, which is, I'm sure, why he did it. "If I'm so awful, why'd you marry me?"

He sucked his teeth and I half expected him to spit on me, but instead, he reached down and held out his hand to help me up. I had no reason to trust him, so I balanced myself in such a way that if he let go, I wouldn't fall. But he didn't. He pulled me to my feet and held me against himself.

"Penny, I don't want you getting yourself

so upset about whether or not we get young'uns. I wouldn't mind a son, sure, but the only thing in this world I need is you." He stroked my back.

Then, just when it seemed like he actually cared, he started in with the insults again. I made a comment he found disrespectful, and before I knew it, his fist cracked against my temple.

Flashes of light blinked around the room, and I dropped to my knees. My ears rang so loudly I couldn't hear what he was saying. Slowly, he and his words came back into focus.

His top lip curled up over his teeth. "Next time I try and offer you a little constructive criticism, don't you dare give me lip. You thank me, understand? I'm your husband and it's my job to look after you. If I don't tell you the truth, who will?"

Truth. I had no idea what that word even meant anymore.

I held my aching head, feeling a trickle of blood snaking its way into my mouth. I knelt on the floor for the longest time listening to him yelling at me to get up. He kicked me once, halfheartedly, but I refused to budge. I was in another time and place. I was the Princess Penny of my childhood, crying out for someone to save me.

God heard, Manny. He always does.

The next morning I woke up early, like I did every day, and fixed your father eggs. One bite was too runny, the next overdone. I apologized for not being a better cook, a better homemaker, a better . . . you name it.

He shoved the tail of his shirt into the back of his work pants and snatched the lunch I'd fixed him off the counter. I handed him his thermos of coffee, wondering what would happen if one day I just forgot to screw the top on. How badly would it scald him?

What a terrible thing to wonder. *Take each thought captive,* I told myself as he walked toward me. I flinched, not knowing if he was about to kiss me or hit me. That morning, I was lucky.

His work boots gave him a couple inches of height, so I had to push up on my toes to reach him. When my mouth met his unpuckered lips, he grunted as though I'd said something he disagreed with.

When he left, I walked to the window, feeling exhausted. The kind of tired that seeps into your marrow and makes your bones feel like lead. It was all I could do to keep my eyes open as I watched our rusty mopar tear out of the driveway and screech around the bend.

When it did, I noticed smudges of ketchup, and who knew what else, streaking down the once-white paint, now stained tobacco-yellow. I ran my fingertips slowly across the coarse living room wall, remembering Trent's promise to paint it whatever color I wanted. Over the years, his dead promises had begun to line up like cars in a funeral procession.

I stood there for the longest time, my palm flat against the chipped paint, knowing I should grab a sponge and clean off at least the worst of the filth. Ought to clean a lot of things. But if the house was spic and span, he would just find something else to complain about, something a bottle of Windex couldn't wipe away.

I was ready to head back to the bedroom when someone pounded on the back door. I had no friends, and my family was almost two hundred miles away. We lived a little out of the way with only two sets of neighbors on our street, both of whom steered clear of Trent, so I had no idea who it could be.

I looked through the open kitchen window, past the torn screen, at a woman who was somehow familiar. It took a few seconds to remember this church lady who'd brought me a cake the first and last time I had visited Sheckle Baptist, nearly six months before.

Trent and his buddies had eaten that cake in one stoned sitting. As he licked the orange icing from his fingertips, he told me church folk were a bunch of hypocritical killjoys that lived one way and expected everyone else to live another. I never went back, but the Bible she gave me to replace the one I'd lost to one of your father's drunken tirades still lay hidden under the bed.

"Long time no see," the church lady said. In the sunlight, her hair shone the color of corn silk and looked just as fine. Tiny wrinkles feathered out from around the corners of her eyes, but the rest of her skin was smooth, making it hard to guess her age.

"Long time," I agreed. There was no way I could invite her in with the house such a mess — not that I wanted to.

As if she could read my mind, she laid the back of her hand over her forehead like she was Scarlett O'Hara. "Isn't it hot as molasses out here?"

"Hot as what?" I wondered if maybe I'd heard her wrong.

"Molasses," she repeated, then blushed as if just realizing what she said. "That's what my mama always said. She didn't make a whole lot of sense sometimes, bless her heart."

I didn't want to lie to her, so I just said, "Ma'am, I'm a little busy. Is there something I can do for you?"

She gave me a look like she didn't much believe me. I didn't care if she did or didn't, so long as she carried herself back to her car.

"Well, I don't want to keep you. I just was wondering if you had ever thought about visiting our church again?"

What did she care? It wasn't like they were hurting to fill their pews or collection baskets. Besides, even if Trent was the tithing sort, 10 percent of nothing would still be nothing. Back then I didn't understand concern for someone else's soul. Your mama didn't understand much of anything except survival, baby.

Inside my socks, my toes curled up tight. "I'm worshiping at home now."

She squinted at me for an uncomfortably long time. "The Bible says you should belong to a church."

I looked past her and the overgrown grass to the tractor tire leaning against a gutted

Yugo Trent had brought home two years before, but hadn't touched since. "No, it don't, neither."

She laughed. "Know your Scripture, do you?"

"My daddy made sure of it." What I didn't tell her was how he shoved it down my throat every time I didn't do things his way. I hated the deity my father presented as a giant principal in the sky, throwing down bolts of lightning and striking women dead for not obeying their husbands, or children their fathers. My mother's version was far kinder. He was the sort that wiped away tears and picked you up when you fell. That's the God I clung to, though I knew precious little about him then.

The lady brushed a strand of hair from her cheek. "Hebrews 10:25 says, 'Let us not neglect our meeting together, as some people do, but encourage one another, especially now that the day of his return is drawing near.' "

A mosquito must have bitten my chin because it started itching like mad. I scratched at the small bump and pondered that verse. After a few seconds I said, "It also says, when two or more are gathered in Jesus' name, he's there with them." I was proud of myself for not only speaking up, but also sounding halfway intelligent for a change.

The strap of her purse slipped down her arm and she pushed it up over her shoulder. I don't know if her blouse was silk or satin, but the shimmery fabric looked so beautiful and cool. I couldn't help but wonder what something like that would cost. Probably more than our house payment.

"Very good. Penny, wasn't it?"

"That's right." How much nicer my name sounded when it wasn't being sputtered like a cussword. I figured I should quit while I was ahead. Besides, my back was getting sore from stooping there at the window to look at her. "Well, thanks for coming."

She turned to go, but then paused and turned around. "I just have one question. *Whom* are you gathering with?"

The question caught me off guard, so I just gaped at her, feeling like the moron I thought I was. After a moment, I finally found my voice. "I *am* married, Miss —" I remembered too late I didn't recall her name.

There was something about her smile that took away my embarrassment. "Mrs. Callie Mae Johnson. You can call me Callie. Your husband — he's a Christian man?"

My face flushed. If Trent knew I was

speaking to her, he would have me looking like a raccoon for sure. "I really have to go."

Her smile faded. "Well, I don't want to keep you, but we sure would love you to come sit with us again. This time bring your husband."

I cleared my throat and studied my dingy socks. "He isn't much on church."

She let out a breath of air like she'd been holding it all her life. "Oh, I see. Well, you tell your husband he may be head over you, but God's head over him. You tell him that."

Although I said nothing, I thought maybe I would tell him. Maybe it would get him to think about a few things; though, of course, I knew better.

"You take care, Penny. Sorry to have bothered you." She turned around and started down the back stairs.

"No bother," I mumbled, wishing my house had been clean. A female to talk to might have been nice. Trent wouldn't have to know.

She slid into a blue sedan that looked like it had just been run through a car wash and drove away. I looked around the kitchen, trying to see how my house might have looked through her eyes if I had let her in. The morning dishes sat on the table and counter, but that was understandable. I'd just fed my husband, after all. Besides the lining of dust along the baseboards, it wasn't so bad if she didn't look too closely. As long as I kept her in the kitchen it would have been fine, but if she had to use the bathroom, and a guest always seemed to have to, she would see what a pigsty I let my husband live in.

Shame warmed my cheeks. Trent was right. I should snap out of it and start being a better wife. No wonder he didn't love me. No wonder God didn't think I could handle being a mother. I hadn't been faithful with what he had provided.

These thoughts should have motivated me to get it together and clean up, but they just sucked me drier. I made my way to the bedroom — blissfully dark — and lay down.

I dreamed that I was a bird. My wide, beautiful wings carried me high above the clouds, high above my troubles, onward toward heaven. The pearly gate was almost within reach when a boom of thunder hurled me back to earth. . . . I rolled over, burying my face deeper into the pillow. The racket grew louder. Rubbing the sleep from my eyes, I sat up.

Someone was pounding on the front door. Maybe the church lady was back. The forcefulness of the pounding told me that was unlikely.

Trent.

He must be home from work and forgot his key. I wondered why he didn't come in the back. I almost never kept that door locked.

Supper! I didn't know what I was going to make. I hadn't even washed the dishes from breakfast, for crying out loud. He was going to kill me. I threw the sheet off and tore out of the room toward the front door. Excuses whizzed through my mind. I was sick, the church lady upset me . . .

The knocking grew more insistent as my trembling hands fought to turn the doorknob. When I opened the door, I almost fainted in relief to find one of Trent's drinking buddies standing there instead of him. It was no surprise Boston reeked of liquor — he never didn't — but he wasn't stumbling for a change. That, along with the brightness of the sun, told me it was not as late as I feared. "Howdy, Penny."

With a curt nod, I acknowledged him. Manny, I could not stand that man. Couldn't stand any of your father's so-called friends. The way I saw it, they were the reason for my constant isolation, our poverty, and in my twisted thinking, even for his affairs. I guess blaming them was safer than blaming your father.

He scratched his chin with those dirty fingernails of his. "I hate to be the one to tell you . . ."

It was like time stood still then. *He's dead,* I thought. *My husband is dead.* And then a strange emotion came over me, one I hadn't felt in a very long time. Hope.

So many thoughts bounced around my mind. What would I do first? Call Mama? Get a job? I could start going back to church proper every Sunday. Find out if my childhood friend, Lucy, had gone to college like she said she was going to do.

And then more somber thoughts. The funeral — how would I pay for it? Maybe I wouldn't. Maybe I would just pack up my belongings and leave before anyone could ask me what kind of arrangements I wanted. But where would I go?

". . . accident."

"Accident?" *Accident* didn't mean dead. The hope I'd been holding seeped out of my hands like grains of sand, quickly replaced by guilt when I realized I was disappointed.

Looking back, Manny, I shouldn't have felt ashamed for fantasizing about him dying. I should have considered myself a woman of exception for not trying to kill him myself. But here's a little marital advice for the future — if you start thinking your only hope for a happy future means the death of your spouse, it's time to get some help.

"What kind of accident?" I asked.

He ran a hand through his thinning brown hair. "He's in the hospital."

Not dead. *Thank God,* I forced myself to think. "What's wrong?"

"He cut through a pipe that still had fuel in it. It exploded in his face." He kicked the doormat. "They took him to St. Joe's. You need to get over there."

A pipe exploded in Trent's face? I feel guilty admitting this, but my first reaction wasn't pity in hearing that. You know what raced through that head of mine? *Great. Now he's going to be even meaner.*

But he wasn't, Manny. It was the craziest thing.

Three

It had been over a year since I'd first set foot in St. Joseph's Hospital. That time, the doctor had told Trent to leave the room, then asked me how I ended up with a broken arm, a black eye, and a gash across my chin. After I repeated my lame story for the second time, she tried to hand me a card for a halfway house for battered women. Just in case I knew someone who needed it.

Thinking of that doctor now as I made my way down the hallway, I wondered what my life might be like if I had taken the card she offered. That, and how your father and I were ever going to pay for all of this if worker's comp didn't cover it.

As I passed a group of nurses, I had to remind myself they couldn't know we were deadbeats, but something about the way one of them eyed me made me wonder.

I forced my gaze off her onto the glass-walled patient rooms to the left. Within each lay a poor soul attached to all kinds of tubes and gizmos I couldn't begin to imagine the purpose of. Nurses hurried in and out of those rooms looking busy and burdened. A dark-haired man sat at the front desk, tapping his knuckles against a phone receiver as he stared at what I guessed to be a bunch of heart monitors. When I told him who I was, he pointed me to the last room on the left.

I hesitated and took a peek before entering. With his eyes patched with squares of white and his body hidden under blankets, I barely recognized him. His hair lay slicked back off his forehead, which was partially wrapped in gauze.

He shifted around in the bed like he couldn't get comfortable. When I stepped into the room, the smell of cheap perfume slapped me in the face. Its source stood facing the window, dressed in skinny jeans, heels that belonged on a street corner, and a pink ribbon tying up stringy black hair. This was not the same woman with the nose ring and pocked skin I was reasonably sure Trent had cheated on me with last time.

I cleared my throat. Trent casually reached for the lidded cup on his bedside table and took a sip from the straw. He either didn't know I had walked in, or else didn't care.

The woman, on the other hand, whipped around like I had screamed her name. The heavy streaks in her makeup told me she'd been crying.

I was suddenly conscious of my threadbare sundress, scuffed sandals, and eyebrows that desperately needed to be plucked. Ignoring her, I went to your father. "Hi, baby."

He jerked his head back in surprise. "Penny?"

I stepped closer. "I'm so sorry you're hurt."

When he felt the air for me, I stepped into his touch. His rough fingers fell first on my face, then down my arm to my hand. From the corner of my eye, I watched the woman's reaction. When she flinched, I knew she was no mere friend or coworker. You could have fried bacon on my face, but there was no way I was going to let either of them know how I felt — she didn't deserve the satisfaction, and I didn't deserve whatever Trent would give me for accusing him of what he was sure to deny.

"Are you hurting?" I asked, trying to keep the emotion out of my voice.

He touched the gauze patch on his right eye as if making sure it was still there. "Not too bad. They're giving me pills every four hours. But I can't see anything."

He smelled of sweat and cigarettes. I wondered how he had managed to sneak a smoke in this place, but knew better than to ask. The question would only be treated like an accusation.

The woman in the corner began to sob. I wanted to yank her by her ugly black hair and run her right out of the room. She had no right to cry over my husband. Let her be sad over her own stinking man.

"I'm sorry, babe." Trent sounded on the verge of tears himself. "I don't know how we're going to make it now."

Before that moment, the only time I ever heard your father say he was sorry was after he'd sobered up and seen the bruises he gave me the night before.

"I could loan you money," the woman whispered. She snuck a glance at me as she rubbed at the place on her arm above a faded rose tattoo. "I already told him I could loan y'all a little money until you're back on your fee—" She cupped her face in her hands and went back to crying.

Since Trent couldn't see me, I rolled my eyes. "Ain't that sweet," I said with a touch of sarcasm. "But we'll get along just fine."

He turned his face in my general direction and patted my hand. "That's my girl. The

Taylors ain't no charity case, are we, One Cent?"

I didn't know why he was talking to me sweet all of a sudden, but I didn't much care. I liked it better than the alternative. "Is it permanent?"

He sighed and gave a half shrug.

The woman wiped the black from under her eyes as she stared down at my hand in his. "The doctor said they don't know just yet. Only time will tell."

I pretended like I didn't hear her. Who was she to be talking to his doctor like she had a pony in this race? "Well, what did they say, *Trent*?"

"Norma's right. Time will tell."

I narrowed my eyes at her. Norma. Suddenly I hated that name.

She walked toward us and stopped at the end of the bed. "He was real bad when he came in. He already looks better."

I couldn't stand it a minute more. "Who are you?" I asked.

She looked to Trent as if he could see the question on her face.

He dropped my hand. "For crying out loud, Penny, don't start. Norma's our new supply clerk."

It was all I could do to stop myself from saying something smart. "You gave him a ride here, then?"

She looked at the doorway as if contemplating making a run for it. "I . . ." She looked at Trent and waited for him to finish for her. When he didn't, she continued. "An ambulance brought him in. I came soon as I heard."

I couldn't stand to hear one more word come out of her fish lips. "That's very kind of you, Norma, but I'll take care of my husband now."

She frowned and looked at Trent.

He reached for my hand again, and I set it in his. Then he did something that made me almost forget she was even there. He brought my hand to his lips like I was his princess.

It was all Norma could do to keep it together as she said her good-byes. When she turned around at the doorway to look at us one last time, I bent down and kissed Trent's lips. I had to fight not to cringe, knowing her lips had probably just done the same.

I listened to the click of her high heels fade down the hallway, then asked, "So how long have you worked with her?"

He dropped my hand and huffed. "C'mon now, Penny. If I had something going with her, would I have kissed you with her in here?"

Yeah, I thought. *That's exactly something you would do, because you like hurting women.*

"We got bigger fish to fry than your paranoia."

I wanted to say my so-called paranoia hadn't been so crazy the night I opened the back door of our car to get a blanket and found him having what looked an awful lot like a lover's quarrel with some bleach-blonde.

But I held my tongue. Trent's eyes might be as useless as his memory, but his hands looked just fine.

FOUR

I hadn't realized the true weight of the boulder I'd been under until it lifted.

During the two weeks your father was in the hospital, the sky seemed bluer, the spring air sweeter, and for once in a very long time, there was peace in our home.

That morning I woke with the sparrows, dusted an already clean house, and even put on a little makeup just because I felt like it. It was afternoon when I decided it was time to give some attention to the flower beds.

I sat Indian-style on the grass I'd mowed the day before, wondering why Trent always made cutting the lawn sound like it was more work than building the Taj Mahal. If I had known how easy it was, I would have been doing it all along. To think, all this time, I was embarrassed about a yard I could have easily been keeping up myself.

Smiling at the realization, I plucked sprouts of rogue seedlings from between a grouping of wildflowers. The rainbow of blooms before me grew vibrant and healthy despite their neglect. I gently pinched the stem of the fullest pink flower, leaning in and sniffing its roselike scent, deciding I would add this one to the bouquet I'd cut for the kitchen table.

After I tamed the weeds, I lay down right in the grass, bent my arms behind my head, and looked up. The underside of the daisies set against the blue sky made for a striking contrast. Sunlight outlined the petals in shades of gold, and I sighed in contentment.

As I wiggled my bare toes on the grass carpet, a butterfly fluttered by, landing on a purple flower I didn't know the name of. I watched it with longing. *How wonderful it must be,* I thought, *to be able to just spread your wings whenever you like without someone following you around trying to swat you out of the sky.* When the butterfly set off and a bumblebee moved in, a feeling of déjà vu washed over me. Scouring my mind, I tried my best to recall the memory fighting to surface.

I stared so long at the sky the sun blurred into a halo, and the memory I'd been searching for finally emerged. It was my thirteenth birthday, and I had insisted I was too old for a party. When the morning came without even the slightest bit of fanfare, I had to blink back the tears.

Sitting outside in my childhood yard, feeling sorry for myself, I had watched a bumblebee land on the honeysuckle vine next to me. He scurried flower to flower, feverishly collecting nectar as if it might be the only chance he might ever get. When at last he flew away, I noticed the vague smell of something freshly baked, and I knew before I even turned around that your grandmother was beside me.

She sat down and wrapped her arm around my shoulder. "Happy birthday, Penny." She wore her thin brown hair pulled up in a ponytail, highlighting the streak of white at the nape of her neck.

I faked a smile. "Thanks."

"Thirteen years ago today, your daddy rushed me to the hospital. You were the easiest birth. I knew you were going be something special when —"

I rolled my eyes in typical teenage fashion. "Not again, Mama."

She untied her apron and slipped it from around her waist. "Too old for public displays of affection. Too old for parties. Too old for memories now too?"

I shrugged her arm off me and picked at a blade of grass.

Your grandmother looked up at the sky, smiled, and said, “I see a pineapple.”

Sneaking a glance upward to see what she was looking at, I said, “Not now.”

She lay back in the grass and pulled at my arm until I begrudgingly flopped down beside her. “All right, your turn, birthday girl.”

I wanted to be left alone, and at the same time didn’t want to be left alone, which I guess is the way kids that age feel most of the time. “C’mon, Mama, I’m not in the mood.”

She puckered her lips and pinched my side playfully. “Well then, maybe I’m not in the mood to give you your present.”

Her touch tickled, but I was too stubborn to laugh. Instead, I huffed. “Fine. I see a porcupine.”

She turned her head toward me and raised her eyebrows. It was then I noticed the fine lines starting to etch into her fair skin. “Penny Elizabeth Carson, you didn’t even look up.”

“Yes, I did,” I lied.

Her mouth twisted into a smirk. “Okay then, show me which one.”

I hurriedly scanned the sky. Not a single puff of white came even remotely close to looking like a varmint, but I pointed to one just the same.

She surprised me by saying, “Huh, I can see that.”

As I turned to see which cloud she was looking at, I felt like my heart would burst. She held her head to the side and squinted so hard it must have been blurring those clouds all together. I had no earthly idea why, but it made me want to cry. You make that same face sometimes, Manny, and it gets me every time.

Your grandma and I lay like that for a few minutes until she sat up suddenly and told me to come on in the house and get my gift already.

When I pushed open the screen door, I was hit with a chorus of family and friends yelling, “Surprise!” I couldn’t get the smile off my face as I scanned the small crowd. The happy smiles of my cousins, grandparents, aunts, uncles, and friends all met me . . . and then my stomach sank. Of course Daddy wouldn’t be here. He’d be out working the field as if it were any other day.

Snapping out of the memory, I looked up at the sky, searching for pineapple clouds, and wondered how my parents could have ever fallen in love. Mama had to be one of the sweetest women to ever walk the earth.

Despite Daddy's barbwire personality, she had done her best to make both him and me happy. Some days I hated him for the way he treated her. Other times, like today, I just felt sorry for them both.

The difference between Mama and me was she would never voice her opinion if Daddy hadn't asked for it, which he never did. At least I called Trent out on his bad behavior most of the time. Not that it made any difference. Maybe my mother had spoken up too, once upon a time. Maybe she just got tired of nothing ever changing, and eventually admitted defeat.

How was he treating her now that I wasn't around to provoke him? Maybe things had gotten better between them. Maybe losing me had helped Mama find her voice or helped Daddy mute his. It had been so long since I'd seen them, they'd become like a far-off dream — the king and queen of a childhood fairy tale I once read.

I wondered if Mama could possibly miss me as much as I did her. And then I had an epiphany.

Trent was blind. He couldn't check the phone records anymore to see whom I called.

My parents had only one phone number all their lives, and I hoped that hadn't changed. I jumped up, brushed off my backside, and raced inside, nearly tripping over the hem of my dress. Resting my hand on the phone receiver, I closed my eyes and prayed for the words to speak.

I dialed their number fast so my mind didn't have time to question my fingers' memory. She picked up on the first ring as if she'd been standing beside that phone all those years, just waiting for me to call. Now that I'm a mother, I think she probably had.

"Hello?" She sounded so old, Manny. So tired.

My heart pounded and I lost my breath.

"Hello?" she repeated.

I think I might have whimpered then.

"Penny? Penny, is that you?"

I don't know why, but I slammed the phone down so hard it should have cracked. When it rang right back, fear paralyzed me. It must have rung a dozen times as I stood there just staring at it.

Finally I found the courage to jerk it to my ear. "Mama," I heard myself say.

My next words were, "Is he there?"

He was in the field, of course, same as always. I have no idea how long we talked, Mama and me, but there had been full light at the beginning of the call, and dusk by the time we hung up.

I told her of my courthouse wedding to Trent, about our little tar-papered house, and anything else I could think of. Of course, I left out the way Trent used his fists to tenderize my face on a regular basis. I suppose when I made her promise not to call me, she might have had her suspicions.

Joy and sadness both flooded my heart as we said our good-byes. There wasn't time to dwell on either emotion, because the second I put the receiver in its cradle, it rang again. With a smile, I snatched it up, thinking Mama wanted to tell me she loved me one last time, but it was Trent hissing that he'd been trying to call me for over an hour. I felt sick to my stomach as I waited for the barrage of questions and accusations about who I was talking to, but all he said was, "I'm coming home."

Five

Trent felt his way through the front door, hesitating with each small step — unsure. I tried to lead him by the elbow like I'd seen others do with blind people, but he kept pulling away from me. Staring straight ahead at nothing, he patted the air until his fingers finally touched the armrest of the couch.

He lowered himself, almost sitting on the copy of *Gone with the Wind* I'd checked out of the library a few days before. With a grunt, he knocked the book onto the floor as he sat. "Why bother cleaning up the place just because your blind husband might trip and break his neck?"

Blood rushed to my face as I picked up the book and set it on the table. "It *is* clean."

He sneered. "Well, I can't very well verify that, now can I?" He kicked off his boots in the usual fashion, then rubbed his stomach. "How about some dinner?"

I headed toward the kitchen intending to find something for him to snack on.

"Penny!"

I whipped around.

"Just because I can't see, doesn't mean I can't hear you walking away from me."

I walked back over — no, slinked was probably more like it. "I'm sorry, baby. I was just going to find you something to eat."

When he stood, I noticed he was wearing mismatched socks — one black and one white.

"The fact I'm blind doesn't mean I'm less of a man. You hear me?"

"I know," I whispered.

He furrowed his brow and glared in my general direction. "You getting smart with me?"

Before I could answer, his balled fist thrust through the air. He intended to hit me, but thankfully I hadn't been standing close enough. He fell backward, looking shocked as his legs went up and butt touched down. To me, his expression was more enlightening than funny.

His rage morphed into embarrassment. "Penny!" he yelled again, but the fight had left him.

At that moment I knew our relationship had changed, Manny. And your father knew

I knew it. "I'm going to go fix you something," I said.

When I brought him a ham sandwich, he surprised me by saying, "Thank you." After he swallowed a bite, he felt around the plate. "You know I always eat two. I lost my eyesight, not my appetite."

I sat beside him on the couch, keeping just out of arm's reach. "I know, but that's it."

He turned toward me. "What's 'it'?"

"That's the last of it."

He licked the mayo from the corner of his mouth. "Round steak would be fine, then."

"We're out of bologna, too." It irritated me to no end he didn't suspect we were out of food. Why wouldn't we be? He hadn't given me grocery money in nearly a month. "I can fix you a bowl of oatmeal or tomato soup, but that's pretty much all we've got."

The color washed from his face. "What've you been doing, feeding the whole town while I was in the hospital?"

I slid a little farther away from him, mashing my hip into the armrest.

His face scrunched up like it always did when he was fixing to lose it. Then, as if remembering the earlier incident, the look melted away again. "That can't be it."

"There's also half a bag of cornmeal," I

offered, "and a can of black olives."

He slid his plate, with the half sandwich, down the cocktail table toward me. "You take it, then."

You could have bowled me over with a feather. Trent didn't do stuff like that — selfless, I mean. The hardness trying to push its way into my heart pushed itself right out again. I slid the plate back to him. "I'm not hungry, but —" I hesitated — "thank you." I couldn't remember the last time I'd thanked him for something out of genuine appreciation instead of fear. It felt nice on my lips.

He leaned back against the couch and turned his face toward the ceiling as if he could see something there. "This is bad."

"What about the money you've been putting away?" Over the past few years, I'd asked him twice where the rest of his paycheck was going. The first time, he told me, "The rainy-day fund." The second, and last, he kicked me in the tailbone and told me I'd better mind my own business if I knew what was good for me.

When he slowly shook his head, I knew his rainy-day fund had been more like a fifth-a-day fund.

I felt like I was going to be sick. "I could get a job," I offered.

"No way." He turned in my direction, looking past me at the door. "Who's going to hire you? I'll think of something."

I hadn't been interested in eating before I knew we had no money. Now I suddenly felt like my stomach was digesting itself. We'd been hungry before, and I had no desire to go through that kind of misery again. "I could go to the food bank. They help people like us all the time."

He reached for me. I flinched until I realized he wanted to touch me, not hit me.

"Don't say it, Penny. The Taylors ain't no charity case. Never have been, never will. We ain't got much, but we still got our pride, darlin'."

And so for the next week, we lived on rations of oatmeal, corn mush, and your father's pride.

When my monthly didn't come on time, I figured stress, weight loss, and caffeine withdrawal had caused it, but just to be sure, I used the last of my pregnancy tests. If I could have afforded a dozen more, I would have taken them. I just couldn't believe I was finally looking at a little blue plus sign after all this time. I wanted to be happy. This was what I had prayed and dreamed of for as long as I'd been married, after all, but the timing couldn't have been worse. I was going to starve my own baby to death.

It was all I could do not to share the news with your father, but something told me I'd better think it out first. So, alone in the bedroom, I got on my knees as I'd seen my mother do so many times, and asked God why. The answer was immediate. This is what I'd asked for. First I ask God why he won't give me a baby, then I ask him why he does? I smiled through tears.

I hate to wish bad things on you, Son, but I hope you get the privilege someday of having no one to lean on but God. It changes a person.

It sure changed me.

Six

The next day, before I even told your father about you, I swallowed my pride into my grumbling stomach and drove to the food bank. Walking in there, I felt defeated and determined all at the same time. When I told Trent I found some money in one of his pants pockets, he told me to pick him up a pack of smokes while I was out.

I hated lying, but when you're starving, somehow a lie doesn't seem as wicked as when your belly's full. I hope you never go hungry enough to understand that, Manny.

A round woman with short, white hair met me at the door. I felt so humiliated at first I could barely look her in the eye, but she had this way about her, this disarming smile and voice that reminded me of my grandmother. By the time she was finished asking me questions, it felt like I was the one doing her the favor by taking the food off her hands.

I was relieved things were going so well, until she ushered me back into the next room. Stacked nearly to the ceiling were shelves and shelves of food, just like a neighborhood grocery store. I could almost taste the Hamburger Helper piled high before me, when I heard a familiar voice say, "Penny, is that you? Penny Taylor?"

My blood turned to ice even as shame warmed my face. Of all the people in the world to be there, it just had to be that church lady. She wore a black apron over her dress, which told me she was there to work, not collect charity.

I pasted on a smile. "Cora Mae, so good to see you."

She looked at the basket in my hands, then for some reason, down at my shoes. Maybe she thought I would be barefoot and filth-toed; I'm not quite sure. "It's Callie Mae, but close enough."

Before my mind could catch up with my mouth, I asked, "What are you doing here?"

She gave me a funny look, then pointed to the sign that said *Sheckle Baptist* in small letters right above *Food Bank.*

I'd never noticed the name of her church being on the sign out front, but here it was in faded brown and green. I felt like the world's biggest idiot. "I'm just here for a friend," I stammered. What was wrong with me? With all the lies flying from my lips lately, I was becoming a regular heathen.

"It's all right, sweetheart. There's no shame in asking for help. We all need a hand every now and then."

The way I figured, the only help those kind of church ladies ever needed was someone to hold their purse while they put on their lipstick. I had a lot of mixed-up ideas about people back then, Manny. About everything, really. "My husband had an accident."

Her thin, blonde eyebrows dipped. "Oh no! What happened? Is he all right?"

"Not really," I said. "He's blind."

After she picked her jaw up off the floor, she snatched up my hand like we were old girlfriends. I'd never felt skin so soft. She led me to a room at the back of the make-shift store. Inside it sat a small table, a microwave, and a bulletin board full of pictures of families I gathered the food bank had helped along the way.

The smell of brewed coffee made me practically drool. She pulled out two ceramic cups from the cabinet and asked me how I took mine. Normally, the answer would be black, but that day, as my stomach grumbled in pain, I asked for extra cream and sugar. Her eyes lingered on me, then she squatted and opened a bottom cupboard and pulled out a box of Little Debbie Oatmeal Creme Pies. "Can't very well have coffee without pastry." She stood and set the box on the counter. "Guess these will have to work."

It was all I could do to keep my eyes off those cakes and on her.

We sat down, and three oatmeal cremes and two cups of coffee later, she knew all about your father's welding accident, our empty cabinets, and even the fact I hadn't seen my parents in years. It felt so good to confide in another human being. It made the weight of my burdens feel lighter somehow.

With her dainty hands wrapped around her coffee mug, she shook her head with a look of pity. "My word, Penny Taylor, I feel like I've been reading the book of Job."

As much as your father hated the idea of charity, I think I hated pity more. In their own way, I imagine both of our responses were the sin of pride. "It sounds worse than it is."

She took a sip from the mug. "Believe it or not, I've been there. I married well, but believe you me, I grew up so poor my brother and me had to ride double on our stick horse."

My gaze moved up her French manicure to the dime-sized rock on her finger. I doubted she'd been within a hundred miles of where I'd walked, but I just smiled.

"You live in that little house covered in tar paper, as I recall."

I could barely look her in the eye. Was she wondering if we were too ignorant to know we were supposed to put siding over that stuff? Was she remembering the overgrown grass, the broken-down car in the yard, or the tractor tire circling around weeds like some kind of redneck planter?

"That's right," I whispered.

She looked off to the side with a hint of a smile playing on her glossy lips. "I'll bet you don't know this, but I stood outside your window for quite a while before knocking that first time I came by to bring you the cake and invitation."

A feeling of panic came over me as I wondered what she might have seen or heard. Trent had been home that day, so there was no telling. "Oh?"

"You were singing my daughter, Sara's, favorite song." She looked at me as if I should remember too, but I didn't. As awful as it was to learn she'd been listening to me squawking like a crow, it was far better than some other things she might have heard.

I stared at the dried brown drip on the side of my coffee cup, waiting for her to either continue or change the subject.

"You have a pretty voice." She cleared her throat.

I pushed my empty cup to the side and intertwined my fingers together atop the table just to give them something to do. "I'm guessing your hearing ain't what it used to be."

One thin eyebrow shot up. "Penny Taylor, are you suggesting I'm old?"

If my eyes were half as wide as they felt, I must have looked an awful lot like an owl right then. "I didn't mean that. I just meant I can't sing, is all. Please don't think —"

"Honey, you need to relax. Don't you think I know I've got enough wrinkles to hold a week's worth of rain?"

Other than a few fine lines around her mouth and eyes when she smiled, her skin was as smooth as mine. Realizing she was using the same self-deprecation on herself that I'd just used on me, I decided then I liked her. Despite the fact she had more class in her thumb knuckles than I had in my entire body, maybe she and I weren't all that different after all.

When I left there, I had three bags stuffed

full of groceries, two job offers, and one new friend.

Callie Mae carried one of those bags out to the car for me. The air outside was warmer than it should have been for that time of year, and it brought to mind Trent and the heat I would be in if I didn't produce a pack of cigarettes. The last thing in the world I wanted to do was to ask for one more thing from Callie Mae. She had already done so much.

"Now, Penny, you best be calling me tomorrow and telling me yes to one of those jobs we talked about. You tell your husband he has got to swallow that pride of his. It's not about just him anymore. He's got himself a wife to feed. If I were you —" she paused and looked over her shoulder like someone might be listening — "I would take the cleaning job. You don't want to work for Mr. Henry. He's a prickly old cactus. Believe you me, you want the job cleaning houses. I'm a good boss. It's not glamorous, but the work's steady, I pay on time, and you'll love Fatimah. She's who'd be training you." She put her hand over her heart, and it looked for a second she might cry. "Oh, and she will love you. She surely will. After all that poor girl's been through, she needs a friend, and I think maybe you do too."

I wanted to ask what Fatimah had been through, but if things went the way I hoped they would, I'd have time to find out for myself.

When she opened the passenger door, it creaked so loudly it made her jump. Laughing at herself, she propped the bag of groceries against the back of the seat, pausing to consider the wooden cross dangling from my rearview mirror. When Trent lost his eyesight, one of the first things I did was replace the Playboy bunny air freshener he had hanging there. Thank goodness I had. The embarrassment of Callie Mae seeing that nasty thing would have killed me for sure.

She closed the door and looked over the top of the car at me. "Now, if there is anything else I can do for you — anything at all — you let me know. I mean it, now."

I put my second bag in the backseat and shut the door. Flecks of rust rained down as it latched. "Callie Mae, you're an angel."

She wiped at her brow as she shot the sun a dirty look. "Better hold your judgment on that one. Anything, now. Hear me?"

I wrapped my fingers around the door handle so tightly my knuckles lost their color. "I guess maybe there is one thing." It was a horrible thing to ask. And of a woman of God, too. "My husband, he smokes. It's an awful addiction, I know. It's just . . ." My voice trailed off.

It made me nervous that I couldn't read her expression. She didn't look disgusted like I thought she would. Instead, her thin lips disappeared as she tried to read something in my eyes. "It's against our policy to give money, Penny. I'm sorry."

I tried to smile, but it just refused to come. "I understand." Wanting nothing more than to disappear, I opened the driver's door. "Thank you so much for everything. I'll call you tomorrow and give you my answer on the job after I discuss it with Trent."

"Oh, wait!" she exclaimed. "Don't go anywhere. I'll be right back."

I sat in the driver's seat and closed the door. The ignition turned over on the first try, which was unheard of for Old Sally, as Trent liked to call our car. She almost always took at least three turns before rattling to life. I watched the thermostat creep up as the car idled. The temptation to drive off and never have to face Callie Mae again was overwhelming, but of course, I couldn't do that. Not after how nice she'd been to me.

After a minute, she came out carrying an

oversize canvas purse. She walked over, leaned it on my open window rim, and unzipped it. I hated myself so much right then. I didn't just feel like a beggar, I felt like one of those bums you hated giving money to because you just knew they would only blow it on drugs or booze.

She reached into her bag and pulled out a green and white soft pack of Salems. Shocked into silence, I just stared at her.

It was she now who couldn't make eye contact. "Don't you dare go telling anyone I smoke. The last thing in this world I need is another well-intended lecture on what these things make the inside of my lungs look like. I was planning on quitting again tomorrow, anyway. I'll just do it today."

Not knowing what else to do, I took the cigarettes from her hand. This pack was not only missing a few, and not your father's brand, they were menthol. He hated menthol. But I didn't want to hurt her feelings, and beggars couldn't really be choosers. "I don't know what to say. Thank you, Callie Mae."

She waved me away. "Don't mention it. And I mean that literally. You had best not show up to church on Sunday thanking me for those things, neither, understand?"

The look on her face tickled me. "No,

ma'am. I wouldn't think of it." It felt almost as good to laugh as it had to eat. I guess I'd been starving for both.

As I drove off, leaving an oil stain behind me, I caught a glimpse of my smile in the rearview, and at that moment, I remembered how life was supposed to feel.

Seven

I found Trent in the same spot I had left him — in front of the TV. The only difference was now he was lying down instead of sitting. He had the couch pillow doubled under his head and the avocado-and-brown afghan wrapped around him like it wasn't eighty degrees outside.

With my arms still full of groceries, I started to ask what he was watching, but caught myself just in time. Instead I said, "What are you listening to?"

With a sigh, he pushed the cover down to his waist, revealing a shred of green yarn stuck to his chest hair. "Stupid news. Nothing good ever happens to nobody. Ever."

I wanted to blurt out that simply wasn't true. Lots of good stuff happened in the world — just today, in fact, to us — but I couldn't show my hand too early, not if I was going to get to take the job that would keep food on our table. First, I needed to butter him up good. "I'm going to make salmon cakes for supper." My hand was starting to hurt where the plastic handles of grocery bags had twisted around my knuckles.

He turned in my direction. "Don't toy with me, woman."

All nerves, I faked a laugh. "With fried potatoes and pole beans. If that's all right with you."

The look on his face was priceless. It must have been the same one I wore when Callie Mae pulled out those oatmeal cremes and offered me one.

After walking the bags to the kitchen and setting them down on the counter, I rubbed at the indents they had left on my palm and returned to your father.

I hadn't shaved him in two days, so his facial hair was starting to sprout up in spotty patches along his jaw. Something about the way he looked past the television at the wall behind it with his hair all spiked up every which way made my heart skip. Despite everything he had put me through, I loved your father. And now I was going to have a baby. His baby.

I walked over and bent down to where he lay. When my lips brushed his scruffy cheek, he turned to give me his lips. It had been so long since he'd done that, I had forgotten how soft they could be.

He smelled like cigarettes, which was interesting because he had run out of them the day before. He threw the afghan off and sat up. His pajamas pants, which I could have sworn had been on right when I'd left, were now inside out.

Jealousy rushed through me, making my face feel hot enough to melt. Crossing my arms, I was glad he couldn't see me. "Where did you get the cigarettes?"

Judging by the pinched look on his face, I gathered my question irritated him. "I picked through the butts in the ashtray like a hobo. Where do you think I got them?"

I chewed my bottom lip, trying to decide if he might be telling the truth. It made me crazy that every time he opened his mouth, I started second-guessing myself, but there I was trying to remember if I'd left the ashtray empty or full, and if maybe his pants hadn't been on right when I left. "You didn't find a pack somewhere?" Calling his bluff never worked, but that didn't keep me from trying on a regular basis.

He huffed. "What are we, the Rockefellers, with money and stogies hidden all over our fancy mansion? Dag, One Cent, use your brain for something other than keeping your skull from caving in."

"Your pants are inside out," I said coldly.

He looked down as if he could see for himself. "Then you must have handed them to me that way this morning."

I was pretty sure I hadn't, but the only way that crow would have known to come over was if Trent had called her, and even then they couldn't have known how long I'd be gone. Still, as usual, a shadow of a doubt lingered.

He bent his head back and scratched at his Adam's apple. "Speaking of smokes, tell me you remembered to pick me up some."

"Yes, baby." I tried to lace my words with honey to counteract the bitterness he was sure to feel.

The familiar crease formed between his eyebrows. "You being smart again?"

"Stop assuming the worst of me. I'm talking sweet. You used to like it when I did that." I headed back to the kitchen.

If he responded, it must have been under his breath, because I didn't hear it. I went to work putting away the food Callie Mae had loaded me up with. All the meat and vegetables were canned, other than the bag of pole beans a local farmer had dropped off that morning, but I certainly wasn't complaining.

I was elbow deep in the second bag of groceries when I heard something hit the floor. I ran into the living room to see Trent standing in the middle of the room and the end table turned on its side. His knees were bent as he groped the air. He looked lost and scared.

I rushed over and put my hand on his arm. "What happened? Are you okay?"

He grabbed my hand and pulled me tight against his chest. At first, I tried to wriggle away, until I heard a whimper. I didn't know how to respond to his crying. He'd never shown that sort of weakness in front of me. Patting his back, I kept telling him it was going to be okay.

"I was coming to get my Winstons from you, but I can't see nothing, Penny. I can't do anything but sit on that stinking couch, wondering what those voices inside the TV must be doing. The screen is black and it's always going to be black. This is no kind of life." He wiped his wet face against his bare shoulder and held my arm the way I'd been trying to get him to do since he got home from the hospital. "You don't got anything to drink in those bags you're crinkling around in there, do you?"

By drink, I knew he meant booze, but of course Sheckle Baptist was not about to hand out whiskey chasers along with instant mashed potatoes. "No, but I got you cigarettes."

His face relaxed as I led him by the arm to the kitchen and planted him near the fridge. He patted the wall, then leaned against it. I walked over to my purse. My heart pounded away as I retrieved Callie Mae's Salems.

I gathered up his hand from his side and set the pack in his palm.

He squeezed along the top of the pack, stopping to feel the exposed filters, and made a face. "You smoke a few?"

I went back to putting groceries away, keeping a watchful eye on him from my periphery. "No, of course not. They gave them to me for free since the pack had been opened."

You would have sworn he could see me by the daggers he shot my way. "What are you talking about?"

I set a can of store-brand tuna in the cabinet, trying to sound casual. "We didn't have enough money at the register and I was going to put back the —" I hesitated as I looked in the grocery bag — "bag of rice, but the check-out lady pulled out a pack of Salems from under the register and said she couldn't sell them, but I could have them if

I wanted."

"Salems are menthol," Trent said, his face all twisted in confusion.

"I know, but they were free."

He had the weirdest look on his face as he felt his way to the kitchen table and sat down. "You mind grabbing my lighter? I left it in the bedroom next to the ashtray."

"Sure, baby," I said, relieved he'd bought my story and didn't seem mad. I went to the bedroom and found a bunch of cigarette butts smoked down to the filter lying in and around the dirty ashtray. It turned out he hadn't been lying after all, and I was doubly relieved for that.

I brought him his lighter and figured now was as good a time as any to tell him about you. "Maybe you should smoke that on the porch."

He tapped a cigarette out of the pack, slid it between his lips, and spoke around it. "Just light the thing, One Cent. It's my house. I'll smoke where I like."

I held out the lighter but stopped short of running my thumb over the steel roller to ignite it. "Secondhand smoke's bad for the baby."

"What baby?"

I set a hand on his cheek. "I'm pregnant." It felt so good to tell him and so scary at the same time.

The cigarette dropped from his mouth.

I sat down at the table beside him. "Say something."

"Are you sure?" he choked out.

"We can't afford to go to the doctor to get a second opinion, but the pregnancy test says yes, and so does my body. Yeah, I'm sure."

When he grinned at me, I let myself breathe. "Are you serious? We're having a baby?"

I laughed. "Yes, a baby. A baby!"

His hands were shaking when he picked the cigarette off his lap and put it back in his mouth. "You need to light it now, Penny. I'll start smoking outside after this. Promise."

I lit his cigarette and watched him wince at the taste he wasn't accustomed to. He took another drag. "Well, don't this beat all." His smile suddenly faded, and I knew it hit him then that he was blind and we were broke.

"I know what you're thinking," I said, "but it's going to be okay. Don't worry."

He exhaled a plume of white. "I can't even support us. How am I going to —"

I turned my head to keep from breathing in the smoke. "God will provide."

"Like he provided that pipe full of gasoline that left me blind? No offense, but I think we might need a plan B."

There was no arguing God with that man. He didn't believe in anything he couldn't control.

"I was offered a job cleaning houses today."

Before I even got all the words out, he was shaking his head.

"Now don't start. I'm not going to stand by and let my husband and baby die because of your pride."

One hand held the cigarette, the other balled into a fist and pounded the table, sending vibrations through me. I pushed my chair back, fixing to get away from him, but the look on his face told me I wasn't in danger of anything but feeling sorry for him. This time when he cried, he hid his face from me.

"I hate being blind," he finally said as he swiped the heels of his hands across his eyes.

"I hate it for you," I said, but it was just another lie. I was beginning to see what he could not — his blindness was turning out to be the best thing that had ever happened to us.

Eight

I don't know if it was all in my head, but it seemed like the minute I found out I was pregnant, the nausea started. Wanting to make a good impression on my first day of my first-ever job, I woke up early, intending to make up my face and put a few curls in my hair, but I spent most of the hour leaning over the toilet.

Every time I retched, your father gagged in response. "Dagnabbit, Penny," he yelled from the living room, "keep it up and you're going to make me puke too."

"I'm not doing it on purpose," I called back as I cupped my hand and filled it with water from the faucet. It tasted so sweet compared to the bile I rinsed away. After a couple of swish-and-spits, I grabbed my toothbrush from the holder, wet it, and dipped it into the baking soda we were brushing our teeth with.

I don't know if it was that paste or the

bristles against my tongue that got my stomach trying to turn itself inside out again, but somehow I managed to keep myself from starting the heave cycle all over.

I left your father sitting at the kitchen table looking miserable. He wouldn't even acknowledge my good-bye, but I was too excited to care. I had a job, Manny! That might not seem like such a joyous thing to most, but to me, it meant release from a very long sentence of house arrest.

Twenty minutes and two wrong turns later, I'd finally found my way to the address Callie Mae had given me and pulled up in front of a large stone home on a Mercedes-lined cul-de-sac. When I rang the doorbell, the door flew open and Fatimah Wek, the Sudanese woman Callie Mae had put in charge of training me, waved me in.

"You are late," she said, adding an annoyed tongue click for good measure. Although she wore her hair cut tight around her head like a boy's, there was nothing else boyish about her. She had the most magnificent features, strong but feminine. With her long face, wide brown eyes, and the highest cheekbones I'd ever seen, she looked like an African princess.

"You stare at me." She set her caddy of cleaning supplies by her feet. "I am dark.

You never see a woman so dark. True?"

I opened my mouth to say that wasn't true, but it was.

"My husband is not so dark. My family were not so dark. I am blackest in my family, even my village. Even the refuge camp."

"Your skin's beautiful," I managed through my embarrassment.

She looked down at the ground. "Beauty is inside." She glanced at me. "What of you? Are you beautiful?"

I blushed, but said nothing.

She pulled two sponges out of the caddy and handed me one. "You clean counters, sink. I sweep and mop floor." She studied me to make sure I understood.

"Why do you get the good jobs?" I asked with a wink in my voice. It felt good to joke. I learned early on with Trent that ribbing, taken the wrong way, could have painful consequences, but something about Fatimah made me feel safe.

"I give you the good job!" She looked really put out by my teasing, until she registered my smile. Deep and full, her laugh was so contagious, I couldn't help but laugh too.

"You play with me. Good. I like to play too."

When I lifted an empty wine bottle from

the counter, she grabbed my hand. "We do not take up mess. We clean, but we do not tidy. Truth."

I was confused. "Picking up trash is part of cleaning."

She let go of me and shook her head. "No, they take up. We clean. You take that up today, tomorrow we must only take up more." Although I'm sure she didn't intend it, her words held a double meaning I still remind myself of to this day.

She eyed the room, sizing it up. "We have only two hour to clean this giant house."

I followed her gaze. Oak cabinets stopped about ten feet short of cathedral ceilings. White leather stools sat in front of an enormous, brushed-steel island. The floor was a larger version of the turquoise counter tiles. My entire house could fit inside this kitchen. I wondered what profession paid enough to afford a home like this.

Side by side, Fatimah and I worked, scrubbing floors and toilets, counters, and appliances. Before I knew it, we were done and she was packing up our supplies for the next job.

She insisted we ride together to the next house to save on gas, and in my financial situation, I wasn't about to argue. I sat beside her in her old Chrysler LeBaron, trying to name the spice the car reeked of. The fabric roof was held up with pushpins every inch or so, giving it a coffin-liner appearance. The console on my side was torn, offering a clear view of the yellow foam under the hard plastic. As she drove, she threw me a glance. "I make purchase of this car for two hundred dollar."

Not knowing what to say, I nodded.

She thrust two fingers at me. "Two hundred dollar. Imagine!"

I wasn't sure if she thought that was expensive or cheap. So I went with a generic, "Wow."

"Two hundred dollar would feed my village." The look she gave me told me I should find the humor in that, but I didn't get it. "I almost forget." She leaned over, opened the glove box, pulled out a rectangular piece of paper, and handed it to me. "Callie says it is advance. You will get the other portion in two weeks."

I looked down at the check made out to me and almost cried in relief. This was half of what she'd promised to pay bimonthly. It touched me that she trusted I wouldn't just take the money and run. It was a good reminder that not everyone was as cynical as Trent.

I folded the check, slipped it into my back

pocket, and picked at the hole in the knee of my jeans. "Was it hard living there — at the refugee camp, I mean?"

She sighed. "I make many friends who became my family, but I still missed my own. My sisters and brother. They are mostly gone except my father, who I am dead to, and only one sister. She is married to . . ." Her shoulders shimmied and her lips puckered like she tasted something bitter. I took it she wasn't a fan of her brother-in-law. "I tried to buy her here, but I won't buy for him, too. He is one of the men who . . ." She couldn't finish, and by the haunted look in her eyes, I wasn't sure I wanted her to.

She jerked the steering wheel hard and fast as if remembering her turn a second too late. I slapped my palm against the door just in time to prevent the side of my head from hitting the window. We nearly took out a buzzard pecking at roadkill as we screeched around the bend. The bird shrieked, stretched out its enormous wings, and flew away from the flattened fur in the nick of time. My stomach, which had settled since that morning, started to roil again. I took a deep breath and focused on the road ahead.

A wave of warmth rushed through me and

I pulled at my shirt collar. Hot air streamed from the dashboard vents. I rolled down my window and let the spring air hit my face. "You don't like your sister's husband."

"Yes, I do. I like him very much — in a pot of stew." This got her laughing. "With potatoes and carrots," she added.

For all I knew about the world back then, they really might have been cannibals in Sudan. She must have seen the uncertainty on my face because she pulled in front of a house half the size of the first, shut off the engine, and bared her teeth. "I eat you, too!" When she chomped in my direction, I jumped in my seat.

This got her to laughing again. "We eat cows and vegetables, not white people. Do not worry."

"What about squirrel?" I asked.

"A squirrel is a rat. So, yes, I would eat one."

We both chuckled at that one, though I still didn't understand her humor enough to know if she did eat squirrel and rat, or didn't. It didn't much matter to me what she ate, where she was from, or how she mispronounced my name, I liked her. Staring at her beautiful profile, I smiled. Callie Mae was exactly right.

I sighed in contentment. *Now I have two*

friends, I thought with a lightness in my heart. *Two friends, a husband who hasn't hit me in weeks, a job, a little money, and a baby on the way.* Just when I thought my life would never be anything but misery, everything had changed.

Nine

Callie Mae met Fatimah and me at Mountain Man Deli for what she called a working lunch. I hadn't been out to eat in eight years, and that was only if you counted the fast-food lunches your father would occasionally treat me to in our early days. Callie Mae insisted the meal was on her, and it's not like Trent would even know, since it was during the workday. But still I couldn't shake the feeling I was doing something wrong by being there.

The place was noisy with chatter, clanging silverware, and plates slapped down by rushed servers. It smelled of baking bread, dill, and raw onion, which didn't help my morning sickness in the least. It was odd to feel both ravenously hungry and sick to my stomach all at the same time, but I refused to complain. For you, Manny, I would have lived my whole life leaning over the toilet. You were worth every saltine and ginger ale

I had to choke down.

I was so anxious to share the good news about you with my new friends, but afraid at the same time it might cost me the job Trent and I so desperately needed. Callie Mae seemed to be in a good mood, but your father had taught me well that a smile could change on a dime, so I decided to wait and feel her out.

Callie Mae wore her thin, blonde hair pulled up in a clip, making her seem ten years younger than I would have guessed at the food bank. Her fine features made her look as delicate as a china doll, but I would soon discover the woman was anything but fragile.

The waiter set down our sandwiches and asked if we needed anything else. Callie Mae wanted a refill on her iced tea and Fatimah asked for extra napkins. I eyed the brown mustard on the booth behind us, but as usual, said nothing.

Callie Mae must have seen me looking because she scooted out, grabbed the bottle, and set it in front of me, then retook her seat. It was such a simple act, but it made me feel like such a loser that she found it easy to take what she wanted when I couldn't. I was so busy feeling sorry for myself I didn't hear Fatimah speaking to me.

"Peeny, where are you?" she asked.

Jolted out of my thoughts, I was surprised to find both women staring at me expectantly. "What?" I asked, confused.

A group of businessmen passed by us, and when I looked up at them, the oldest winked at me in a way that made me uncomfortable. Without responding, I turned back to my lunch dates.

"I'll get this one," Callie Mae said. "You get the next."

I thought she meant the check. When she grabbed my hand in one of hers, and Fatimah's in the other, I was relieved to find she was talking about the one thing I could actually afford — grace.

"Lord, thank you for bringing these beautiful ladies into my life. Bless this food to our bodies and this fellowship to our souls."

Her prayer made me want to cry. As far as I knew, no one had ever thanked God for me before. After we added our amens to hers, Callie Mae picked the top bun off her turkey sandwich and scraped off the hot peppers with a butter knife. She let them plop to a slimy mess on her plate beside her potato chips.

My stomach roiled. "Why did you ask for

them if you're just going to take them off?"

She gave me a librarian stare. "You sound like my late husband. For your information, I like a hint of peppers in my mayonnaise. Is that all right with you?"

"I . . . no . . . it's okay. I was just curious." *Great,* I thought, *I've offended her already.* Eating at me was the same feeling as when I'd earned Trent's disapproval.

The way Callie Mae squinted at me made me feel exposed. I turned away, but still managed to see her and Fatimah share a private look. Trying to deflect the weakness they had just discovered in me, I threw out a joke. "Didn't your mama ever tell you there are starving children in Af—" My eyes must have become the size of plates when I realized what I was about to say. I jerked my head toward Fatimah, who sat beside me. Unaware, she ate potato chips as she watched a baby throw his sippy cup onto the floor.

Callie Mae touched my arm, making me jump. "Penny, it's okay. Calm down. You're with friends." The way she looked at me with that sweet expression touched me to my soul, and I knew she was right. I was with friends. I was safe. Still, my face was hot with embarrassment. "That was a stupid thing to say."

With a raised hand, she summoned our waiter back to the table. "Excuse me, young man, do you think you could find me an envelope?"

He gave her a tired look, but left and returned a few minutes later with one of the long, check-holding kind. "Will this do?"

"You don't happen to have one that's insulated with dry ice, do you?"

He slowly shook his head with a weary expression. "Sorry, all out. Anything else?"

"That's it. Thank you very much," Callie Mae said.

He set the envelope down on the edge of the table. When he left, she picked the peppers off her plate and dropped them, mayonnaise and all, into that envelope. The liquid bled right through, making an oil stain on the front. She peeled back the flap, gave it a lick, and sealed it up. "Fatimah, what's the address for Africa?"

Fatimah turned around, looked at the envelope, then at Callie Mae. "For the last time, woman, we do not want your scraps." A crumb of potato chip clung to the corner of her mouth, moving up and down as she spoke until she brushed it away.

I sat, stunned, looking back and forth between the two of them.

Fatimah took a sip from her drink, then

looked at me. "She tells me mothers here tell their children to finish everything on their plate because there are starving children in Africa. There are hungry children here too, true?"

Callie Mae sighed. "You couldn't tell my father that. When I was growing up, he was forever chiding me at dinnertime about those starving children in Africa." She rolled her eyes. "As if that would encourage me to gluttony. One day, I couldn't finish the five pounds of meatloaf my mother heaped onto my plate, so I put my leftovers in an envelope and asked him for Africa's address."

"What did he say?" I asked.

"He gave me a tail whooping I'll never forget and sent me to bed."

I pictured a little blonde Callie Mae with pigtails, alone on her bed crying her eyes out. "That's terrible. He thought you were being a smart aleck."

"I was."

Fatimah clicked her tongue. "You were a terrible child. He was a wise man to give you the rod. Being hungry is not joke."

Callie Mae's smile faded. "No, it's not. But how is a chubby American girl being forced to overeat affecting anyone in Africa or anywhere else for that matter? Every time I opened my mouth to ask a question or speak my mind, my folks shoved food down my throat to shut me up."

It was clear then that Callie Mae was more than just the church lady with the smart clothes and well-to-do late husband. She had her scars just like the rest of us. I wondered what others she bore and if we'd be friends long enough for me to find them all out. I hoped so.

In one fluid motion, Fatimah ripped open the short end of the envelope and dumped the hot peppers onto her roast-beef sandwich. "On behalf of the great people of Africa, we thank you for your contribution. Feel better?"

I choked on my salami sandwich.

"Are you all right?" Callie Mae asked.

I took a sip of root beer and nodded.

"You know," Callie Mae said, looking at Fatimah, "I liked you better when you didn't have a bun in the oven. You used to be a lot more fun."

Fatimah clicked her tongue again and waved her hand like she was trying to shoo away a fly.

"You're pregnant?" I asked, surprised.

Fatimah gave her flat belly a rub. "Two months tomorrow."

"How could you not know?" Callie Mae asked, scooping up bits of shredded lettuce and tomato off her plate and putting them back onto her sandwich. "Jiminy Crickets, that's all the woman talks about."

I turned to Fatimah. "You didn't say anything to me."

Fatimah shrugged like the conversation bored her and swallowed what was in her mouth. "I have baby, yes. We had other things to talk about, true?"

"That's why I wanted this meeting." Callie Mae picked up the napkin from her lap and wiped her hands across it. "I was going to split you two back up after Penny's training, but I think until Fatimah has her baby, I might keep you as a team. I'd rather not have her working with certain chemicals like bleach or ammonia if we can help it. And since Penny is now with us, we can."

As soon as she said it, I could almost smell the ammonia burning my nose. I hadn't even considered that cleaning houses could be dangerous for you, Manny. It scared me to think of all the damage I could do to you just by being ignorant. "Do they hurt the baby?"

Fatimah blurted with her mouth full of bread, "Pftt! She worries too much. She thinks sneezing hurts the baby."

Callie Mae raised an eyebrow. "Keep it up and I'm going to hurt *you.*"

The sight of that mush in her mouth hit me right in the gut, and what little I had eaten started to push back up my throat. "I have to get up. Now." The look on my face must have told Fatimah I meant business, because she jumped out of that booth so fast she almost fell onto the floor.

I ran to the bathroom, making it just in time.

After relieving my stomach of what little I'd eaten, I rinsed out my mouth and looked at myself in the mirror. My skin, which had been clear even in puberty, was now breaking out in small pimples around the bridge of my nose. I wasn't sure if it was the fluorescent light or if my skin really was taking on a greenish hue, but at least I felt better now, even if I did look awful.

When I was younger, I remember stuffing a pillow under my shirt and examining my profile to see how I might look pregnant, as if the only thing about my appearance that would change would be the shape of my stomach. Boy, was I unprepared for reality.

I made my way back to the booth to explain, but the smiles both women wore told me they already knew.

"You are with child too, Peeny?" Fatimah asked with a silly grin.

"What?" Unsuccessfully trying to play coy,

I was unable to force down my own smile.

"She is!" Callie Mae exclaimed, slamming her drink down on the table, adding emphasis to her exclamation. "Well, I'll be. Fatimah said she thought you might be, but I didn't believe her."

Fatimah slid out and let me back into my seat. "You see? I am never wrong."

"Except when you are," Callie Mae said.

"How did you know?" My stomach was flat, and it's not like I was going around wearing a T-shirt with the word *baby* and a down arrow.

Fatimah held the round end of the spoon to her face and bared her teeth, I assumed checking for poppy seeds. After running her tongue across her mouth, she set the spoon back on her plate. "You have a girl inside you. She is stealing your beauty."

The smile left my face when my brain caught up with her mouth.

Callie Mae gave Fatimah's hand a motherly slap. "Now don't you say that, Fati. She's beautiful." She squeezed my hand. "You're beautiful, Penny. Don't you listen to her."

I wanted to crawl under the table. "No, it's okay. I know I've looked better." I just didn't know how Fatimah could know that, having just met me. For all she knew, I never had any beauty to steal.

"I told Callie you have a fat pimple face," Fatimah added, unaffected by Callie Mae's reprimand or my frown. She took a gulp of sweet tea and spoke between crunches of ice. "I have a boy. See, my skin is still very good." She touched her cheek as if to prove her point.

Once I got my mind off my hideousness, I began to wonder if what she said about a girl stealing her mother's beauty had any basis in truth, or if it was just an old Sudanese wives' tale. It seemed I might have heard the same thing once from one of my mother's friends. I certainly didn't like the idea of my daughter stealing my beauty, but the thought of a baby girl was kind of nice.

While Fatimah and Callie Mae chatted, Manny, I had a dozen pink dresses, ruffled rubber pants, and patent leather shoes picked out for you in my mind. I was picturing a cherub-faced little girl with ringlets and pink bows, and regardless of your sex, I fell more and more in love with you.

In her delicate, Southern way, Callie Mae put her manicured fingertips in front of her face to hide her full mouth. "So, Penny, do you know when you're due?"

I broke off a piece of french fry I wasn't sure if I was brave enough to eat. "I think sometime in January."

"My Sara was a New Year's baby. Who's your OB?" she asked.

Not having the slightest clue what she was talking about, I shrugged, feeling as stupid as I probably looked.

Ironically, it was Fatimah who translated. "She asks to know who is your doctor."

My face must have turned scarlet as I looked down at my plate.

"Ha-ha, she has same doctor as me!" Fatimah shouted, then bellowed that deep laugh of hers, bringing way too much attention to our table.

Callie Mae's lips disappeared into a thin line. "Don't encourage stupidity. She needs a doctor."

Fatimah snapped off a bite of pickle. "I be your doctor, Penny. I deliver a hundred babies in my village. Maybe more."

"Really?" I asked, surprised. "You know how to do that?"

Callie Mae shook her head. "This isn't the boondocks, ladies. We do have hospitals here."

Fatimah shrugged as if she couldn't care less what anyone thought. I wanted so badly to have that kind of confidence.

Callie Mae set down what was left of her sandwich. "And how many of those babies died, Doctor Fati?"

Fatimah huffed. "I lost only three babies in two years."

Callie Mae nodded. "Oh, only three?" She turned to me. "And, Penny, you're willing to risk your child's life? Ninety-seven percent odds good enough for you?"

My head was spinning with numbers and options. "I don't have health insurance." I didn't like the idea of taking any kind of chance with your life, of course, but my options seemed limited. Fatimah at least knew what she was doing, which was better than leaving myself in Trent's hands. He'd never delivered anything other than a litter of kittens and a stillborn calf.

Sitting back, Callie Mae crossed her arms. "And how many of the mothers did you lose, hmm?"

"Only two," Callie Mae said proudly. "One from blood. One from the infection." She looked to the side and twisted her mouth as though the memory tasted bad. "Her husband would not wait like I told him to. He was a filthy hog."

It took me a second to get what she was saying. "That's disgusting," I finally said. I stirred the straw around my soda, looking at it instead of them. "How long do you have to wait?" There was so much I didn't know about taking care of you, Manny, and it terrified me.

"A month at least." Fatimah used her fingers this time to pluck out another ice cube from her glass. "Two is better." She popped the cube into her mouth and crunched away.

Callie Mae raised her hand in the waiter's direction and mouthed she was ready for the check before turning back to us. "You're both going to the clinic right after we leave here. My cousin is the office manager. I'll ask her to fit you in. They work on a sliding scale, so it shouldn't cost much at all. I'll ask Michelle to clean your last house, which frees up the afternoon."

"You will not give my work away. That is food from my mouth!" Fatimah said.

Callie Mae wagged a finger at her. "Yes, I certainly will, Miss Thing. You'll just have to take one of her houses tomorrow."

Fatimah huffed and mumbled something in her native language that didn't sound very nice.

The tension made my stomach tight, but Callie Mae was content enough with the outcome to eat the last few bites of her sandwich. "You may get to see the baby on the ultrasound we talked about." She wasn't looking at either one of us, but since I knew she hadn't talked to me about any ultrasound, I figured she must be speaking to Fatimah.

"I will see the baby?" Fatimah grinned. "Seeing a baby inside his mother. Imagine!"

"I thought they didn't do that until you were further along," I said.

Callie Mae gave me a look that made it clear I was to shush.

Picking up the check the waiter had set down, she threw me a glance. "And you, Penny, should get to hear your baby's heartbeat."

I smiled, overjoyed with the fact I was going to be seeing a doctor and even more that I might actually hear your heart beating. "I want to see the doctor," I said, hoping I didn't make Fatimah mad. "I want to do everything I can for her — or him."

"I know you do," Callie Mae said. "And you will."

Ten

The doctor squeezed in a quick visit with me for Callie Mae's sake in exchange for a promise I would set up an appointment for a full workup before I left. Fatimah got cold feet at the last minute and, despite Callie Mae's threats and pleading, insisted she could and would doctor herself just fine. When she plugged a finger in each ear and started making a loud whooping sound, Callie Mae got embarrassed enough to let it go.

The doctor squirted cold jelly on my stomach and kept sliding what she called a Doppler farther and farther down until I blushed; then she slid it back up, stopped several inches below my belly button, and smiled at the steady *whoosh-whoosh* sound she located. "That's the baby's heartbeat."

I closed my eyes and listened. I couldn't believe that was your little heart beating inside of me. It made it all so real, so wonderful, and so scary.

All I could think of as I drove home to Trent was that we were going to have a Christmas baby! Of course we both know now it didn't work out quite that way. I drove home to your father, wanting to get there as fast as I could. It seemed like that fifteen-minute ride was two hours long. Finally, I pulled into the driveway. Carrying a glossy black-and-white picture of a blob the doctor assured me was you, I raced toward the house.

When I opened the door, I knew right away he was drunk. There he sat, as usual, slouching on the couch with his eyes drooping into those telltale slits. The television was blaring, and there were half a dozen crushed beer cans at his feet, along with an empty whiskey bottle.

The last thing I would have done is left that man alone with hard alcohol, so I knew one of his buddies or girlfriends had been over to supply him.

His hair stuck straight up like a lunatic's, and his white T-shirt had a mustard stain smeared across the shoulder like he had wiped his mouth on it, which, knowing him, he probably had.

With one arm draped over the back of the couch, he turned toward the door and belched. It was all I could do not to run to the bathroom and get sick again.

"Well, well, Mrs. Taylor. You finally decided to carry yourself home," he slurred in my direction.

I could smell the booze and cigarette smoke clear across the room. So much for not smoking in the house. The good news about your due date would have to wait until I had time to assess his mood. Trent could be a mean drunk just as soon as a friendly one. Only time and conversation would tell which way the wind blew that day.

"I see you've been busy." I made my way to the beer cans and started plucking them off the floor. When I picked up that glass whiskey bottle, I'm not proud to admit it, but the thought of smashing him over the head with it did cross my mind.

He wiped his forearm across his mouth. "You don't have a pair of lips for your loving husband?"

I exhaled. Happy drunk today. *Thank you, Jesus.* "Hi, baby." With my hands full of cans, I leaned down. Holding my breath, I kissed his scruffy cheek. He'd had so much to drink he was actually sweating alcohol. I wanted to fuss at him and tell him every six-pack he slammed down was a pack of diapers we could have bought. But he was happy, and so I was going to pretend to be happy too. Nothing mattered now except you, Manny. Over the following months it would be a constant battle to remember that around your father.

"I'm so hungry I could eat the butt end of a hobby horse," he said, making the whole sentence sound like one long word.

I took the cans and bottle to the kitchen and let them clank down into an already-full trash can. I knew Trent couldn't see, but the garbage can was right outside the back door. Surely if he could feel his way to the fridge to get a beer, he could find his way out there to empty the trash. How badly I wanted to say his loss of vision was not an excuse to lie around the house and do nothing. Why was it when he had worked I was expected to have the house clean and dinner made, but now that the shoe was on the other foot, he couldn't even be bothered to pick up his own filth?

"What are we having?" He pointed the remote at the TV, let out another belch, and kicked his feet onto the cocktail table.

You don't know how much I wanted to leave right then. Let him worry about his own stinking dinner and deal with the cockroaches sure to take over the place if I wasn't there to clean. But what kind of woman would leave her blind husband?

Rummaging through the cabinets, I eyed the stack of dirty dishes in the sink and called back to him. "What do you feel like?"

Something slid across my waist and I screamed. I hadn't heard him come into the kitchen, but there he was, puffing his beer breath onto my neck. Apparently, he was getting around the house on his own pretty good. Just not enough to find his way to the trash can or kitchen sink.

"Dag, One Cent, why are you hollering? You tryin' to wake the dead?"

Stumbling backward, he grabbed onto my shoulder for support. The weight of him almost knocked me over. I hadn't realized my nausea had subsided until it came back.

"I was just coming in here to tell you I know what I'm in the mood for." He leaned in to kiss me, but I turned so he caught my ear. This didn't deter him one bit. He just started grabbing at me.

Just coming from the doctor, I was in no mood to be groped. "Baby, leave me be so I can fix you some supper."

The familiar crease had found its way between his thick eyebrows, which told me a rant was finding its way to his lips. I backed away.

"This job of yours has got you so high-and-mighty now you don't even want your own man. What, are you turning gay now?"

I sighed and grabbed the washcloth off the faucet. "Come on, don't start. I love you. I don't want no one but you." *No one, including you,* I thought. "I'm just tired, is all."

He slapped the air, maybe intending to hit me, maybe not. He was too drunk and sloppy for me to tell which. "If this job is going to make you too tired to —"

"It's not the job making me tired. It's your baby growing inside of me."

"So now it's my fault?"

I wet the rag and wrung it, then wiped the counter crumbs into the sink. While he stumbled back into the counter, trying to play it off like he meant to lean there instead of fall, I walked over to the freezer and yanked out a pack of hot dogs. If he wanted something better, let him cook it himself. "I saw a doctor today."

"We got a money tree growing out back now?"

I had gotten good at rolling my eyes, now that he couldn't see me. I wondered if he would like me asking that same question about his eye doctor's visits if his job wasn't picking up the tab.

I slapped the hot dogs on the counter and grabbed a knife out of the drawer. "It only cost me five dollars. They work on a sliding scale. Since I don't make much, they don't charge much." On the way home I'd prepared myself in case he started on the "Taylors ain't no charity case" thing again. The way I figured it, a sliding scale arrangement wasn't charity. It was just an even playing field for a change. I was prepared to put my foot down if he tried to insist I couldn't go back, but my fears turned out to be unfounded.

"What did he say? It's a boy, ain't it?" Your father's ignorance didn't seem to bother me when I wasn't pregnant, but now that I was, it plucked my last nerve.

Pressing the tip of the knife through plastic, I worked four hot dogs away from the others. "They can't tell until I'm further along."

"What'd they tell you? Is he okay? Are *you* okay?"

Something told me to look at him, and I did. The expression on his face knocked the chip right off my shoulder. He cared if you were okay. Even more surprising, he cared if I was.

I went to him and told him all about what I saw on the ultrasound. The blob I thought was you, but turned out to be just my bladder, your strong little heartbeat, and saving the best for last, I asked him if he wanted to sit down for the most exciting news of all.

"Twins?" he asked wide eyed as I led him to the table and pulled out a chair.

I laughed. "No, thank goodness." I waited for him to sit. "I'm further along than we thought. She's due on Christmas day."

His mouth dropped open. "He is?"

I stood there in silence a moment as I let him collect his thoughts.

Finally, he snapped out of whatever place in his mind he'd been visiting and shook his head. "Christmas day? This is a sign, Penny."

"A sign of what?" I sat beside him, giving him my full attention.

His words were still slurred, but even so, there seemed to be a soberness about him I hadn't seen in years. He pulled his pack of cigarettes from his shirt pocket, then realized what he was doing and put it away again. "I've been thinking today that maybe God striking me blind was his way of punishing me for the way I've been treating you." He paused. "And I told God I was sorry." He gently squeezed my hand. "I meant it, too. And now I find out we're having a baby, and on Christmas day?"

He shook his head at the ceiling. "Don't

you get it? This is God's gift to me. His reward."

I'd never heard your father talk about God except to complain about all the things he thought God should be doing for him, but wasn't. I had no earthly idea if any of this was a gift to Trent, but it was definitely one to me. I'd been praying for your father's soul since the day I'd married him, and I had begun to give up hope. It was so overwhelming, I began to cry.

Trent wrapped his arms around me and kissed my tears in a way I'd only seen men do in movies. *Whose life is this?* I wondered as he kissed my face and promised that, from this day forward, he was going to be the man I deserved.

Eleven

The next morning, I awoke feeling like I hadn't slept in weeks. After showering and throwing my damp hair into a ponytail, I dragged myself to the kitchen to fix Trent's lunch so he would have something to eat when I was at work. To my astonishment, he was already up making breakfast. The smell of coffee and frying eggs hung in the air.

With the spatula in one hand, he turned his head as if he could see me. "Good morning, mother of my child."

"Good morning," I practically stuttered, coming closer to see what exactly was in the pan. Bits of white shell swam among yellow slime. I almost said something, but stopped myself in time. Hadn't I just complained he wasn't making an effort to do anything around the house?

He used a metal spoon to stir the eggs and put scratches in a Teflon surface I'd been babying with wood and plastic for five years. "When I woke up this morning, I could see light."

My heart stopped. "You can see?"

"Nothing but smudges of light, but the doctor said if my sight was going to return, that's how it would start."

"That's great news," I said with as much enthusiasm as I could muster. "You'll be back to normal in no time." No time soon, I hoped.

"I fixed your lunch," he said proudly. "It's in the fridge. Bologna and cheese."

"Wow, baby," was all I could say, wondering how in the world he would know when the eggs were done when his vision was nothing but a blur of color.

"You might notice that a little piece of the meat on your sandwich has a bite taken out of it. It's how I checked to be sure what I was making you."

He scooped up a spoonful of egg and brought it to his mouth. After knocking off the steam with his breath, he ventured a taste. "A little runny, just the way you like them."

I didn't like eggs at all, never had. On the rare occasion when I actually did eat them, they had to be bone dry. But, again, he was making an effort and I didn't want to discourage that.

Throwing a glance at my watch, I said, "Baby, sit down and let me serve us up." I only had fifteen minutes to make it out the door, so I didn't really have time for him to painstakingly feel his way around in search of dishes. Thankfully, he turned the stove off and made his way to the table.

Swallowing back the nausea, I forced down a few bites of runny eggs mixed with crunchy shells.

He took his first bite, made a face, and picked a piece of white from his mouth. "Guess I need a little practice." He set the debris on his plate and pushed it away.

"They're delicious," I said. "Listen, I'll clean up when I get home, but I really have to get going or I'm going to be late."

"Wait a minute, Penny. There's something I want to talk to you about. I want us to start going to church. I don't want my child to grow up a heathen like his old man."

My eyebrows shot up. "Church?" Callie Mae had been begging me to come back to Sheckle Baptist. It was going to feel so good to finally say yes. Knowing how Trent's ego worked, I didn't want to act too eager, though. He had to feel like he was laying down the law and I was submitting. "I guess you have a point."

"Daggone skippy, I do."

"This Sunday?" I was so happy I'd forgotten all about my nausea and fatigue. I couldn't wait to get to work and tell Fatimah we would be joining her family and Callie Mae this Sunday.

"No, next Christmas," he said, looking annoyed.

"Service starts at ten," I said.

"No, it don't, neither. I called myself. It's eleven o'clock sharp."

Setting my fork down, I looked at my watch again. I really needed to get going. "You called where?"

"I can't remember the name of it. Beginnings something. You've seen it. We pass by it every time we go to the Piggly Wiggly."

I did remember the church he was talking about — New Beginnings. A mid-sized, warehouse-looking building with a lot of fancy cars parked out front. I'd never been inside, but it looked nice enough.

Callie Mae would be disappointed, but at least we were going to church. Another miracle among a string of many lately. "Okay, eleven o'clock it is." I walked over and kissed him, then picked up his plate along with mine, and set both on the counter. "How did you pick out that place, anyway?"

He slid his hand under his T-shirt and scratched his belly. "I called 411 and asked them to pick out a Christian church within ten miles of us, and that's the name she gave me."

I doubted he prayed before he'd done that, but the last thing I was going to do was ask. At least we were going.

Grabbing the lunch he'd made me from the fridge, I said, "See you tonight. Thanks for breakfast and lunch."

"Don't be late," was his reply.

Twelve

Fatimah and I had an uneventful morning. After finishing our first two houses in record time, we ate our packed lunches in the car, then made our way through the ritzy historic section of town to the last house on our itinerary. I stood behind Fatimah on the covered front porch of a large, baby-blue Victorian.

She grabbed the brass knocker and slammed it down several times. Shooting the empty driveway a dirty look, she knocked again.

I studied the ornate posts that joined the railing to the shingled roof. A large stained-glass panel hung by thin chains in the front window. The design appeared to be some sort of coat of arms — a multicolored shield surrounded by an urn on each side overflowing with ivy. Sunlight glimmered off the red of the shield, bringing to mind rubies.

Fatimah tapped her foot. "She is better

answer this time." She sat on the top stair and checked her watch again. "I give her five minute only."

I sat beside her, looking out at the picket fence lined with rows of yellow roses and taking in their sweet smell carried by a warm breeze. "Fati, can I ask you a question?"

She turned toward me.

"How did Callie Mae get into the cleaning business? Was that how her husband made his money?"

She occupied herself by checking the levels of cleaning fluid in the caddy. She picked up a can of Ajax, shook it, and slipped it back in. "He was attorney and left her wealth enough to live on. She do not need the money."

I waited for her to elaborate. Instead, she picked up the Windex bottle and turned the nozzle, then set it back in the caddy.

"So," I said, leaning my elbows on my knees, "why does she do it?"

"I come to this country with no education. With some English and no money. She sponsor me through her church and try to get me job, but no one would give to me. So she make this one. Callie is a very good woman with kind heart."

"So, we're kind of charity cases," I said,

knowing what Trent would think about that.

She shrugged. "We make money for work. She make money. She is happy. Is good arrangement for everyone."

"That's really nice of her." I picked a pebble off the step and rolled it between my fingers.

"Yes, is nice," Fatimah said. "What is not nice is this woman. If she do not come, I spit on her house."

Just then a long red convertible pulled into the driveway. A pretty forty-something brunette rolled down her window. Fatimah crossed her arms and glared at her.

"Oh, ladies, I'm so sorry. I forgot." She stepped out of the car, pulled several department store bags from the backseat and slammed the door. "I've got company coming in a few. We're going to have to reschedule."

Fatimah stomped so hard the wood planks beneath my feet shook. "I tell you last time you must provide twenty-four-hour notice."

The woman transferred two of the bags she carried to her other hand, evening out the load. "Try to remember you work for me, not the other way around. You tell Callie Mae I'll discuss this with her privately."

Fatimah's eyes narrowed. "I tell her you cancel again without proper notice."

The woman's expression turned to stone as she walked toward us. "Maybe over in the jungle it's acceptable for the help to talk to their bosses that way, but here in America, we have a thing called etiquette." Her disdainful gaze moved slowly down the front of me. "If you speak English, maybe you could explain it to her."

I couldn't believe she actually said that. My face grew hotter than a frying pan.

Fatimah marched down the stairs, meeting her in the center of the closely clipped lawn. My stomach dropped, thinking there was going to be a smackdown. Stopping abruptly a few feet from the woman, Fatimah stomped her foot again. "You are a rude woman. I will not come back to your house again."

The woman threw her nose higher into the air. "That's right, you won't." She stepped around Fatimah, then stopped and turned around. "Here's some friendly advice for you. If you want to make it in this country, you need to know your place."

Before my mind could catch up with my mouth, I pointed a shaky finger at her. "And here's some friendly advice for *you.* The Union won the war."

She sneered at me. "What's that supposed to mean?"

"It means slavery was abolished in this country."

She opened her mouth to say something, but I cut her off.

"If I were you, lady, I'd shut it," I said.

Her face turned paler than the whitewalls of her tires. Fatimah chomped her teeth at the woman for good measure, then grabbed my hand and pulled me toward the car.

"What was that about?" I asked as I buckled my seat belt. My anger melted, and all I could think about was the possibility I might have just cost myself the job. A job I needed in so many ways and for so many reasons.

She turned over the ignition. "This is the three time she does this."

I stole a glance at the woman as she set her bags on the porch, freeing her hands to unlock the front door. "You're kidding."

"True." She slid the gearshift into drive. "This is a woman who, all her life, never been tells no or given the whip." She hit the brakes and glared back at the house. "I give her the whip if I ever see her again!"

Fatimah's temper reminded me of Trent's right then, and it made me want to flee. When she turned to me, my stomach knotted as my fingers reached for the door handle. A peculiar look came over her as she studied me. "I not really give her the whip, Peeny. Do not be worried. I just say words. I do not do more than yell. Promise. I never do."

I hadn't realized I was holding my breath until I exhaled.

When we started down the road, she reached over and patted my arm. Her fingertips were rough as sandpaper. I made a mental note then to buy myself some latex gloves so my hands wouldn't end up the same way. "Do not ever be afraid of me, Peeny. I am good woman. I have my temper, true, but it does not have me."

We drove to the food bank, where Callie Mae stood out front sweeping debris from the walkway. As we pulled along the curb, she gave the car a double take. When Fatimah leaned toward me, I rolled down my window so they could speak.

Callie Mae dropped her broom on the grass and headed toward the car. "Let me guess."

"She do it again!" Fatimah yelled so loudly it made my ears hurt.

Callie Mae leaned into the window. "Well, that's that. Three strikes, she's out. Please tell me you didn't spit on her house." Her breath smelled like she'd just chewed a piece of spearmint gum, and her skin glistened with perspiration.

Fatimah hung her head in shame. “No, I do not. But I should!”

Callie Mae’s expression remained neutral. I figured now was the best chance I’d get to admit what I’d said before she found out from the woman. With my eyes focused on my wringing hands, I forced out the words before I could lose my nerve. “She said something about Fatimah and the jungle. . . . I’m so sorry, Callie, but I lost my temper and told her to shut up.” I closed my eyes and waited for the guillotine to drop.

Surely not even Callie Mae was so understanding as to allow her customers to be treated that way.

After a few seconds of silence, I snuck a glance at her.

Her expression remained unreadable. “Listen, ladies, I appreciate you not yanking out her hair, which is what I might have been tempted to do.”

When I think of grace, Manny, I always remember Callie Mae’s response that day.

You’d have thought Fatimah would have been satisfied with not getting fired or fussed at, but the look on her face was indignation rather than relief. “You will make her pay. I and Peeny should not have to miss money because she makes rude behavior."

Callie Mae scratched her eyebrow. "I agree. But I hate to tell you, Fati, I can't make her pay. We can only refuse to work for her."

Fatimah grabbed the steering wheel and stared straight ahead through the windshield at the tree-lined road.

Callie Mae glanced down at her watch, then at Fatimah. "You know, it's only one. No sense in y'all going home so early."

Fatimah looked at her askance, the beginnings of a smile forming. "We bowl?"

"We bowl," Callie Mae said, turning her gaze to me. "Penny, you like bowling?"

The only thing going through my mind right then was that if Trent found out I'd been bowling instead of working, I'd never hear the end of it. I unlatched my purse and peeked in to make sure my car keys were still there. "I should probably go home."

Callie Mae leaned her elbows on my open window. "Why? You're scheduled for another three hours, anyway."

I felt myself flush as I stammered, "Trent's vision still isn't good and . . ."

She stared at me for an uncomfortably long time. "He'll be fine, just like he is when you're working. Besides, a wife who lets herself unwind now and again makes for a better wife. You'd be doing it as much for him as you. You're wound up tighter than Ginny Elizabeth's girdle."

"Who?" I asked, confused.

Callie Mae gave her own cheek an admonishing slap. "Never mind."

"She cannot bowl," Fatimah blurted. "Look. She is too skinny to hold up a ball. It will tip her."

I scrunched my mouth at her. "I do so know how to bowl, and I'm not that skinny." I was no pro, but I could hold my own.

"You come," Fatimah stated. "You come or we will know you are too gentle for games."

Even though I saw through her ploy, I still took the bait. "I'm going to kick your butt so bad, you won't be able to sit down for a year."

Fatimah narrowed her eyes at me, then gave Callie Mae a questioning look.

With a grin, Callie Mae said, "That means she's in."

Thirteen

Just in case Fatimah wanted to stay longer than I could, I drove my own car to Lucky Lanes. Callie Mae said she had to take care of one last thing at the food bank and then she'd meet us.

I scanned the front of a long brick building with two giant bowling pins stuck to the side of it. My gaze paused on a public phone beside a newspaper vending machine. For the umpteenth time, I wondered if I should call Trent to tell him where I was, but decided against it. As long as I made it home the same time as always, it shouldn't matter. Even with the decision made, I couldn't shake the sick feeling in the pit of my stomach that had nothing to do with pregnancy.

Sliding the key out of the ignition, I watched for Fatimah.

As her Buick rattled into the sparsely occupied lot, I stepped out of my car and waited for her to park. When the brightness of the sun suddenly faded, I glanced upward, surprised to see that a blanket of clouds had blown in, when just moments ago there had been none. It never ceases to amaze me, Manny, that life, just like the weather, can change on a dime. Mama used to say, hope for sunshine, but pack an umbrella.

Fatimah pulled alongside me, waving as if we hadn't seen each other in days.

"Nice of you to show up," I said as she shut her door.

"Why is that nice? I tell you I come." With a twist of her key, she locked the door.

"It's just a joke," I said.

"A not funny joke."

Eyeing the clouds, I rubbed my arms to warm them from the sudden chill.

She just stood there staring at me as if I were the one who'd been here before and should take the lead.

"Well," I said, "we're here."

She blinked at me dully. "Very good. You are as wise as you are beautiful."

Considering she'd just called me a fat pimple-face the other day, I was beyond the ignorance of taking that as a compliment. "And you're as . . ." When I couldn't come up with anything witty to finish my sentence with, she laughed.

"I'm glad I'm so amusing."

This made her laugh harder. "I am glad too. You make days shorter."

She walked to her trunk, opened it, and pulled out a pair of bowling shoes. Slamming the trunk, she said, "I do not make use of shared footwear. My aunt become very ill from foot worms."

I'd never heard of such a thing, and still haven't, but I figured they probably dealt with all sorts of things in Africa we didn't have here. "They spray the shoes with Lysol or something to kill the germs," I said, mostly to make myself feel better since I'd be the one renting.

She wrinkled her nose. "I do not make gamble with my health."

I could have said not using a doctor for her pregnancy was a bigger gamble, but I was in no mood for listening to her make loud yelping sounds with her fingers stuck in her ears.

When she started toward the building, I followed. We passed a group of white-haired men in matching polyester team shirts. When one of them smiled at me, I looked away.

Fatigue was hitting me more and more often each afternoon, and that day was no exception. Unfortunately, I made the mistake of mentioning it to Fatimah.

She turned around and pooched out her bottom lip. "Poor Princess Peeny. You should not have to work so hard. Please, have a sit in your car and rest. I will roll your ball for you, then bring you here a snack and return with news if you have won the game."

I stopped abruptly, planting my feet on a painted white parking line. "Oh, I knew you'd understand, Fatimah. Thank you. If they have burgers, I take mine well done."

She swung around. "You cannot sit in car!"

Finally, it was my turn to laugh. "See, Fati, you're not the only one who can be funny."

Her eyebrows dipped and then she shocked me by plopping down right there on the pavement. As I gawked at her, she set the shoes she carried on her lap and crossed her arms in defiance.

I glanced around to see if anyone was watching, then looked down at her. "What are you doing?"

She turned her face toward the road, away from me.

Sitting there like a child, in the middle of the blacktop, she looked ridiculous. "Get up. You know how stupid you look?"

She jerked her head toward me, her eyes full of fire. "I will get up after you make apology."

Someone honked from the road. I turned, relieved it was aimed at another vehicle rather than us. "What do I have to apologize for?"

"For insulting me," she said coldly.

"Insulting you? I was only making a joke, just like you did."

She shrugged. "My joke was funny. Yours was unkind."

"It was not unkind. It was funny."

"The most not-funniest joke I have ever been told," she said. "When I was a child, my schoolmates ridiculed me, and now you do so too. You are no friend of mine, Peeny Taylor. I will not bowl with you or work with you ever again. Leave from my sight."

Stunned, I stared down at her, unsure what to do. I needed this job. She'd worked under Callie Mae for years. If one of us had to go, it was going to be me. Still, I'd spent most of my adult life telling Trent I was sorry for things I didn't do. The thought of doing so now to her was more than I could bear. "I'm not apologizing." I sat down beside her, crossing my arms right back.

She said nothing for a moment, then finally stole a glance at me. Red veins marked the outermost corner of her eyes. "Look at yourself. You are like baby."

"And how do you think you look?"

She slapped her knee and grinned. "Ha! I got you again, Peeny. I am the winner. You cannot beat me, true!"

I felt like the biggest fool when I realized she'd been joking. I squinted at her. "I hate you."

Pushing herself off the ground, she said, "I do not care so long as you hate me while you bowl." She reached out her hand to help me up.

With a spring in her step, she practically skipped to the entrance. We hadn't seen Callie Mae pull up, but somehow she was already inside, opening the door for us.

"How did you get in here?" I asked, confused. "We didn't see your car pull in."

Third Eye Blind belted out "Semi-Charmed Life" from the loudspeakers while balls hitting pins sounded like cracks of thunder in the background.

"Side entrance. What were you two clowns doing out there?"

The place smelled of Lysol and feet. I gently elbowed Fatimah. "Determining I was funnier."

Fatimah voiced her disagreement with a "Ha!"

My eyes slowly adjusted to the darkness as I surveyed the long row of lanes. A family with two small boys occupied one lane, another two were taken by college-age couples, and the final being used was by a group of half a dozen guys about my age.

Callie Mae's gaze settled on me. "If I were you, I wouldn't get into a spitting contest with that woman. She can't stand to lose." She nodded toward an empty lane in front of us. "We're number eleven." I glanced over at where she indicated. The lane was lit and ready to go, with a long black bumper spanning the length of each gutter. My eyebrows lifted. How bad did she think I was?

"You will pay me for a full day," Fatimah demanded rather than asked.

Callie Mae rolled her eyes. "Fine. Now I've sunk so low I have to pay friends to play with me."

I cringed at the thought of losing part of a day's pay, but it wasn't like it was Callie Mae's fault that lady cancelled last-minute. I couldn't let her think she needed to buy my friendship. "You don't have to pay me for the last house. It wasn't your fault."

The smile she gave me melted my heart because I could see in her eyes that I'd touched hers.

"I knew you would say that, sweet Penny.

Do you know how I know? Because we're cut from the same cloth, you and me." She turned to Fatimah. "That goes for you, too. That means we're the same."

Fatimah twisted her mouth. "Yes, clearly we are twins of three."

Callie brushed something only she could see from her jeans. "They're called triplets, Einstein, and I mean on the inside."

"You barely know me," I whispered around the lump trying to form in my throat.

She set her soft hand on my cheek the way my mother used to. "Believe me, Penny, I know you."

For reasons I couldn't wrap my mind around until much later, my eyes began to well. Manny, no one had even pretended to know me in a very long time. The Bible says in heaven we'll know just as we're known. Guess that desire he created in us makes us all long to have someone really "get" us, or at least try to.

She gave my cheek a soft tap. "You two pick yourselves out a ball."

When Callie Mae walked toward the lane, I joined Fatimah at a rack by the door. Without even bothering to test the holes out, she snatched up a bright orange bowling ball.

After getting my finger stuck in half a dozen, I finally found a medium-weight black one that fit well enough. When I brought it over to the lane, Callie Mae was standing there looking as serious as I've ever seen her with a sweatband across her forehead, gleaming white bowling shoes, and a hand towel shoved into the back pocket of her jeans. She rolled her head and shook her arms like she was getting ready to either run a marathon or remake Olivia Newton-John's "Let's Get Physical." "Ladies, go grab your shoes; I'm going to warm up. Mama's fixing to bust a rack today."

Feeling like I was in the twilight zone, I walked over to the shoe rental counter. An oily-haired girl asked my shoe size without so much as looking up from her magazine. Before handing over my ugly red-white-and-blue size sixes, she pulled out a large aerosol can and sprayed the foot holes so long a cloud shrouded her. I had to turn my head to keep from choking on the fumes. I set the tennis shoes I'd been wearing on the counter for collateral.

As I picked up the rental shoes, someone grabbed my wrist and I jumped.

"Listen, Peeny," Fatimah said, looking over her shoulder like someone might be listening. "You must let Callie Mae win. She is crazy for this game, but she plays more awful than someone born with no limbs. I tell you the truth, she must win."

"Why?"

She let my hand go. "For same reason my Edgard sends poetry to magazines. She does not know she is no good."

"That's silly. She's a grown woman — she can handle the truth."

One of the men from the group of guys asked to exchange his shoes for a half-size larger. When he winked at us, Fatimah gave him a lemon face and ushered me farther down the counter away from him. "Why must she know? She spends up her life making for other people's happiness. This makes her happy. Understand?"

I didn't really. It seemed out of character for Callie Mae, and downright bizarre, but I certainly didn't want to upset someone who'd been so good to me. "So, the bumpers aren't for me?"

"She thinks they are for me." She headed back toward the lane, and I followed. Twenty feet or so from Callie Mae, she stopped and turned around. "Tonight, neither of us will make fifty." She gave me a severe look. "True?"

I paused to do the math. That would be about four pins a frame. It would take some really bad bowling to pull that off. "I'll do my worst," I said.

Fatimah and I set our balls on the holder and sat down at the small desk in front of the lane. While Fatimah typed in our initials on the digital scoreboard, I watched Callie Mae's ball ricochet wildly from bumper to bumper and take down the center pins leaving a 7-10 split.

Fatimah smiled. "Wonderful!"

Callie Mae blushed. "Well, it wasn't a strike, but I've done worse."

When she walked over to us, Fatimah gave her a high five so loud it had to have stung.

Callie Mae slid a small pouch of chalk from her front pocket and rubbed it between her hands. "Okay, Penny, warm-up's over. You're up first."

I hit the reset button, then picked up my ball. Not only did I have to manage to hit half the amount of pins I normally would, but I'd have to do it without the option of a gutter ball. Without bothering to put my fingers in the holes, I bent my knees like a child would do and rolled it as softly and off-center as I could. What seemed like a half hour later, the ball finally crept its way to the pins. It barely tapped them when the front two slowly teetered back and forth and eventually fell. Relief filled me. Two. If I could keep that up, Callie Mae would *have* to beat me.

The Bee Gee's "Night Fever" started to play as I aimed to take my second shot. Hands slipped around my waist, and I screamed. I turned to find the same guy from the counter standing behind me. "Easy there." Dimples sunk deep into his cheeks as he smiled. He reeked of cigarettes and beer. "I was just going to help you improve your aim."

Manny, I didn't see a flirtatious young man who might have only drunk once a year at his get-together with old college buddies. I saw Trent. I thought of all the times he was out with his friends, and how he probably came on to some unsuspecting woman just like this man was doing to me. "Get your hands off me," I said. "You think you can just smile at a girl and that gives you the right to touch her?"

He backed up. "I was just trying to be helpful. You look like —"

I gave him the dirtiest look I could manage. "I don't care how I look to you."

That poor guy slunk back over to his group of friends, who were now howling with laughter.

My heart beat a mile a minute as I turned to sneak a glance at Fatimah and Callie

Mae, who both stared at me, unblinking. Feeling ashamed and more than a little frightened at my reaction, I licked my lips and threw my ball gently against the bumper. By the grace of God, I managed to knock down the farthest pin, rendering me a total of three for the frame.

Callie Mae squeezed my shoulder as I sat. "That was quite a reaction to Casanova."

I couldn't look at her. How could I explain it? "I don't know what came over me. I should probably go apologize."

She hooked my chin, forcing me to look her in the eye. "You could have said it nicer, sure, but you weren't wrong. You bet he'll think twice about touching a woman without her permission again."

It made me feel better to hear her say he'd crossed a line in touching me that way. Setting boundaries was something I hadn't done a whole lot of before then. Changing the subject, I said, "Good thing we have those bumpers or I wouldn't have gotten any pins."

She pulled the towel from her pocket. "You'll get better. I've been at this for years. It takes time and practice."

I bit my tongue. "It's not really my game."

She chuckled. "Obviously it's not mine either." With a nod of her head, she motioned to the bumpers.

Fatimah jumped up. "Yes, it is your game!"

A devilish grin slithered across Callie Mae's lips. "You think you're the master prankster, but guess what, Fati? The laugh's on you this time. I've been pretending to be terrible all these months just for this moment."

Fatimah's eyebrows dipped in disbelief. "You lie."

After Callie Mae scored her fourth strike in a row, Fatimah was livid. "You play the most horrible joke I ever had seen." Her lips disappeared into a thin line. "I will get you for this."

With a wink in my direction, Callie Mae laughed. "Why don't we just call it even? You've been getting me for years, after all."

"I have something to admit too." I stood to take my turn. "I'm actually not pregnant, and my husband isn't blind."

Callie Mae's and Fatimah's jaws hit the floor.

I walked to the arrows and lifted the ball in front of my nose to aim. "Just kidding." When I threw the ball, I managed to get a strike of my own, making my joke seem a little less lame. I looked back over my shoulder at them. "Who's the master now, ladies?"

After five games, my arms were ready to fall off. Callie Mae had broken 200 each game, Fatimah averaged just under, and I came in last place, only breaking 150 once.

The three of us walked to the parking lot together. Callie Mae stopped and turned around. "Leaving this place always makes me feel like I'm burying Matthew again." She looked at me. "This was our place." Her gaze moved to Fatimah. "I really miss him."

"I know you do. He was good man." Fatimah held her arms out.

When Callie Mae stepped into them, Fatimah waved me into their little huddle. We hugged Callie Mae as she quietly wept. After a moment, she rubbed her eyes against the shoulder of her shirt, leaving a dark streak of wetness. "It's silly, I know. He's been gone three years. It's really time to let the poor man rest in peace."

"We should bowl someplace new," Fatimah said.

With a grimace, Callie Mae nodded.

Fatimah patted her shoulder. "I think is very good idea. It is time to say good-bye."

I felt a little like an interloper, knowing Fatimah was privy to so much of Callie Mae's life I hadn't been around for. I comforted myself with the thought that I'd been around for this moment and, God willing, would be for all the rest, too.

Callie Mae wiped her eyes again and looked up at the gray sky. "See you on the other side, Matthew."

"You make right decision," Fatimah said, looking at me for agreement, then back at Callie Mae. "You cannot grab hold of tomorrows when you hold the past with both hands."

FOURTEEN

At last the weekend came, and I was off for two whole days. I probably should have been resting, but I had a compulsion to begin turning the spare room into your nursery. When we moved into that house on Abraham Street, the previous owners had left a few gallons of paint down in the root cellar.

After I peeled off the latex skin from the top, mixed the layers of goo back into one solid color, and got over the stinky-foot smell, they, and I, were ready to go. I wasn't crazy about the lime-green color, but the price was right. Besides, I read infants liked vivid colors. If the paint was half as bright dry as it looked wet, I should have the happiest baby in town.

Wearing one of the face masks Callie Mae had given me to work in, I painted like a woman possessed as I rolled out the final coat on the last wall. My arms were sore from reaching over my head, but the closer I got to being done, the easier it was to ignore the pain. Ignoring your father was another matter entirely.

I figured by now he would have forgotten all about his drunken proclamation to be a better man and go back to treating me like a doormat. But once again, he surprised me. Having come in for the tenth time to check my progress, he stood leaning against the doorjamb staring in my general direction. "You shouldn't have to be doing this in your condition. What was wrong with the way it looked before?"

I set the roller back in the pan, letting it soak up what little paint there was left clinging to the aluminum ridges, and rested my aching arm at my side. "You may not remember, but the walls were full of nail holes and scuff marks. Our baby should have better than that."

"I just wish you didn't have to work so hard. It ain't right you're shouldering a man's share."

I swiped my forearm across my brow and pulled down the mask. It felt so good to breathe without that thing on. "I'm not doing anything more than other women my age."

With a grump on his face, he mumbled

something I couldn't make out, and didn't really want to.

I walked over to him, touched his cheek with my paint-speckled finger, and kissed his lips. It was the first time in a long time he didn't smell like booze. "Taking care of my family is an honor. Don't take that away from me."

His eyes glistened. "You don't know what it's like to be so useless. I wouldn't wish this on nobody."

Your father could be tougher than a two-dollar steak, but he had his tender side too.

"I know, baby." I wrapped my arms around his narrow waist.

"I hate my wife has to work. It ain't right," he repeated.

"It's just for a season." I hoped that season would be a lifelong one. Now that I had a taste of freedom, the thought of going back to the way things were was unbearable.

He rested his head atop mine. I could feel his chin moving as he spoke. "Darlin', it's lonely out there in the living room. I've been missing you all week. I was hoping you could come lay with me on the couch and watch some TV. You can tell me what those streaks of color are doing."

I looked at the walls. They were as green as they were going to get. I just needed to peel off the masking tape from around the windows and edges. "You go on out. I'm just going to clean up and then I'll join you."

"How's it look?" he asked.

"Kinda like a big square lime," I said, pulling my mask back up.

He chuckled. My word, your father was a good-looking man, and never more so than when he laughed. I'm grateful to say God blessed you with all of Trent's looks and none of his disposition.

It used to make me sad to wonder how differently things might have turned out if his upbringing had been better. Funny how bad parenting echoes through the generations. That will stop with you, though, Manny. You'll be the father to your children your daddy wanted to be. As I watch you sleep in a crumpled ball with your thumb in your mouth and tattered Pooh bear hugged tight against your chest, I know that as surely as I know your name.

After cleaning up and showering off the grime, I joined Trent on the couch. He lay behind me, pressed against my back, holding me tightly around my middle like he was afraid I might run away.

His warm breath on the back of my neck didn't set my nerves on edge, and I didn't have one eye on his fists. For the first time in a long time, I felt safe in his arms.

He flipped through the channels until an old rerun of M*A*S*H came on. "I won't have to guess what they're doing tonight," he said happily. "I've seen this one."

And there I lay with him, content as a kitten. Trent talked through the entire show, telling me, from memory, what the actors were doing. "Colonel Potter's petting the horse now, ain't he?"

"That's right," I said.

"His eyes are tearing up now. I remember that."

I pulled the afghan up over our shoulders. "They are."

"Radar hugging that teddy bear?"

"No, it's laying at his side."

"Our son should have a teddy bear."

"He will," I said.

"Not a little sissy bear, neither. One of those giant kinds you have to win at a carnival."

I laughed. "That would be a little tough to snuggle with."

"He don't need to snuggle. He's going to be tough like his old man."

Little did your father know I was praying every morning and night you *wouldn't* be tough like him, but tenderhearted like me.

Straining my neck, I looked back over my

shoulder at him. “He or she is going to be born a baby, you know, not with hair on his chest.”

He cleared his throat. “You don’t need to argue with me over what my son will or won’t do or be.”

A commercial for a truck we couldn’t afford the hubcap for blared as we lay silent.

His tone softened. “You hear me, One Cent?”

“I hear you,” I said.

He grunted that way he does when he’s in agreement with himself. “He needs to understand who the boss is. If you’re questioning everything I say, he’s going to, too, and I can’t have that. The Bible says I’m the head of the household. Try to remember that.”

As if I could forget. I found it interesting he only knew the parts of the Bible that seemed to justify his distorted viewpoint.

When the show was over, he pushed against me to let me know he wanted to sit up. I hated that our snuggling time was over already, but grateful he didn’t just push me onto the floor like he might have before his coming-to-Jesus moment.

He patted the table in front of us, feeling for his Coke. “Speaking of the baby, I’ve been thinking. With my sorry excuse for a father being in jail and my mother probably on some street corner, our child ought to have a set of decent grandparents in his life."

Your father's words stopped my heart as I hoped against hope. I had wanted to pick up the phone a hundred times and call your grandma to tell her I was going to be a mother myself, but I knew it would just rip her heart out to know about you, but not be allowed to see you.

As I held my breath, Trent took a long, leisurely drink from his soda can. Finally, he set it down. "I may regret this, but I think you should call your folks and tell them about the baby."

Unable to contain my excitement, I hugged your father, pulled back then hugged him again harder.

He put his hands up as if in caution. "They need to understand, though, this is my kid, not theirs. They're going to need to abide by my rules if they want to be part of his life."

Here we go, I thought, but said nothing. He was giving me my parents back. I'd negotiate the details later. "I'll make it clear, baby. They won't cause no trouble. They'll just be so happy for us."

"Well, go on, then. Call them. Don't try to put me on the phone, neither. Just tell them about the baby and let them know you'll call when he comes."

It was all I could do not to break out into a moonwalk, I was so thrilled. Experience told me not to overdo it, though. He didn't mind me being happy now and again, just not too happy. "Mama might want to stay with me when I go into labor," I said without thinking.

He puckered his mouth as if I'd said something stupid, and I realized I'd played my hand too soon. "You'll just have to tell her you've got your doting husband here to help. She's welcome to come visit, but she ain't moving in."

Mama was not going to take that lying down. Every woman in my family, for generations, stayed with her daughter when she gave birth. At least for a week or two. It was just what the womenfolk did. A new mother needed help, and even with the change in Trent, he was still about as much help as a toddler.

With my heart in my throat, I dialed my parents' number, but it just rang and rang. Looking back, I think maybe that was God's doing. Trent didn't know I'd spoken to Mama recently. Since I wasn't much of an actress, I doubt I could have pulled off the performance needed to both communicate effectively with my folks, and not give myself away to him.

When the answering machine came on, I weighed every word carefully as Trent listened in. "Mama, Daddy, this is Penny, your long-lost daughter. I have wonderful news. Trent and I are going to be parents. I'm due on Christmas day. Can you believe it?" I left the number I knew they already had, and hoped they would read between the lines they weren't to mention our previous phone call.

Fifteen

Not an hour after I called my parents, the phone rang. Running from the kitchen to answer it, I tripped over your father's foot. Luckily I caught myself just in time. I'm sure the sight of it would have been something to see if there had been anyone there who could.

"I'm fine," I said, not that he'd asked. I grabbed up the phone. "Hello?"

"Peeny, dat you?" Fatimah asked. Trying as I might, I couldn't keep the disappointment out of my voice. "Oh, hi, Fatimah. What's going on?"

"I and my husband, Edgard, would like invite you to dinner with us tomorrow night."

I looked at Trent. He pulled his sock off and rubbed his foot. I could see from where I stood why it was bothering him. A bruise spanned the length of his toes. My stumbling into them couldn't have helped. "Dinner?"

"You and your husband, Tent, come here and eat. I will make for you Sudanese food. You never eat so good!"

"His name is Trent, Fati, not Tent." There was no way in the world your father was going to agree. Not unless there was a keg involved. "And that's really nice of you. Hang on just a minute and let me make sure he doesn't have anything else planned." I put my hand over the receiver, pressing my palm tight against it. "It's my coworker. She wants us to come to her house tomorrow night for dinner."

Trent looked up. "I think you know the answer."

I uncovered the phone. "I'm sorry, Fatimah. He's not up for it."

"Good. You come."

I turned around and brushed the dust off the top of a wood-framed picture of your grandparents resting on the shelf. "I wish I could, but he needs me here."

"For what he need you?" She didn't bother to try to hide her annoyance.

"Um, it's not like he has a seeing eye dog, you know?"

"You are not a dog, Peeny."

"I know I'm not."

Suddenly I felt the phone yanked out of my hand. Trent jerked it to his ear. "This is Penny's husband."

I strained to hear what she was saying on the other end, but couldn't.

"That's very nice, but —" He made an annoyed face. "It sounds delicious, but I'm not much of a —" Another pause. "I know Penny isn't my dog. I never said she was." He shot a dirty look in my general direction. "I'm sure it would be. I'm just not that social. . . . No, I ain't telling her she can't go. She can go." He thrust the phone out for me to take.

My hand shook as I did. "Hey, it's Penny again."

"I tell your husband you come tomorrow at seven."

Forgetting he couldn't see very well, I mouthed I was sorry. "What can I bring?"

"You bring yourself fully dressed."

"I wasn't planning on coming naked."

"I did not know. I have never had an American for dinner."

"Well, don't think you're having me for dinner," I said.

She laughed that wonderful laugh of hers. "I don't want you, but I bet your husband taste good in stew."

"You'll never know," I said. "I've got to

go. See you then."

I had one eye on Trent the whole conversation. The anger on his face told me he'd wanted to do more than just grab the phone out of my hands.

"What was so funny?" he demanded to know.

"Nothing. I was just —"

"Fine. Don't tell me. 'Seeing eye dog'?"

My mind whirled trying to figure out what exactly had offended him. "I was just saying you can't see. How was I supposed to get us out of it? I can't come up with excuses on the fly like you." I hated the power he had to turn me into a driveling idiot.

"Oh, so now I'm a burden and an accomplished liar?"

He was no longer close enough to reach me, but I was ready just in case he decided to lunge. I glanced over my shoulder to see if the front door was locked. It wasn't. "You're not a burden. I was just trying to get us off the hook."

The crease between his eyebrows sunk so deep it looked like his face was splitting plumb in half.

"I'm a joke to her and obviously to you, too." He groped at the end table, making me wonder if he was searching for something that could be used as a weapon. All that was there were his socks, the remote, and an empty soda can. He grabbed up the can and start shaking it in front of him. "Go on, Penny, put some change in it for your pathetic, blind husband."

I didn't know where his mind was, but I tried my best to backtrack. I'd have all the time in the world to analyze the conversation later during the silent treatment sure to follow. "Baby, you can't help what happened to you. You're not a burden. You're my . . . ," I had to choke the word out, but I knew it was what he needed to hear, "hero."

His face relaxed. "Don't," he said, but his eyes said do.

"Who else could lose their eyesight and take it like a man the way you have?"

He looked to the side the way he did when he was embarrassed but eating it up at the same time. Relief filled me when I realized a little ego stroking was all it would take to make things right this time.

"What do you mean?" he tried to sound indifferent, but his vulnerable expression gave him away.

"You were up fixing me eggs," I said. "I mean, you can't even see, and there you were cooking breakfast."

His lips started to turn up, then shot back down again. "I don't want you talking that way about me to your friends, you hear?"

I wasn't quite sure what way he meant, but I agreed just the same. A waft of cumin, beef, and onion floated by. "Come on, love, dinner's ready. Taco soup, your favorite."

"Steak's my favorite," he grumbled.

Feeling confident his rage had passed, I ventured over. He allowed me to hold him, but didn't hug me back. That was his way of saying there was a tentative truce, but further buttering up would be necessary to ensure an end to the battle.

"If I had the money, you'd be eating steak every night," I said.

He frowned. "No, if you had the money, you'd buy me a monkey suit and set me on the corner with a harnessed dog and can of pencils."

"Please, don't." I snuggled up closer to him. He felt so warm and smelled of soap. "I love you. I'm having your baby, and you are every bit the man you always were."

Finally his hands came up to rest on my hips. "What time you fixing to go to dinner with that African loudmouth?"

"Seven. Don't worry. I'll fix you something before I go."

"Believe it or not, I still remember how to use a can opener."

He followed me to the kitchen. With the

ladle, I scooped two bowls of soup from the Crock-Pot and set them down on the table. Normally, he wouldn't join me in saying grace, but I figured with the change in him, it might be a good time to try again. I took his hand. "Lord, thank you for this meal and for providing for us through this trial. Please let Trent know how much I love him and how much you love him. Bless this food to our bodies. In Jesus' name, amen."

"Amen," Trent added, already with a spoonful of soup halfway to his mouth.

I watched as he took the first bite to see if this batch turned out all right. His expression didn't change, which told me it must be okay. "Are you praying for my eyesight to come back?" he asked.

His question caught me off guard. I wasn't about to pray for things to go back to the way they used to be. "What do you think?"

"You're a good woman," he said, taking another bite.

Guilt came down on me like the Holy Spirit at Pentecost. You know, Manny, God has the funniest way of using people you think are so beneath you spiritually to convict you. I guess that's one of his ways of keeping us humble. Well, I was feeling meek as a mustard seed right about then.

"Let's pray, the two of us together, for

that," I said, fighting with myself to not cross my spiritual fingers.

He swiped his hand across his mouth. "If you've been praying, that's enough. I know God hears a good woman like you."

My heart turned to jelly. There are moments of truth in life. I saw then that even though your father acted like he despised me, something about my Christian walk must have been right if he thought my prayers were reaching God's ears.

"The Bible says when two or more are gathered in his name, he's there with them. I'm only one person, baby." With that, I took his hand and prayed for his vision to be restored. For God to bless him, me, you, my parents, his, and everyone else that came to mind. Silently, I added a prayer that the change that had begun in your father would continue, with or without his sight.

I could have gone on praying, but Trent's hand left mine, telling me he'd had enough.

We ate silently for a while until he tilted up his bowl to his mouth and slurped the last bit of liquid. He set it on the table and leaned back in his chair, giving his belly a satisfied rub.

Poking at a piece of floating corn, I asked, "Do you want another bowl?"

I figured if he did, I'd just slide mine over

to him. My appetite had left me when he lost his temper.

"Maybe later. You are one good cook, One Cent. If I hadn't married you for your body, I'd have married you for your vittles."

Now, every woman likes to hear she has a nice figure and is a good cook, but I don't know a single one who wants to be married because of either. It might not have bothered me if I didn't think it was really true. I couldn't say anything, though. I married him for his swagger, which I guess is just as shallow and stupid. "Thanks."

He felt around for his napkin, then brought it to his lips. "You know, I've been thinking of names for the baby."

My stomach knotted as I braced myself for the worst. "And?"

"Trent Junior if it's a boy, of course."

I cringed. A name might not seem like such a big deal so long as it's not something that'll get the child shoved on the playground, but for a mother wanting her son to be so much more than his father, it meant everything. "What about Tommy, after my mom's brother?" My uncle had passed away from a heart defect when he was just a baby. I know she would have loved to have you named after him.

"He ain't his kid. He's mine."

I swallowed a spoonful of soup, not really tasting it. "What if he's a girl?"

As he scratched his chin, an idea came to my mind. Trent couldn't turn down a bet. "What if we flip for it?"

"Why should I flip for it when I'm his father?"

"You know, I'm the one who fills out the birth certificate, and last time I checked, 50 percent of her DNA is mine. Are you chicken you'll lose?"

I knew that would clinch it. That man didn't back down even when the challenge was idiotic.

"How will I know if it's heads or tails? You can say anything you want."

"Have I ever lied to you?" I asked.

"Just because I haven't caught you, doesn't mean you haven't done it."

His words stung. Despite years of devotion, he still refused to trust me even on the simplest matters. "Remember how you said you were going to be the man I deserved? I deserve your trust. I've earned it."

He huffed. "Fine. Tails."

I hated calling heads because it seemed to me tails came out more often, but I prayed God would let me have this one. I picked a nickel out of the bottom of my purse and returned to the kitchen table with it. Balancing the coin on top of my thumbnail, I said, "Here we go. Tails, you name the baby; heads, I do."

He slapped it from my hand and it clanged to the floor.

I watched it roll under the table. "What was that for?"

"This way I know it's fair."

Gracious, that man could make me so mad. Never mind that if I wanted to cheat, I still could. It's not like he could see which way the coin ended up.

"Where'd it go?" he asked.

"Under the table."

"And?"

I squatted down and looked at it. "It's heads."

"Of course it is."

I picked up the coin, along with a piece of eggshell that had somehow made its way under his chair. "I didn't cheat."

"Sure, you didn't." His tone was dripping with sarcasm.

I took my bowl over to the sink and dumped the remainder in. "I said I didn't cheat."

"You're not naming him after your mom's brother," he said.

"I won the toss."

He practically growled. "You're not naming him after some dead baby."

Blood rushed to my head so fast it felt like it would shoot off my shoulders. "I don't believe you just said that. He wasn't some dead baby; he was my uncle. Have some respect."

He crossed his arms. "So, what's it going to be? It better not be one of those names a girl can have too, like he's some kind of transsexual."

I liked those kinds of names — like Charlie, Addison, Jordan, and such — but if you couldn't be named after family, I wanted you to have a biblical name, so I let him think I conceded. "It won't be."

"So what's it going to be? Dagnabbit, Penny, don't toy with me."

"Leah if it's a girl," I said. "Emmanuel if it's a boy."

He scowled. "No way. That's —"

"Manny for short," I quickly added.

The scowl left his face as he scratched his chin considering it. "Manny," he repeated. "I don't hate it."

Sixteen

Your father surprised me for the hundredth time that week by honoring his word to go to church. I didn't have to prod or plead or anything. The church he had picked out was as charming on the inside as it was warehouse-like on the outside. Men in suits stood holding open the doors for us and thanked us for being with them that Sunday.

Inside, the foyer was adorned with bouquets of fresh flowers and gilt-framed oil paintings. It smelled like coffee and a department store perfume counter. I led Trent by the elbow past the lingerers who seemed to go out of their way to block the path into the sanctuary. After your father bumped into a few people and stepped on a child's foot, we took our seats on the aisle in the very last row of pews.

The choir, dressed in majestic purple robes, sounded like angels from heaven. One song I remembered from my childhood church; the other I mostly just lip-synched the words as they flashed on the overhead screen. Poor Trent just stood there with his head down as though he were praying. I don't think he'd ever been in a church before, except for his brother's funeral and once at Christmas when we were newly-weds.

While everything seemed the way it should, the place made me uncomfortable. If it had been up to me, I wouldn't have gone back. There was something about the way the pastor preached the whole sermon without the giant smile leaving his lips that gave me the heebie-jeebies. Even when he spoke of damnation, the man was grinning. But he read straight from God's Word, and so I figured that was all that really mattered.

Your father sat at my side with his arm draped over my shoulder. The weight of it irritated me, maybe just because I was pregnant, or maybe because it seemed to me like he was trying to appear to be something he wasn't — a loving, Christian husband. I chided myself for being so suspicious of his motivations. He was a changed man or, at the very least, changing. The public display of affection might have more to do with that than keeping up appearances. I hoped it did, even as doubts lingered.

At the end of the service, churchgoers milled about. I shouldn't have cared, but I admit I was grateful Trent wasn't the only person sporting jeans. My own dress was old and faded, but I figured God couldn't care less and so I tried not to, either.

Still smiling, the preacher came up to us, and with a once-over I'd have missed if I had blinked, he thrust out his hand toward Trent. "Pastor Nathan Harold."

"He lost his eyesight," I said, hoping that wouldn't set off your father. "He's trying to shake, honey."

Trent held out his hand. "Trent Taylor."

The pastor slid his grip into it and gave his hand a pump, then turned his eyes to me.

I could feel my face flush. Something about the way he held my gaze with that giant smile of his made me self-conscious. "I'm his —"

Trent broke in. "And this is my wife, Penny."

"Nice to meet you, Penny." He held out his hand to me. I didn't like shaking hands. It always felt so inappropriately masculine. Your grandpappy used to say you could tell a lot about a man by his handshake. I don't know how he would have interpreted this man's too-firm, sweaty grip.

"Nice to meet you, Pastor Harold," I said.

"Please call me Nathan, or Pastor Nathan if you must."

Trent talked to him as I excused myself to use the bathroom.

As I washed my hands under lukewarm water that kept shutting off every few seconds, I snuck a glance at myself in the mirror. The dark circles around my eyes were starting to resemble a panda bear's. I don't know if that was pregnancy hormones at work or just fatigue, but if Fatimah was right that a baby girl would steal her mother's beauty, I figured I should be buying pink.

When I returned to Trent, he was still talking to Pastor Nathan, or rather the pastor was talking to him. "We're holding a class in a couple weeks for those new to our church. You and the missus think about coming if you can."

"We sure will." Your father sounded like a happier, more-refined version of himself.

I slid my hand into his to let him know I was back. Pastor Nathan waved good-bye and was off to talk with another couple.

On the drive home, a frown replaced Trent's smile.

My partially open window let in the warm spring air. "What's wrong?"

He shrugged, but I knew he wanted me to probe.

"Something's obviously upsetting you. Please tell me." A minivan sped up to pull in front of us, then slowed down once it got there. I was glad Trent couldn't see it, or he would have been cussing and carrying on. I just flipped my blinker on and pulled to the middle lane.

"Is Fatimah married?" he asked.

My mind whirled, trying to guess what he was getting ready to fuss about. "Yes."

"What's her husband look like?"

I wondered why it mattered what he looked like, but the question told me he'd been brooding about it and probably inventing all sorts of scenarios to work himself up to jealousy. Either that, or he was just looking for an excuse to pick a fight so I wouldn't go to dinner that evening.

"I've never seen him."

He pulled at a string on the pocket of his jeans. "You told me she was beautiful."

"She is."

"So she probably has a good-looking husband."

I turned to look at a field of cows and spotted a calf nursing on its mama. The smell of fresh manure floated in. "Not as good-looking as mine."

"I don't want you to go tonight."

"I already said yes."

"Well, say no."

The last place I wanted to get into it with your father was on a main road with our car just inches from oncoming traffic, so I kept my mouth quiet until I pulled into our driveway.

I led him into the house and walked to the kitchen to fix us some leftovers for lunch. After heating up two bowls of soup from the night before, I called him to the table.

I waited for him to finish eating before I said, "I'll fix you a couple of chicken salad sandwiches for dinner and leave them on the top shelf of the fridge. There's a bag of chips on the counter and a whole crisper full of Granny Smiths."

He wrinkled his face at me. "I told you I don't want you going."

"I know you did, but I already said yes."

"You're not going without me. We don't know anything about that man."

"Then come with me if you're worried."

He refused to talk to me the rest of the afternoon. Flipping channel after channel, he just sat there in front of the television until it was time for me to go.

When I bent down to kiss him good-bye, he grabbed my arm. "You're not going without me."

By turning my wrist and yanking at the same time, I was able to break his grip. "Come with me or don't, but I'm going." I could feel my heart slamming against my rib cage, but it felt good to be finding the courage to stand up to him after all this time.

When he followed me out the door, I knew it was going to be an interesting night.

SEVENTEEN

I called Fatimah right before we left to ask her if it was okay if your father joined me. While I could hear the sigh in her voice, she couldn't have said no without being rude.

She lived in a historic apartment building downtown. Of course, our downtown consisted of nothing more than a half-dozen stores, a couple of apartment buildings, and Marty's Feed and Seed, but still Trent complained the whole ride over about how much he hated going "into the city."

Getting to Fatimah's was simpler than I thought, and I was grateful for that. She lived just two turns off Main Street, and her apartment happened to be on the first floor, which made getting your father inside a whole lot easier than it could have been.

I'd never seen her in anything but her self-imposed uniform of sweatpants and T-shirts, but that night she wore an ankle-length cotton dress covered in bright red and purple flowers and a head wrap of the same fabric.

With her blinding grin, she ushered us in. I noticed a line of shoes beside the front door and Fatimah wearing house slippers. "Peeny, Mr. Peeny, come in!" She was practically yelling, she was so excited.

I leaned into Trent and whispered that we needed to leave our shoes at the door. He made an annoyed face, not knowing, and probably not caring, that Fatimah was looking right at him. I was embarrassed, but couldn't say anything without running the risk of setting him off. He slipped off his boots and pushed them to the side with his socked foot. Taking mine off, I remembered too late I had a hole in the heel of my left sock.

Fatimah caught me trying to hide it. "I see you are with air-conditioning. This is good. You will need. Edgard's blood runs too cold. He makes it hot as Nubian desert in here." As usual, her smile put me at ease.

The smell of cloves and some other spices I couldn't put a name to filled the air as she closed the door behind us. She picked up two small glasses filled with a pink liquid off a buffet table and handed one to each of us. I could tell by the exaggerated enthusiasm in Trent's thank-you he assumed we were being given predinner cocktails. Bless his heart, that man loved his alcohol. Without so much as smelling it, he slammed it down like it was a shot of whiskey . . . and promptly started choking.

I rubbed his back. "You okay?"

It took him a few seconds to catch his breath. "Grapefruit juice?"

He couldn't see the look of amusement on Fatimah's face, and I was glad for it. "Yes, juice. Refreshment for your long journey."

He swiped at his mouth. "What long journey? We live fifteen miles from here."

"Baby," I gently chided, squeezing his hand.

I drank mine down, doing my best not to pucker at the bitterness. "That was very refreshing. Thank you."

She took our empty glasses and set them back on the table. "You are most welcome. Let us come and meet Edgard."

Trent cleared his throat. "That name doesn't sound very African."

She looked him over slowly, not bothering to hide her disdain. "Edgar*d,*" she enunciated, so hard she almost parted his hair.

We followed her to the living room, where a man sat with his hands folded in his lap. When he saw us, he stood. Manny, I had never seen anyone that tall before. I'm sure I was probably gawking, but since he'd been tall his whole life, I'm guessing he was used to that kind of reaction. He had to be at least six and a half feet.

He wore a suit and tie, which also surprised me. I guess I figured he would be dressed, like Fatimah, in some sort of African garb. Trent still wore the dungarees he'd gone to church in, and I was no better in my old brown dress and air-conditioned stockings.

Edgard's smile was every bit as charming as Fatimah's as he held his hand out to Trent. "Welcome, brother — please allow me to shake your hand."

I thought it clever of him to let your father know he wanted to shake without bringing attention to his disability.

Trent held out his hand. When Edgard clasped it, Trent's jaw dropped so far down he looked like one of those giant clown faces on a putt-putt course. "How big *are* you?"

"Trent!" I couldn't believe him. Sometimes he could be downright Yankee.

Edgard's laugh was even more contagious than his wife's. "Your hand feels like a small child's in mine, true? My wife should have warned you I am a very tall man. Two meters, nearly."

It was all I could do not to laugh when Trent must have realized his face was pointed at Edgard's middle instead of his eyes. He bent his head back as if he could actually see him. I don't know why it struck me so funny, but I had to tuck my lips in to keep from laughing.

Edgard turned his attention to me. "Penny, I've heard very good news concerning you and your husband. Is this correct?"

A proud smile crept across my mouth. "It is. We're expecting too."

"And I am told your baby is to come one month after mine. Perhaps they will be good friends."

The scowl left Trent's face. "You too, man? That's great. Congratulations."

I told your father more than once Fatimah was pregnant, which proved how good he was at tuning me out.

Edgard gave Trent a hearty slap on the back that sounded like it might have hurt. "We all have very good reasons to celebrate tonight. Let us begin!"

I was grateful the tension had broken, and your father actually seemed to be warming up to them. Edgard led us to a dining room filled with shelves of carved wood statuettes and a wall covered in family photographs — a slew of smiling faces set against the backdrop of a dusty landscape. In the center of the room sat a table that looked like it was made for preschoolers. It stood just a foot or two off the floor, surrounded by oversize, colorful pillows in place of chairs. It was what I would have expected to see in China, not Africa, but then, I knew nothing of any culture other than my own. In the center of the table sat half a dozen miniature ceramic bowls filled with different-colored sauces, surrounded by half circles of flatbread.

"Tonight you get the Sudanese experience, my friends," Edgard said. "I hope you have come hungry. My wife is an excellent cook. Not as good as my mother, but much better than my sisters. I would be a very fat man if I were not so tall."

Although Fatimah was too dark to see the blush in her cheeks, the way she averted her eyes with the hint of a smile told me it was there.

I whispered in your father's ear that the table was low and we were going to be sitting on pillows. Prepared for a snide remark, I was shocked when none followed.

After we situated ourselves at the table, Fatimah took my hand and her husband's. Edgard and I each took one of Trent's.

Edgard closed his eyes. "Lord Jesus, you

are so good to us. You have given us so much for which to be thankful. You have filled our stomachs with food, our minds with knowledge, our souls with love, and now our women's wombs as well. Thank you for these friends you have brought safely to our home. May we show them every kindness you have shown us."

"Amen," we all said.

Fatimah carried out the first course on a large copper platter. She knelt beside the table like I imagined a geisha might do, and set before each of us a bowl. Although it looked like vegetable soup with chunks of carrots, cabbage, green beans, and white rice, it smelled heavily of garlic and peanuts.

Our hosts waited for Trent and me to go first.

I put a spoon in your father's hand and told him it was hot soup. He sniffed the air wearing an expression that looked like someone had just passed gas. I was determined to make up for his reaction no matter how bad the stuff tasted, or how it affected my queasy stomach.

I scooped a spoonful of vegetables and liquid and blew the steam from it. My tongue was in shock at the combination of tastes I'd never experienced before. It took me a few seconds to decide whether I liked it or not. It was definitely not something I would have ordered again in a restaurant, but it wasn't bad, exactly — just different.

I smiled and hummed as though it were magnificent. Halfway through my serving, I glanced over at your father, surprised to find him scraping his bowl.

Fatimah slipped a piece of flatbread into Trent's hand, which he promptly used to sop up the rest of the broth.

"Penny, I think your husband has a river of Sudanese blood in him," Edgard said.

"Everything is delicious when you're starving," was Trent's backhanded compliment.

"It is called shorba," Fatimah said. "I will teach Peeny to cook for you." A smirk found her lips, and I suspected correctly what was coming. She turned to me. "You make the stock with either lamb, if you prefer savory, or husband, if you prefer bitter."

The comment went right over Trent's head. More than likely, he wasn't really listening to her anyway.

Edgard, however, did not miss it. "Fatimah, watch your tongue. We speak blessings, not cursing."

She hung her head.

"You're all right, Eddie," Trent said. "I

like a man who can put his woman in her place."

Edgard picked up a piece of bread from the platter and dipped it into one of the small bowls of sauces. "God holds me responsible for my family. I am the shepherd."

Trent turned in my direction. "You hear that, Penny?"

I just stared down at my bowl.

Fatimah glared at Trent, then gave me a look that made it clear what she was thinking. She addressed him with a voice far too sweet to be genuine. "There is a difference between a godly husband who leads his family to righteousness and one who leads them by the teeth."

Edgard's jaw clenched.

Fatimah gave him a nervous glance, then added, "I am glad for we who have husbands who do not yank. For God will deliver the prey from the mighty."

Edgard relaxed at this. "This is correct, wife. God will deliver the oppressed. Praise the Lord!"

Trent sat silent a moment, hearing what he wanted to hear and filtering out the rest, I'm sure. Finally, he said. "Well, that was a good meal. Not much to it, but tasty."

Edgard laughed. "That was just course

number one. We still have three to go, my friend."

After we ate a salad that seemed to me a lot like coleslaw without the mayonnaise, Fatimah brought out the main course. Another copper platter filled with whole fish — heads, tails, and all — covered in some sort of tomato sauce. I didn't know how I'd be able to keep it down with their glassy eyes watching me.

Once again, Trent gobbled up every bite as though he hadn't eaten in weeks — this from a man whose favorite food was Spam. I wondered if he would have been quite so hungry if he could see what he was eating.

I tried to help Fatimah clear between courses, but that stubborn woman wouldn't hear of it and kept pushing my hands away.

For dessert, she brought us a bowl of what looked like a nest of spaghetti. She served us each a portion, giving Trent double what she'd given me. With anticipation written all over his face, he brought it to his lips, made a face and spit it back out into his napkin.

"You do not like?" Edgard asked, looking concerned.

"I'm just not used to eating my spaghetti with sugar on it."

"So, our guest is not Sudanese after all,"

Edgard said. "We like you anyway, brother. I do not like all American cuisine either. When I first moved here, I became so skinny before I married Fatimah. I did not understand how to eat your food. I thought butter was the worst cheese I ever tasted."

Fatimah looked at him lovingly. "This is true. One day I found him crushing potato chips into a paste."

When everyone else laughed, I let myself too.

"It is a confusing country at first. I am still unsure by many things," Edgard said. "Christmas, for instance. A tree is taken from its home in the forest, dressed in lights, and displayed in a window. I do not understand what that has to do with the birth of Jesus."

"I thought everyone in your country was Muslim," I said.

Edgard nodded. "Most are, but not all. Fatimah's family was, and they would not approve of our union. Nor my family. But she is my sister now, as well as my bride. I am a lucky man. And she is lucky too."

Trent patted the table. "I'm apparently not lucky at all. I can't even find my dag-gum drink."

"We do not serve with dinner." Fatimah ran a damp cloth over the spot on the table where the bread and sauces had been. "Would you like me to serve you a glass of water?"

"What I'd really like is for you to serve me a twelve-pack." Trent grinned like we would all share his joke.

Edgard furrowed his brow. "You wish to drink twelve waters?"

Trent folded up his napkin full of discarded noodles and set it on the table beside his plate. " 'Water' nothing. I'm talking about beer."

Edgard's smile disappeared. "I do not drink alcohol."

"Is that a Sudanese thing? Surely y'all got booze over there," Trent said.

Fatimah looked at her husband as if seeking permission to speak. Whatever look passed between them must have told her it was okay. "Edgard came to this country two years before me. He was very lonely. It was difficult time. Very difficult."

Edgard rubbed at the face of his watch nervously. "I was accustomed to being surrounded by friends all the time. We played together. Slept together. Ate together. It was a very close community in my home country. Here, I was in a flat with one other man only. I worked too-long hours. He worked too-long hours. I saw no family. I had no time for friends. Lonely and sad, I drank so much then that I cannot drink at all now."

"That must have been hard," I said.

Fatimah put her hand atop her husband's.

"It was a hard life in the Sudan for my family," Edgard continued. "Two of my brothers were taken from my mother's house and forced to join the militia. Made to kill their own people. Leaving my mother and friends behind in this terrible situation was too difficult, but now I can send money. Now I can help them to live a better life."

Although Trent was listening, as usual, he wasn't hearing a word. "Well, at least you're here now, and no matter what everyone else says about immigrants, I think you've got as much right to be here as anyone. The American dream, man — it's for everyone willing to work for it."

Edgard ran his thumb over a scar running across his knuckles. "My dream, my friend, is neither American or Sudanese. It is —" he pounded his heart — "the Christian dream. My responsibility is to my people second, to my God first. True?"

I fell in love then, Manny, not with my best friend's husband, but with his godliness. It was just beautiful. I was so jealous of Fatimah at that moment. Not of what she owned — she had nothing — but she had everything a woman could want.

EIGHTEEN

"How did you get so lucky?" Standing beside Fatimah at the bathroom sink of another McMansion we were hired to clean, I squeezed the nozzle of the spray bottle. A mist of droplets spread like dew across the bathroom mirror as the smell of vinegar filled the air.

She stopped scrubbing the cleanser from one of the bathroom sinks long enough to answer me. "It was not luck. I prayed for an Edgard."

"That must have been some prayer." I pressed my fingertips into the damp paper towel, rubbing hard against a stubborn streak. "You've got a wonderful man. He is so in love with God."

The bright row of vanity lights shone across her face, making her eyes appear more amber than their normal shade of mocha. "He is a good man and I am good woman, too. What of your husband? He is harsh man, I think perhaps."

After wiping away the last bit of lint left by the paper towel, I balled it up and let it drop into the small garbage can beside me. I grabbed the toilet brush from its holder and began to scrub at the ring running along the perimeter of the porcelain bowl. "Not every woman gets a man like Edgard. I hope you know how blessed you are."

"You would not have thought me blessed when I listen to him complain this country allows one wife only."

I stopped scrubbing long enough to turn and look at her. Her cheeks were becoming full from the pregnancy, but the extra weight agreed with her much better than mine did with me.

"Maybe not," I said. As if being second to the TV and his drinking buddies wasn't enough, I couldn't imagine also having to compete with another wife. Suddenly I wasn't quite so jealous.

She brushed a streak of cleanser from her cheek and shrugged. "It is just the way over there."

"So, how did you two meet, anyway?"

She turned the faucet handle and began rinsing white paste from the sink. I had to strain to hear her over the sound of running water.

"Through our guide. His name was Tarik. It was his job to show us about this country's customs when we were relocated. He liked Edgard, as everyone does. Knowing of his loneliness, he introduced us."

I knocked the water from the toilet brush and flushed. Watching blue water swirl down the drain, I asked, "Was it love at first sight?"

She turned around and leaned against the sink. A little smile pulled on her full lips and her eyes lit up. My word, she looked so beautiful, Manny. It hurt to look at that expression because I wanted so much to feel that way about someone. "No. When I first set my eyes upon him, I was very frightened. He was so big. I thought a man that tall can kill me with one punch."

My insides knotted. Now there was a feeling I didn't have to envy.

"I wanted to run away from him and wait for a man not so big." She turned back around, picked up her rag, and went back to scrubbing. "But it did not take me long to see he was a different kind of man. Not like the militia. Not like my father. Like Jesus."

"He is different," I agreed.

I stood and watched her through the bathroom mirror. "Peeny, he is the kind of person I wish to be. Nothing frightens him.

Nothing makes him too angry . . . except disobedience to God. He loves me not because of what I give him or because of my beauty, but because God gave me to him for care." She searched my eyes intently. "Do you understand?"

I didn't, but I wanted to.

She moved to the other sink and sprinkled cleanser over it. "Is your husband a Christian man like Edgard?"

I didn't know what to say. Your father had changed since his accident. He had spoken of God punishing him, but did he really understand what it meant to follow Jesus? I knew he didn't. Not really. "He says he is."

"Men can say many things with their mouths their hearts do not agree with."

"He's having us go to church together now."

Fatimah grinned back at me through the mirror. "Oh, Peeny, that is wonderful. To where you go?"

"New Beginnings over on Oakwood Lane."

A shadow passed over her face.

Pulling the shower curtain back, I looked to see how much work the tub was going to be. A narrow soap scum ring encircled the perimeter, and a wad of red hair lay entrenched in the drain grate, but everything else looked pretty clean. I picked up the can of cleanser from the ledge Fatimah had set it on. "You know the church?"

"I know it." She turned on the second faucet.

"Isn't it a pretty place?" I asked, feeling defensive and a little hurt. I guess I sensed her rejection of the church your father had picked out, and for some reason it felt like a rejection of me.

"Yes, it is pretty," she said, "in same way your husband is pretty."

I wasn't the brightest bulb, Manny, but I wasn't the dimmest, either. "What's that supposed to mean?"

Still scrubbing, she shrugged as if the conversation no longer interested her. "Ask Callie Mae. I do not wish to talk anymore."

My face blazed with anger, but I held my tongue. If there was one thing living with your father had taught me, it was that.

On the drive home from work, I stopped at the food bank to see Callie Mae. Worry filled her face when she saw me walk in. "What is it? Are you okay? Is Fatimah?"

The shelves, which had been overflowing with food the last time I had been there, now stood nearly bare. An overhead incandescent light flickered like it was getting ready to blow, and the place smelled like insecticide. "What's wrong with my church?" I asked.

Callie Mae looked nervously at an elderly man with a patchy white beard filling his bag with what groceries were left, and put a finger over her lips to shush me. She walked over and whispered, "What are you talking about? You look like you've been crying."

I lowered my voice. "I told Fatimah that Trent and I started going to New Beginnings. I asked her what she thought of it. She said it's pretty . . . like my husband is pretty. What's that supposed to mean?"

She brushed a rogue strand of hair from her face. "How should I know? That woman has a language all her own."

I could tell by the way she wouldn't look at me that she understood Fatimah's language just fine. "She said I should ask you what she meant."

She huffed. "I'm going to kill that woman."

I crossed my arms to let her know I wasn't going anywhere until she spilled it.

The shopping man brushed something off the knees of his pants and carried his bag over to Callie Mae. He handed her a voucher, which she examined, scribbled something on, and slipped into her apron pocket. When she offered to take the bag to his car for him, he gave her a look that made it clear the offer offended him. When he left, we were alone.

"What did she mean?" I asked again, hating the quiver in my voice.

Callie Mae's eyes filled with pity. "I think what Fati is saying is that the church is pretty on the outside, but the hearts of some of the people attending there are anything but."

"How would she know?"

"She went there a time or two with Edgard. I don't think either of them felt welcomed with open arms by the congregation."

"Everyone was nice to me," I said.

"You're not exactly all that different-looking from them, now, are you?"

"They weren't like that. There were all kinds of people there."

She shrugged. "Maybe things have changed."

I pushed my purse strap up higher on my shoulder. "So Fatimah is saying my husband is pretty, but not on the inside . . . or what?"

She sighed. "Let's go outside. I need a cigarette."

"I thought you quit."

"I have, and I will again tomorrow."

I followed her out to the back of the building and sat on the steps. Above us, clouds were trying hard to crowd out the sun.

Callie Mae stood on her tiptoes and felt around the inside lip of the canvas awning covering the stoop. Her hand emerged with a pack of Salems and a lighter. She tapped a cigarette out of the pack and looked over her shoulder before sitting down and lighting it. The stench of smoke filled the air as she sucked in a drag. "Let me know if you hear or see anyone." Wisps of gray accompanied each word from her mouth.

"What is she implying about my husband?" I asked again.

She turned her head away from me and blew out a plume of smoke. I stared ahead at the old church van parked at the farthest end of the small lot. Someone had traced the words *mystery machine* onto its dusty back doors. "She doesn't like your husband, Penny."

Even though I already suspected as much, it still hurt to hear it spoken. "Why not? He hasn't done anything to her."

She used her free hand to rub at the center of her forehead as if she were fighting a headache. "She thinks he abuses you."

I felt my muscles tighten. "Do you two just sit around talking about me when I'm not around?"

She gave me a weary look. "Fatimah and I have been friends a long time. We talk. That's what friends do."

"I thought I was her friend."

She took another hit off her cigarette. "You are, sweetheart, and you're mine, too. No one's out to get you here. Did she tell you about her past?" She didn't wait for an answer. "She knows a thing or two about being abused. When she refused to marry the one her father chose for her, a man who was old enough to be her grandfather, he beat her within inches of her life while her brother-in-law held her down."

I flicked an ant off my shoe and watched it scurry into the grass. "That's awful for her, but she doesn't know the first thing about me." Cringing at the thought of what Fatimah had been through, I deluded myself into believing the abuse I'd suffered was somehow more justified. Trent had put up with as much from me as I did from him — jealousy, insecurity, and emotional outbursts for starters.

She knocked the ash off the end of her cigarette onto the concrete step. "Well, she's got it in her mind he's abusive."

I don't know how I got from the offensive to the defensive, but it seemed like it was always that way with me. "Is she just making up stories in her head? She's never seen him lay a hand on me. The only thing he's done is tell her he didn't like her dessert. That doesn't exactly make him Attila the Hun."

Callie Mae gave me a look that made me think she might agree with Fatimah.

"Well, she's wrong," I said.

She stared at me for an uncomfortably long time. When I broke her gaze, she simply said, "Okay."

"He's not," I repeated.

"Okay, he's not abusive. But Fatimah thinks he is."

A car alarm blared in the distance. I turned to look toward the street, but a house and a row of pine trees blocked my view. I stood. "Is that what you think too?"

She took another drag of her cigarette.

"I see."

"She cares about you, Penny. So do I."

The car alarm fell silent. "If she cared about me, she wouldn't spread rumors about me and my husband behind our backs. That's not what friends do."

She smashed what was left of her cigarette against the step. "Friends don't always say what you want to hear. They tell you the truth. 'Faithful are the wounds of a friend.' "

“Thanks,” I said, “but I’ve got all the wounds I need.”

She started to say something else, but the sound of a snapping twig stopped her. We both turned to see a woman coming up the side of the building. She stopped a few feet from us, staring at Callie Mae with a hand dug into her plump hip. I recognized her as the woman who interviewed me the first time I’d come there for help. “You were smoking again, weren’t you, Callie? Don’t you dare even try to deny it this time. I can smell it.”

Callie Mae opened her palm and thrust the wrinkled butt at the woman. “That’s right, Ginny Elizabeth Perfect, I’m smoking. I’m a grown woman. If I want to smoke, I will.”

The woman shook her head in disapproval, making her double chin jiggle. “Do I need to remind you again we are supposed to be God’s temple?”

“Yes, we are,” Callie Mae said. “You try to remember that the next time you pile up a third helping at Lovely Palace Buffet.”

The woman looked at me as if I might step in to defend her from Callie Mae, then looked back to her. “Well, maybe I won’t come out to eat with you anymore if my eating habits offend you.”

Callie Mae shrugged.

The woman turned on her heel, stomped up the back steps, and slammed the door behind her.

"Was that your idea of a faithful wound?" I asked her.

She pulled another cigarette from her pack and lit it. "As a matter of fact, it was."

Nineteen

Work was miserable that week. I planned on giving Fatimah the silent treatment for as long as it took to elicit an apology, but that woman was pure stubbornness. It didn't seem to bother her one iota I wasn't talking to her. She just hummed church hymns and cleaned as if I weren't even there.

It was driving me absolutely crazy. After about day three, I was ready to cave. "So, do you want me to take the upstairs?" I asked.

She picked up a dining room chair from the rug and moved it to the hardwood floor so she could vacuum. "Am I your mother that you should answer to me?"

I gave her a dull look. "You don't need to be rude. I was just asking a simple question."

She picked up a second chair and walked around me with it. As she passed, her familiar scent of unfamiliar spices wafted by. She set the chair in the hall under a framed watercolor of James Dean. "I am not rude. I asked you simple question in return. At least I answer you. That is more than you have done."

I snatched the broom from against the wall. "I'm supposed to answer the question of whether or not you're my mother?" I held out my arm next to hers to compare our skin colors. "Um, from the looks of it, I'd say probably not."

With a blank expression, she picked up another chair. I was so mad I wanted to spit, Manny. But as much as I wanted the tension between us to be gone, I was not about to give in when she was in the wrong. She'd been talking about your father and me behind our backs. She could have come to me and asked me straight up if he was using me as a punching bag — not that I'd have answered truthfully. But then, as far as I was concerned, it was none of her business.

"Fine," I said. "I'll take the kitchen."

She bent over and plugged the vacuum into the wall socket. "I knew you would."

The way she said it was pure ornery. "What's that supposed to mean?"

"I am speaking your language, yes? I have

not reverted to Arabic, true?"

I narrowed my eyes at her. "Just don't talk to me again until you're ready to apologize."

She stood and worked a kink out of the vacuum cord. "Why should I make apologize to you?"

My mouth dropped open in disbelief. "Are you kidding me? You talk about me behind my back to Callie and accuse my husband of being a wife beater. I think that's pretty awful."

Ignoring me, she hit the on button with the toe of her shoe and pushed the humming machine back and forth slowly over the Oriental rug as if she didn't have a care in the world.

That kitchen probably had never been so clean as I worked out my aggression with Pine-Sol and elbow grease on every last crevice, mumbling to myself, arguing with what I imagined Fatimah would say if we were speaking.

I hadn't realized how long I'd been working until she came in with her cleaning caddy all packed and stood there glaring at me.

"What do you want?" I finally said.

She clicked her tongue in irritation. "While you have enjoyed a leisurely cleaning of this one room, I have completed the entire house."

I looked at the digital clock on the microwave, shocked to find I'd been at it for nearly two hours. Embarrassment filled me, but I did my best not to give her the satisfaction of knowing it. "Well, at least they can't say the kitchen isn't clean."

"If it were not for me, that is all that *would* be clean."

That did it. I'd had quite enough of her. "I am so sick of you, Fatimah."

She ignored my comment, grabbed the broom with her free hand, and started for the door. I was so furious I grabbed her shoulder to get her attention. She jerked around and looked at me with a ferociousness that paralyzed me.

I let go.

"You do not ever touch me again," she whispered.

"I was just trying to get you to stop."

She pointed the broom handle at me. "You touch me like that again, and you will lose your hand. True."

"I'm not scared of you," I said, but of course, I was.

When she set the caddy on the floor and the broom against the wall, I thought she was fixing to whoop me.

My adrenaline started to flow as I watched

her, fists at my side ready to defend myself.

Her eyes were wild as she pointed her finger inches from my face. "I was beaten. I was raped. I was spit on. No one will put their hand on me ever again. Do you understand?"

I nodded.

Manny, in life there is a time and place to stand up for yourself, but always walk away from crazy if you can. That's just what she was at that moment.

"Just because your husband puts his hands on you does not allow you permission to put yours on me."

"Why do you think that?" I asked, partly to de-escalate the situation, partly just really wanting to know how she had come to the conclusion I was a battered wife.

"I do not think it. I know it."

"You don't know anything," I said. "You shouldn't have said that to Callie."

The wild look in her eyes left as quickly as it had come. "I do not know many things, Peeny. I am without education, but I can read the fear of a wife whose husband beats her. He hits you, yes. But the bruises that cannot be seen are the most painful of all. True?"

I couldn't breathe. Why was it now when things were improving with Trent I should be called out? He was doing better. I didn't want to talk about it now. The abuse was history. A history I didn't want to relive. "You're wrong, Fatimah."

She grabbed the handle of her caddy. "Your husband is blind, but I am not."

I grabbed the broom, pushed past her, and got into the car. I sat staring out the window at a half-dead willow tree that looked as defeated as I felt. Expressionless, Fatimah put the cleaning supplies into the backseat and slid behind the wheel.

"We have one house more only. It is a good thing, too. It is the giant house that ate all the other houses on the street."

"Why are you talking to me?" I asked, still staring out the window. A robin disappeared behind the crumbling brown-and-green curtain of willow leaves.

She turned the ignition and backed out of the driveway. "Why shouldn't I?"

I gave her an annoyed look. "Are you for real?"

"I am real," she said as if my hypothetical question really needed an answer. "Are you?"

I whipped my head back toward the window and watched houses and cars blur by. The neighborhood we were driving to was a good twenty-minute ride. Fifteen minutes in, I broke. "You're wrong."

"About the house?"

"About Trent."

"No." She pulled off the ramp onto the next main road. When a traffic light blinked from green to yellow, she slammed on the brakes. I threw my palm onto the dashboard to catch myself. Apparently no one told her a yellow light meant gun it, not come to a screeching stop.

"He did hit me — you're right about that. But he doesn't do it anymore."

She gave me a dull look. "When does he stop?"

I tried to mentally form my answer so it didn't sound so pathetic when it came out of my mouth.

"I will have guess." She tapped a rhythm against the steering wheel with her thumbs. "When he lost his eyes."

The truth of what she said struck me. "So what? He's changing. That's what matters."

The light flashed green, and Fatimah punched the gas, pushing me back into my seat. "If he never lost his sight, he would still hit on you."

I didn't want to believe she was right. After all, his eyes were improving each day. What if his vision came back completely? I shuddered to consider it. "But he did, and he doesn't."

"Heart do not begin to see just because eyes no longer can."

I was so sick of her philosophical mumbo jumbo. "You don't know everything. Why can't you admit you don't know Trent's heart? Only God does."

"God give me discernment, and I see him for who he is. You are his wife. You see too, even if you will not make admit."

I turned my head so she couldn't see the tears filling my eyes.

"You cry because I am honest. It is not your fault, Peeny. It was not my fault my father beat me. It was not my fault I was raped. The shame was theirs, not for mine. The shame is your husband's. Not yours."

"He's better now," I said around sniffles. "People can change. He's changed."

She pulled along the shoulder of the road and rolled to a stop in front of a black mailbox affixed to a splintered piece of timber. A bald man watched us from his porch swing.

Fatimah just looked at me for the longest time. Finally, she said, "I do not know how many times your husband has beats you. I only know no man hits a woman just once."

Twenty

I couldn't wait to get home to your father, lie with him on the couch, and forget about my awful day. Of course I wasn't about to discuss with him what Fatimah accused him of. I didn't want to listen to him curse her out and guilt me into quitting the job. Lying beside him would have to be comfort enough. As it turned out, even that was too much to ask.

The smell of booze and a cloud of marijuana and cigarette smoke hit me as soon as I opened the door. Trent sat on the couch beside that black-haired woman from the hospital. A dozen empty beer cans littered the cocktail table and carpet, and a mound of cigarette butts overflowed the ashtray. Some were smoked down to the filter, while others had been lit and forgotten — nothing but a long gray ash.

Trent and Norma were laughing so hard they didn't even hear me come in.

"What's going on?" I asked.

Through slit eyes, they clamped their mouths and looked at me . . . then started laughing again.

I'm not proud to admit it, but I felt one chuckle away from ripping that woman's straggly hair right out of her head. Lucky for both of us, she shut her mouth real quick and looked at your father. Funny how I used to blame all the wrong people for my troubles. Guess it felt safer that way.

He fought to catch his breath through the laughter. "Penny, you remember Norma from work."

My mouth said nothing. My eyes, I hoped, said all that needed saying.

Tripping all over herself trying to get to me, she put a hand out for me to shake. Her long nails wore a coat of chipped fire-engine red. I just looked down at her hand until she withdrew it. "I'm sorry, Penny. I know how this must look, but believe me we were just —"

"Oh, shut up, Norma." Trent took a gulp from the beer in his hand, then crushed the can between his palms and dropped it to the floor. It clinked against another empty. "Penny, don't be rude. Norma here brought us good news. Very good news, as a matter of fact. We're just celebrating. Come have a beer with us."

Us. To my ears, the word sounded like fingernails scraping across a chalkboard. "What news?" I asked coldly, eyeing the woman. With her beak of a nose and beady black eyes, she looked like a crow, but she had curves where I didn't. Trent always said I had the body of a tomboy. The way he said it made it clear he wouldn't mind more. And once again, he had it.

He reached into his pants pocket and pulled out a check, then snapped it. "I'm back on the payroll, baby. Our money worries are slam-bam over."

"What are you talking about?" I watched her watch him.

Norma stood in the middle of our living room in her painted-on jeans and spiked heels, high as a weather balloon, fidgeting with her hands as if she couldn't figure out what to do with them. "I talked Ralph into putting Trent back on the payroll until his disability goes through."

"That right?" I asked, wondering why it was okay for him to take charity, but not me.

"Turns out all she had to do was tell him I'd been talking to a lawyer," he said.

"Stanford Gourdfest." They both vomited the name at the same time and started laughing again like it was the funniest thing they'd ever heard.

Trent caught his breath. "She couldn't make up a name like John Smith, no —" he gave her a side glance — "she had to come up with Stanford Pumpkin-Party."

She feigned an indignant look. "Hey, it worked, didn't it?"

I searched her and Trent for signs they'd been together. Their clothes weren't disheveled. Their hair didn't look a mess. I started to relax . . . until I noticed a smear of pink grease by Trent's left ear — the same shade as Norma's faded lipstick.

My stomach bottomed out as I fought to keep my voice steady. "You've got lipstick on your face."

He rubbed at the wrong cheek with his knuckles. "There you go, jumping to conclusions again. She kissed my cheek; so what? Your mama never kissed your cheek? Was it sexual?"

I pushed my purse up and crossed my arms. "I want her out of here, right now."

Norma's bloodshot gaze ping-ponged between us.

"Now you wait just a minute," Trent started to say, but she cut him off.

"No, it's okay. I've got to go. I don't blame her. I wouldn't like to come home and find some strange woman in my house with my husband."

When his jaw clenched, an idea came to me. He was as jealous as they came, so I decided to test their relationship.

"I'm sorry," I said. "Norma, is it? Thanks for doing that for us. You're a godsend. I just had a bad day, is all. I shouldn't take it out on you. Please stay and have another beer."

She looked at Trent, unsure, then picked up her purse — a zebra print that had started to turn the same shade of yellow as our walls. "I really have to get home."

"I'll bet a pretty woman like you has got some kind of man to go home to," I forced out.

No crinkles formed around her eyes as she smiled.

I watched Trent's face turn shades of red.

"What's your husband do?" I asked.

She looked at him as if needing permission to answer. "He's a welder, like Trent."

I set my bag on the entry table, but hung on to the car keys, just in case. "Oh, so he works with you?"

She shifted from one foot to the other. "He has in the past. Now he mostly don't work nowhere."

I faked a look of pity. "Why is that?"

"He says he's too pretty to work."

My laughter sounded as phony as it felt. "With a gorgeous woman like you, I bet he is," I practically choked on the compliment, all the while watching your father from my periphery.

"Penny, stop giving her the inquisition," he growled.

"I'm just being friendly. Sheesh. You tell me not to be rude, and then not to talk nice. Can't have it both ways, darling." My boldness was uncharacteristic for me. My counselor likes to say a person only changes when their belly finally gets full, and I think that night mine had begun to.

"Nothing wrong with having a pretty man," I said, relishing the flush in Trent's neck and the squirm in Norma's stance.

I imagined that this woman had a very definite type — good-looking, lazy alcoholics.

"Well, Penny, it was nice to see you again, but I really ought to get home." She started for the door and turned around to look at Trent. "I hope that helps. I'll make sure those checks keep coming until your disability rolls in, okay?"

"Whatever. Run on home now to your pretty husband." His icy words answered every question I had. Although I wasn't surprised, I still managed to feel devastated.

"You know you shouldn't be driving in your condition," I said as her hand reached for the doorknob. I wasn't worried about her as much as the unsuspecting people she might come in contact with. "Why don't you call your husband to come get you?"

She waved her hand in dismissal. "Shoot. I drive better this way. It's the only time I'm too afraid not to do the speed limit."

Lovely, I thought. Silently, I asked God to keep her from hurting anyone and wished I had it in me to pray for her too. You know, Manny, I still find myself thinking about that opportunity I missed to pray for her protection, and I can't help but wonder if that one prayer might have changed everything. Guess even now, I like to take the guilt of the world on my shoulders, as if anyone besides Jesus could bear that weight.

When Norma finally left, I went to the window and watched her crawl into the beat-up Honda across the street.

"What was that?" he demanded.

"What was what?" I tried my best to sound indifferent, but inside I was full of hatred. I left him standing there with his jealousy and walked to the kitchen.

"Don't you walk away from me," he called. "Get your skinny rear back in this living room and tell me why you think you have the right to talk to my friends like they're trash."

Turning the water on, I drowned him out as I started on the dishes he had left for me in the sink. Two plates. Two forks. Two cups — one with her lipstick all over the rim. And of course, I was expected to wash it off.

The image of them together played in my mind. Her lips kissing his cheek, then mouth, then neck. Rage filled me. I slammed the plate to the floor. With a loud crack, it smashed to pieces.

Trent hurried to the kitchen with a look of concern. "What happened?"

I picked up a plastic cup from the sink and threw it at his head, nailing him in the forehead. His hand flew up to protect his face a second too late.

Grabbing the other plate, with every intention of hurling it at him, I froze when I saw him cowering. It took the fight right out of me. My grandmother used to say if you kiss a frog, he doesn't turn into a prince; you turn into a frog. I realized then, that's exactly what was happening to me.

I set the dish back in the sink. "I'm sorry," I whispered.

"Dag, Penny. What's wrong with you today?"

I wrapped my arms around myself, feeling suddenly cold and scared. "You slept with her."

"What?" He made an annoyed face. "Don't even start —"

Before I could swallow them back, sobs wrenched from me, and I sank to my knees. "I'm having your baby and you're sleeping with that woman. My baby's not going to have her father." I was crying so hard I could barely breathe.

I felt his hand fall on my shoulder, but I didn't even have the energy to flinch. I think I wanted him to beat me then. Feeling the physical pain was so much better than the anguish eating me up inside. But he didn't raise a hand. Instead, he knelt beside me on the linoleum and wrapped his arms tight around me. "No, Penny. No. Shhh. I'm not sleeping with her. She's just a coworker. Why would I want that weathered old thing, when I've got a trophy wife like you?"

As stupid as it was, his words made me feel better. I knew it was a lie. I was no trophy, and she wasn't all that weathered, but I needed to believe it. I was having his baby. I was his wife. My choice was to believe it or leave, and I wasn't ready to do that.

"And you're smoking in the house," I said around tears. "You promised you wouldn't. Our baby's breathing in secondhand smoke right now!" The thought made me cry even harder.

"I'm sorry." He nuzzled his face into my neck. "You're right. I'm done. I won't let her in here anymore if it upsets you this much. And I won't smoke in the house again. I swear it." He wiped at my eyes, getting more of my eyebrows than lids. "Shhh, now. Calm down. This has got to be hurting the baby more than a little smoke. Come on, now. I love you. I love our baby. That woman don't mean nothing to me."

After a few jagged breaths, I'd calmed down, feeling more pathetic than ever. I hated it that I cared so much what he did or who he did it with, but despite everything, I loved him, Manny. Or rather, that's what I told myself. Truth was, I was just trying to control my world in a way I wasn't able to as a child. Like my father, Trent hurt and rejected me, and I realize now I was still trying to right that wrong. Trying desperately to get a man to cherish me who didn't have it in him to.

I sat beside him on the couch, wiping at

my eyes and watching the evening news as he listened. Two burglaries and three murders later, he turned to me and said, "You know what this means, don't you?"

I laid my head on his shoulder, taking in his warmth. "What *what* means?"

"My check."

I suspected what he was going to say, but played stupid, hoping I was wrong. "What?"

"You can quit that job now."

I had no intention of quitting even if I was mad at Fatimah and Callie Mae. If things were bad when he was working, I could imagine how much worse they would be with him home all the time.

"We'll see," I said.

His voice lowered an octave. "I said you can quit your job."

I stood and started picking up his empties. "Trent, please. I'm not up for this right now. I've had a terrible day all around."

"Well, now you don't have to worry about any more bad days."

As if that were so. "We're going to have a lot more bills when the baby comes," I said. "Diapers, formula, college."

"You ain't farming my kid out to some two-bit day care."

"I'll quit when she comes, okay?"

He didn't say anything, just sat back with

that crease between his eyebrows.

It dawned on me what life was going to be like for you. Whether I worked or not. Your father might worship the ground you walked on and treat you like a prince or princess, but if he was demeaning me in front of you, what would you grow up to be like? A man who would do the same to your wife someday? Or maybe a woman like me and Mama, who would put up with it?

I tried to push the thought from my mind, but it refused to budge. There was nothing I could do about it, I told myself. It would all work out. I would pray like I never prayed before for your father to change. And somehow, some way, things would be all right.

Twenty-One

Isolation is an abuser's best weapon. If a woman has no friends or family around, then who can tell her that what she's putting up with at home isn't normal? Where will she go if she decides she's finally had enough? Who will build her up so she starts believing in herself enough to say no to what she knows, in her heart of hearts, isn't right? The abuser tells her that he should be enough for her, but one person can never be all things to someone else.

Most women have sisters, friends, or mothers in their lives to teach them about their bodies. I'd been a teenager when I met your father, and completely isolated until getting the cleaning job. I knew nothing about what was or wasn't normal for pregnancy.

When I finally spoke to my mother about you, she recommended I pick up some books from the library, but I hadn't gotten around to it yet. I so wished Trent would go out somewhere and leave me alone in the house so I could call her again. There were so many things I wanted to ask her.

One morning at work, Fatimah and I were just getting started on cleaning our first house when I discovered I was bleeding a little bit. I didn't know enough to be worried.

Fatimah wore her face mask as she mixed up a new batch of bleach water in the kitchen sink. The smell burned my nostrils as I approached her.

"Where is your mask?" she asked.

I backed up a few steps. "Is it a problem if I'm bleeding?"

She screwed the cap back on the bleach bottle and set it on the tiled floor. "You are bleeding?"

I fidgeted. "It's just a few spots."

"You should not have blood." She set the bottle on the counter beside the toaster and turned around. The look in her eyes worried me. "Have you tell it to your doctor?"

"It's just a few drops," I repeated.

"I call Callie Mae." She used the house phone to relay what was going on. When she hung up, she said to me, "She will meet us at the clinic."

As we gathered our supplies, the frantic

pace at which Fatimah worked troubled me. Here was a woman who delivered babies. She knew a lot better than me what was and wasn't of concern.

At the clinic, we were led to a small room that smelled of rubbing alcohol and lotion. Several chairs faced a wall of thick procedural manuals and one rough-looking *Woman's Day* sitting atop a rolling chair. After what seemed like forever, a redhead dressed in scrubs walked in, holding a clipboard. She picked up the magazine to free the chair, and sat down across from us. "How far along are you? When did the bleeding start? Do you feel cramping?" and the questions continued until her form had been filled out to her satisfaction.

After she finished gathering information, she led me to a room across from the one I'd gotten my ultrasound in. Fatimah waited outside the door while I replaced the clothes I wore with a thin paper gown. I sat on the examining table listening to overhead music and the sound of wax paper crinkling beneath me as I fidgeted. When I told Fatimah she could come back in, Callie Mae was with her.

She rushed over and gave me a hug, smothering me in her warmth. "Oh, sweetie.

It's going to be okay."

I was already so in love with you, Manny. Losing you after everything else I'd lost in my life would kill me. "It's not me I'm worried about," I said.

"Your baby's going to be just fine." Callie Mae guided my head to her shoulder and stroked my hair like my mother used to do.

"What if she's not?" I dared to ask.

Fatimah took my hand and held it. Hers was so cold. "I see many women bleed in my country. Having blood sometimes is a very bad situation, but sometimes is nothing."

Very bad. Those words hung in the air like a guillotine ready to crash down on me.

Callie Mae frowned at her. "That's not helpful."

Fatimah gave her a perturbed look. "I said sometimes is nothing."

Instinctively, I held a hand over my belly as if that could protect you somehow. Callie Mae laid her hands over mine. Fatimah added hers to the pile, and the three of us took turns praying you would be okay.

After a while, the nurse returned, along with an Asian man in a white lab coat who looked too young to be a doctor. He put his hand out for me to shake. "Good morning. I'm Doctor Lee."

His hand felt softer and smaller than any man's should. I repeated to him the same things I told the nurse.

"I need to have a look." He turned to Callie Mae and Fatimah. "Would you two please have a seat in the waiting room? I'll call you when we're finished."

Callie Mae must have sensed I didn't want to be alone because she said, "Can I stay with her?"

He looked to the nurse, who nodded, then to me. "Is it okay with you, Mrs. Taylor?"

"Please," I said.

Callie Mae stood at the head of the exam table beside me, holding my hand and looking only at my face. The doctor placed my feet in cold, metal stirrups and asked me to relax my knees. I wondered how relaxed he would be if he'd been the one lying there.

He pulled a vinyl curtain, hiding us from the shut door. Trying to ignore the weird foreignness of what the doctor was doing, I concentrated on Callie Mae's smile. Her thin lips were outlined in peach and filled in with a lighter shade of the same color. Her teeth were small and slightly yellowed. I wondered if they would get whiter if she were to give up the cigarettes.

She made small talk about the weather as the doctor probed around looking for whatever it was he was looking for. He said nothing to give me an indication of what he was or wasn't finding.

"I called Trent," Callie Mae said.

"What did he say?" I asked, wondering if he was sober when she reached him. I figured he probably was, since he only rarely started bingeing before noon.

The doctor pulled out the metal speculum from me and, with a clang, set it in the bowl the nurse held out to him.

The noise made Callie Mae turn her head. "He was worried about you and the baby."

"What did he say?" I repeated.

She fixed her attention back on me. "He's on his way over here. I offered to pick him up, but he said he'd call a cab."

I worried about him trying to navigate his way outside, and if he'd be taken advantage of when it came time to pay. The fact he cared enough to do that for me meant everything.

The doctor told me I could slide my bottom up as he helped my feet out of the stirrups. He threw out his gloves, washed his hands, and asked me to pull up my gown so he could get to my stomach. When I did, he squirted cold goo on my belly button, then pushed around a small Doppler over my stomach until the *whoosh-whoosh* sound of the baby's heartbeat filled the room. When it did, I smiled.

"That's too slow," he said, as if he could read my mind.

He moved the Doppler lower. "That was *your* heartb—" Before he could even finish, he picked up another beat, this one much faster. He looked at me. "This is your baby's. It's strong and steady. That's what I wanted to hear."

A huge weight fell off my shoulders when I heard your little heartbeat, Manny. I could have listened to it all day, but Doctor Lee turned the Doppler off and used a small hand towel to wipe the gel off my skin.

He tossed the dirty towel into a hamper, washed his hands again, and then he and Callie Mae stepped out of the room so I could get dressed. He said he would be back to talk to me in a few minutes.

After I was dressed, I walked to the door, intending to let someone know I was ready. As I started to open it, I could hear your father's voice. He was breathless, asking Callie Mae about me.

When I opened the door, Callie Mae led him to me.

"Trent," I said. "Thank you for coming."

He looked a mess with his wrinkled shirt and scruffy face, but even so, he was a sight for sore eyes. "Why are you thanking me for coming?" he asked. "That's my baby in there. Why wouldn't I?"

Maybe I was being too sensitive, but his omission of me in that statement of concern made my heart hurt.

I hugged him as Callie Mae excused herself to join Fatimah in the waiting room. I pulled up the chair next to the exam table and sat him down.

"We heard the baby's heartbeat," I said. "So she must be okay."

"Why do you keep calling him a she?" he asked.

"Why do you keep calling her a he?"

His brief smile faded. "I was so scared, Penny. If anything happened to you . . ." his words trailed off as he choked up.

Someone knocked twice on the door and it opened. Doctor Lee stepped in, without the nurse this time. He introduced himself to your father and pulled up a rolling stool to sit on. "I think your bleeding is nothing to be concerned about, but until I get you in for another ultrasound, I want to play it safe. Until we tell you otherwise, I want you to refrain from sex, tub baths, and anything strenuous. Light bleeding is fairly common, but the main worry is you might have something called placenta previa."

Trent opened his mouth, I'm sure to ask what that was, but the doctor continued. "That's a condition when the placenta grows in the lowest part of the womb, covering all or part of the cervix."

I felt like such an idiot. I didn't even know what a cervix is and was too embarrassed to ask.

"What if she has that?" Trent asked, leaning forward.

Doctor Lee looked down at the beeper hanging on his jacket pocket, then back up at us. "We'll know for sure when we do the ultrasound. If she does have it, we'll have to take special precautions. I don't want to worry you unnecessarily, so let's try not to go there unless we need to."

"Do you look as young as you sound?" Trent asked.

The doctor grimaced as if he were sick of the question. "I'm twenty-seven, and yes, to answer your question, I look young."

"Thank you, Doctor," I said, trying to get him out of the room before Trent could say something more to embarrass me. "When do you want me back?"

Doctor Lee stood and rolled the stool back over to the side of the cabinet where he'd gotten it. "Tell the front desk I want them to work you in by the end of this week."

Twenty-Two

The five days between my doctor visit and the ultrasound appointment were bittersweet. Callie Mae wouldn't let me work again until my follow-up appointment, so I had to endure nearly a week of being home with Trent. He tried his best not to let me lift a finger, but ended up making more work than if he'd just left me alone.

When he tried to cook spaghetti for dinner, the pot ran over and smoked up the kitchen. When he washed the dishes, he broke a glass and couldn't see well enough to make sure he got all the shards off the floor. And when the phone rang, he tripped more than once trying to get to it in time. I ended up nursing him more than the other way around. He was trying, though, bless his heart, and I was proud of him for that.

After my return visit to the doctor, I relayed to Callie Mae I didn't have placenta previa like we feared, but she made me bring her a note that spelled out my limitations just the same. I felt like a child trying to get out of gym class, or rather into it, but knowing concern was her motivation made up for the aggravation.

It was so nice to be cared about. I hadn't had that kind of love and attention surrounding me since I was a child. I did everything in my power to keep it that way too — ignoring your father's daily drunkenness and the different turns his abuse took. He no longer hit me, but he found plenty of other ways to torment me. I did whatever he wanted, even through tears sometimes, to keep my job, to keep you safe, and if I'm being honest, to hold on to the illusion that he loved me.

In the months that followed, I received the happy news, via ultrasound, that you were a boy. It took a little while to adjust to, since I'd been so sure you were a girl. But I warmed up to the idea quickly when I saw the tiny bow ties and suspenders in the department store. Your father, of course, had known all along you were a boy. But then, in his mind, what didn't he know?

His vision returned so gradually we hardly noticed the difference until the day his doctor okayed him to return to work. That's when the real trouble began.

It was Monday morning, and I was up fixing his breakfast. He strolled into the kitchen in his uniform. "Let me guess, eggs again?"

Now that he could see me, I couldn't just roll my eyes at him as I'd done before. With my back to him, I stirred the eggs in the pan. "We have a little sausage left. I could mix it in and add some cheese."

He huffed. "No matter what you do to them, they're still eggs."

I closed my eyes and begged God to help me hold my tongue. My hormones were raging and my stomach was cramping. "I didn't realize you were sick of them." *How would I realize it?* I wanted to say. *You were the one cooking your own breakfast all weekend.* But as usual, I said nothing.

He yanked the coffeepot off the burner and poured himself a cup. "It's my first day back to work. What does it matter if I go in hungry?"

Turning the stove off, I set the spatula on the counter beside my cup of tea and turned around. "What would you like?"

"What I'd like is a woman who knows what it means to be a wife."

Before I could stop myself, I said, "Like Norma?"

His face tightened into an angry ball. "So help me, if you start accusing me of that again —"

A car horn sounded from the driveway, telling me Fatimah was there to pick me up. Trent stomped to the living room window and yanked back the curtain. "What's loudmouth doing here?"

I slipped my coat on and grabbed my purse off the counter. "I figured you'd be taking the car, so she's going to start driving me." It was only one more week till Fatimah's baby was due, but at least for this week, I was looking forward to not being dependent on Trent for getting to work.

"Tell your little friend I'll take you to work."

"You can't," I said. "That would make you late."

He let go of the curtain and turned around. "You think you're something special, prancing around in those houses all day, don't you?"

Yes, Manny, that's exactly what I thought — fancy me with my fancy sponge scrubbing fancy toilets. Fatimah honked again. I glanced out the window at her. The exhaust from her tailpipe turned to crystals in the winter air. Through the windshield, she stared at the front door, tapping her fingers against the steering wheel.

I walked back to the kitchen and pulled my bagged lunch from the fridge. "I told you I'd quit when the baby comes. It's only for one more month."

He grabbed his mug off the counter and gulped. "I said I'll drive you."

I opened my mouth to argue, but before I could get the first word out, he slapped it right off my lips. The sting of his hand against my cheek brought tears to my eyes. It was the first time he'd hit me since I became pregnant. The fact that it was also his first day back to work didn't escape me.

I set my purse on the counter and gave him a hurt look.

He swiped spilled coffee from his hand. "Go waddle your fat self out there and tell her your husband will drive you."

Fatimah sat in her car with the window down, listening to some talk show. When she saw me, she grinned. "Hurry. I want to finish early today. Edgard has present for the baby."

When I walked over to the driver's side window instead of the passenger side, her smile faded. "What is wrong, Peeny? Why do you not get in?" She looked at my empty hands. "Where is your bag?"

I pulled my coat closed against the cold.

"Trent wants to drive me to work today."

Under a furrowed brow, she eyed my cheek. "What is that?"

I touched my face and flinched from the pain. If I'd realized he'd left a mark, I would have had an excuse ready. As it was, all that would roll off my tongue was the biggest cliché in the book. "I fell."

She white-knuckled the steering wheel. "That filthy —"

"Stop," I said. "There you go jumping to conclusions again."

Fire burned in her eyes. "You have a baby — his baby — in your womb, and he hits you? You make call to the police."

I put my finger over my lips so she would lower her voice. "He's just stressed out. It's his first day back to work. That's all."

When she started to open the car door, I panicked. Between the murderous look on her face and Trent's mood, I knew a confrontation between them would end with someone — most likely Fatimah or her baby — getting hurt. "What are you doing?" I shut the door before she could get out.

She pointed at me through the open window. "No one is going to hurt my friend. I will tell him he is no man."

I turned back to see Trent standing in the window, holding back the curtain.

I lowered my voice. "It's not going to change anything."

She leaned toward the passenger door and unlocked it. "Get in. You stay with me and Edgard."

"Stop, Fatimah. I'm not leaving my husband."

Sunlight streamed in through the windshield and across her face. She was perspiring despite the weather. "You tell me why not?"

"Because I made a covenant before God until death do us part."

She clicked her tongue. "And what of his treatment of you? Is he not required by God to take care of you? To love you as Christ loves the church. This is not love!"

I glanced nervously back at the window, but Trent was gone. "You don't know everything."

"I know he will kill you." She chewed her top lip, looking at the house as if considering her options. Finally she said, "He hurts you because you permit him."

I frowned at her. "I don't let him. He just does."

"When he hurts you, you do not leave. You do not call police. Why should he not hit you? You still cook him dinner and lie in his bed. This is permission." She looked at me for the longest time. "Do you want change, Peeny?"

"What kind of question is that? You know I do."

She nodded as if she knew as much. "Very good. Then change."

Her words made no sense to me then, Manny, but I realize now they were the key that could unlock everything. "Just go," I said.

With lips pressed tight, she rolled up her window. As her car tore out of the driveway and disappeared down the road, it felt like I was watching hope itself drive away.

My head began to throb from confusion. I knew the world would tell me I should leave Trent, but a good Christian woman like Fatimah?

Slowly, I walked up the stairs, ready to face your father again. He was now sitting at the table. The eggs were no longer in the pan, but there wasn't a dirty dish in front of him, or anywhere else, which told me he'd probably thrown them away.

He rattled the change in his pocket. "What was she hollering about out there?"

"She was mad because I asked her to pick me up, then changed my mind."

"Too bad. So sad," was his charming reply. He took a gulp of coffee from his mug. "You better get on those pancakes, or we're both going to be late."

Twenty-Three

Fatimah didn't say a word to me as we worked. She wouldn't even acknowledge I was there until the drive home. My word, that woman could hold a grudge.

"You missed my turn," I said as we whizzed past the drugstore on the corner.

Stone-faced, she stared ahead at the road. "I am not take you home."

"What?" Her words from earlier replayed in my mind. She wanted me to leave Trent. To live with her and Edgard. But we weren't heading toward her apartment. Where, then?

Sunlight stabbed through the windshield, nearly blinding me. Pulling the visor down, I shielded my face.

Fatimah flipped on her blinker. "Callie Mae want to see us. This is where we go."

We turned from the one-lane road onto the highway, and I relaxed. Fatimah's baby was due in a week, and mine soon after. I'd been wondering when Callie Mae was planning to discuss how she would handle our work schedules. Today must be the day. Trent wasn't going to be home for a few hours, so I didn't have to worry about him fussing about me being late.

I stared at Fatimah's profile, wishing she would at least look at me. "Where are we meeting her?"

"Her house."

The car bumped and hummed along the road as I watched my breath turn to frost in the cold air. I reached over and turned on the heat.

Fatimah glared down at my hand, then at me. "You are cold? I am burning alive."

I rubbed at the too-thin sleeves of my coat. "It's like thirty degrees out. How can you be hot?" In my pregnancy, I hadn't experienced any of the hot flashes Fatimah and other women complained about. With winter upon us, I would have welcomed a few.

She didn't answer, so I split the difference on the dial. Heat streamed out of the dashboard vent and I held my hands over it to warm them. After a few minutes, we turned into a newer neighborhood lined with young, leafless trees and huge houses with almost nonexistent yards. Each house on the street was roughly the same size and shape, just a different facade.

"Callie lives here?" I knew she had money. Her husband had been a successful attorney, so I wasn't surprised she would live in an expensive house. I just expected one with a little charm to it.

Fatimah didn't answer. I knew her well enough by then to understand that her silent treatment would last only a few days, so I didn't worry.

We pulled into the driveway of a stately brick house outlined in rows of perfectly trimmed boxwoods. Together, Fatimah and I walked up the paved pathway. The door opened and Callie Mae stood there wearing a pair of jeans, a turtleneck sweater, and a somber expression. She waved us inside.

As we entered the warmth of the foyer, I noticed an arched shelf built into the wall. On it stood a sculpture of a woman with butterfly wings fashioned from pink, purple, and blue stained glass. I stopped to admire it. Standing around six inches tall, her long, wavy hair covered her body like a mermaid's. She reached her graceful fingertips heavenward with such a look of longing, I couldn't help but feel it too. Her wings were spread and ready for flight, but a vine wound tightly around her ankles, binding her to the stone base.

"It's beautiful, isn't it?" Callie Mae said from behind me.

The piece managed to both fascinate and disturb me, though I couldn't put my finger on why.

Callie Mae led us down a wide, white-tiled hallway that smelled vaguely of lemon. I looked back over my shoulder at the sculpture and listened to our footsteps echoing in the open space. I wondered what Callie Mae could possibly want with so much house. It seemed rude to ask, so as usual, I kept my questions to myself.

Fatimah and I followed her to a room that had no television, just some leather furniture centered around a large fireplace. The walls were painted light gray, and the trim a darker shade of the same color. Fatimah plopped on the white sofa as though it were her own and plucked a dead leaf off a small bouquet of pink flowers resting in the center of a glass table.

Callie Mae grabbed a remote off the stone mantel and pointed it at the fireplace. The logs glowed red as warmth emanated from them. I slipped off my jacket and laid it over the back of a chair. Above the mantel hung a large oil painting. I stared up at the field of painted wildflowers, imagining what it would be like to be among them. I hadn't realized I'd gotten lost in it until Callie Mae startled me with a question.

"You like art, don't you, Penny?"

Embarrassed, I averted my eyes from the painting. "I guess I do. I've never been around much of it."

While Fatimah and Callie Mae made chitchat, I snuck another glance at the painting. Layer upon layer of different colors made up the field and sky. It fascinated me that I could make out the swirls and feathering of the brushstrokes.

"A friend of mine gave me that as a gift after Matthew passed away," Callie Mae said.

I raised my eyebrows in surprise. "It's beautiful. I wish I had a friend like that."

She wore a curious smile as she motioned toward Fatimah with a nod. "You do."

When I looked at her, Fatimah was still wearing that same stony expression she had worn all day.

"You did that?" I asked her.

She leaned back against the couch cushions and shrugged like it was no big deal.

My mouth gaped. "You never told me you could paint like that!" The truth was, she never told me she could paint at all. That woman was, and continues to be, full of surprises.

She frowned at me. "I paint. So?"

I laughed. "So, Rembrandt is cleaning houses for a living."

Gesturing toward the empty chair where I had laid my jacket, Callie Mae indicated I should sit. "It's not easy to make a living in the arts."

"Have you tried?" I asked Fatimah.

She gave me a dull look. "Of course I try. I sell paintings sometimes, but they are much work. I give more than two hundred hours for that one. No one wants to pay their worth unless you are famous or have died. I am alive and do not sell my paintings for nothing. I rather give to friends than cheap strangers."

Looking at her bulging belly and beautiful face, it was like I was seeing Fatimah for the first time. I had no idea she was that full of talent, and I was suddenly a little starstruck.

"Can I get you a drink — water, tea, anything?" Callie Mae asked us.

Fatimah shook her head.

"I'm fine," I said.

Callie Mae sat beside Fatimah on the couch and crossed her legs. "Okay, then, let's get this over with. Fatimah is due next week, but we all know by looking at her the baby could drop out tomorrow." She glanced at me. "Penny, hopefully you've got another month, but just in case, I don't want to wait until the last minute to work out your maternity leave."

For the next few minutes we discussed what would happen once the babies came. Fatimah said she would not be back to work because it was her job to stay home with her child. Callie Mae didn't seem at all surprised. "I figured as much, Fati. I think if y'all will be okay financially, you're making a wise decision. They're only young once. But don't think for a hot second you're going to get away from me that easy. I'll be by once a week at least to check on you and . . . what *is* that baby's name going to be?"

Fatimah puckered her lips, looking perturbed by the question. "It is not for you to know."

Callie shook her head. "Fine. We'll just call her Stubborn after her mother until we hear otherwise." Turning to me, she asked, "And what do you want to do when Emmanuel comes, Penny?"

Her understanding reaction to Fatimah gave me the courage to be honest too. "Trent wants me to quit working."

She and Fatimah shared another one of their private looks that always made me feel like a third wheel.

"What do *you* want to do?" she asked.

I felt myself flush. Back then I wasn't used to anyone asking what I wanted, including myself. "I like working. It's nice getting out of the house and having my own money, but —"

"But leaving your baby alone with your husband would be dangerous, true?" Fatimah said.

The accusation in her voice put me on the defensive. "Don't start with that again."

Callie Mae's once-sympathetic eyes took on the same hardness as Fatimah's. I rightly suspected then that I wasn't there just to talk about maternity leave.

"She has a point," she said.

My hands had become so swollen I'd begun to wear my wedding band on a cord of leather around my neck. I ran the ring up and down the cord nervously. "What are you talking about?"

Callie Mae sat forward, resting her elbows on her knees. "I think you know."

"I already told Fatimah he doesn't beat me."

Callie Mae glanced at the bruise Trent had left on my cheek that morning. "Let me guess — you walked into a door." It was the first time I'd ever heard her speak with sarcasm toward me.

I covered my cheek as if I could hide what they'd already seen.

"You lie to protect him," Fatimah exclaimed with more emotion than I'd seen all day.

I don't know if it was the heat from the fireplace, my hormones, or the adrenaline coursing through my veins, but suddenly the heat was unbearable. I grabbed my jacket off the back of the chair and laid it across my lap, intending to leave the first chance I got. "Why are you two attacking me?"

Callie Mae sighed. "We're not attacking you. This is what they call an intervention."

I'd watched enough television to know what an intervention was, and I didn't exactly fit the profile. "I'm not addicted to anything."

"Yes, you are," Callie Mae said. "You're addicted to an abusive man."

I felt my throat closing in. "I told you he doesn't —"

"I know what you told us, but that handprint on your face makes it hard for us to believe you."

I would have jumped up in protest, but I was too big to do anything but slowly push myself to a standing position. I was prepared to walk home if I had to. Trent didn't want me to have the job anyway, and he was expecting me to quit when you came, so leaving a month early wasn't going to matter much one way or the other. I didn't have to take this.

"Do not leave, Peeny," Fatimah said. Her pleading eyes stopped me in my tracks.

Unsure, I looked toward the hallway, then back at her.

"Just you listen to her. Please," she said.

Slowly, I lowered myself back into the chair, cringing as your weight settled on my bladder. The house was silent except for the ticking of the brass timepiece on the mantel. After what seemed like forever, Callie Mae finally spoke. "The butterfly sculpture in the foyer — I would like you to have it, Penny."

"I can't take —"

"I bought it for my daughter, Sara. Fatimah got to meet her, but you never will, this side of heaven."

"She was beautiful," Fatimah whispered, looking at her socked foot, "like an angel."

Confusion clouded my mind. I hadn't known Callie Mae had lost a daughter. She never once mentioned it.

She pressed her lips together as her eyes glistened. "She's right. She was beautiful.

She was so beautiful. But she married a man with a bent for violence. She wouldn't admit he beat her, but I could see it in her eyes. I'd been around enough battered women to recognize the pattern. He took her away from us, isolated her, and eventually brainwashed her against us. For three long years I didn't get so much as a phone call."

Thinking of my own mother, I wrung my hands and swallowed back the guilt. It dawned on me then that Trent had done the same thing to me. First he had a problem with my family, then with the church. The only things he didn't have a problem with me spending time with were him and the vacuum cleaner.

"As soon as I saw that sculpture in the foyer," she continued, "I was like you, Penny — mesmerized by it. I didn't know why I was so drawn to it but knew I had to have it for my little girl. The artist was local. I tracked her down and asked her about its meaning. It turned out she was also once the victim of abuse. Women, to her, were like butterflies — beautiful and free to love and be loved — but sometimes they would tie themselves to someone or something that wouldn't let them be free, wouldn't let them be the women God created them to be.

"Without words, that piece said all the

things I couldn't seem to articulate. Before I could give it to Sara, he beat her to death."

I had to look away from the rawness of Callie Mae's pain. "I'm so sorry," I said. "I didn't know."

She dabbed at her wet eyes. "I have to live with the fact I never confronted her about my suspicions. I mentioned them to Matthew, but he couldn't help but think the best of everyone. I knew, though, Penny. In my heart, I knew she was in trouble. I was so afraid of speaking up and losing her. I should have told her I knew. I should have told her allowing it is encouraging it. I should have said *something.*"

I leaned over and laid my hand on her arm. "You can't blame yourself. Believe me, she already knew all of that."

"What are you going to do if he starts hitting little Manny?" she asked.

"He wouldn't," I said, feeling sick to my stomach. "He loves him so much. You should see the way he —"

Fatimah's hand sliced through the air like a karate chop. "What if he do?"

It was a question I'd asked myself a hundred times, but I honestly didn't believe he would ever harm a hair on your head, Manny. Looking at the concern in my friends' eyes and hearing the question asked out loud forced me to consider it anew. There was no hesitation in my answer. "If he did, I'd leave him."

Fatimah stomped her foot. "Why is your baby worth more than you? You should leave him now!"

The loudness of her voice made my stomach jump. Callie Mae, on the other hand, didn't so much as flinch.

"You're supposed to be a Christian," I said, trying to keep my tears at bay. "You know what the Bible says about divorce."

"It doesn't say you have to stay with a man who abuses you." Callie Mae sounded eerily calm next to Fatimah's hysterics.

I shook my head. "Yes, it does. God hates divorce." I thought about my parents' marriage; it had suffered ups and downs, but never once was there talk of divorce. No one in my family had ever divorced, as far as I knew. You made it work. That's what you did. No one was perfect. Men sometimes strayed or lost their temper. Sometimes wives did too. That's just the way it was.

Callie Mae locked eyes with me. "I'm pretty sure God hates what Trent is doing to you even more than he hates divorce. For your own safety — and Manny's — you need to get away from him."

"Then what?" I asked, tears now streaming freely down my cheeks. "I spend the rest of my life alone?" Didn't the Bible say that if someone divorced their spouse and remarried, they would be committing adultery? Leaving Trent was one thing; staying alone for the rest of my life was another.

"You will find a man like Edgard," Fatimah said, "who will love and show you kindness."

"If you can show me where in the Bible it says I can remarry, I'll leave tonight, but you can't because it's not there." I was practically shouting. "You're trying to sentence me to a lifetime of loneliness."

Callie Mae walked over, sat on the arm of the chair, and took my hand. "You wouldn't be alone, Penny. God makes a fine husband — I should know — and you'll have Manny and us."

I considered her words. Leaving Trent was an option, just not an appealing one. I had read the Scripture for myself that hadn't condemned separation. But then what? I knew myself well enough to know I wouldn't be able to tolerate being alone for long. I would crave another man in my life, and then I would fall. Besides, I loved Trent. He wasn't perfect by any means, but he was my husband. Your father. And Callie Mae was exactly right; I was addicted to him.

Callie Mae drew my head to her shoulder like she'd done in the hospital and kissed the top of my head. "If you had a daughter, and she came to you and told you her husband was treating her the way Trent is treating you, would your advice be to stay with him?"

I covered my face and wept into my hands, thinking of you, Manny. The answer was all too clear when she put it that way.

She rested her forehead against mine. "The Bible says God loves us even more than a mother loves her child. Do you really think he would tell his daughter to stay and be abused?"

"You don't understand," I said. "Trent needs me."

Fatimah stood and stomped her foot. "He do not need you. He only need air, food, and water like all people. If you stay, you are a fool! He will kill you. And your son."

"I'd like to go home now," I whispered.

On our way out, Callie Mae lifted the winged statue from its arch. "I won't say another word to you about this. Whether you stay or go is your choice alone. But I'm going to pray my heart out that God will open your eyes. This isn't his plan for your life, Penny."

She held out the statue, and reluctantly I took it.

"Every time you see this, I want you to think of my Sara. Promise me you'll put it where you can see it every day."

Wanting to get out of there as badly as I did, I would have promised anything.

Twenty-Four

Unable to face Callie Mae or Fatimah, I called in sick the next day, and the next, until I didn't bother to call anymore. I did, however, put the statue Callie Mae had given me in a place where I would have to look at it every day — on my dresser in front of the mirror. Each time my gaze fell on it, my reflection stared back at me. I knew that kind of longing. I was that woman with the wings of glass.

Trent was pleased as punch I was no longer working. He was back to behaving like the man I'd married, and I tried hard to convince myself it would last. Norma came around less and less, and each time she did, she looked worse and worse. She was becoming nothing but scabs and bones.

I worried she might have HIV, but calmed myself with the knowledge that I'd been checked for that as part of my pregnancy lab work. I reasoned that since I didn't have it, then your father also didn't, which could mean if Norma did, I'd been accusing him of cheating for no reason. If they gave out degrees for denial back then, I was well on my way to earning a PhD.

Being due in just a few weeks, my thoughts were more consumed with you than with what Trent may or may not be doing with Norma, anyway. I spent at least an hour a day lying in bed, watching your elbows and knees push out around my navel, as I wondered what kind of parent I'd be and what you would look like. Would you have his eyes and my demeanor? Or, heaven forbid, would it be the other way around? I prayed more during that time than I ever have before or since.

As I browned hamburger to make tacos for dinner, I started having contractions. Slowly, I took in a deep breath as my stomach, with you inside it, hardened into a tight ball. The doctor told me false contractions were called Braxton Hicks, which sounded to me more like a country music band than a medical term. I'd had plenty of them in recent days, but they were few and far between and always went away after a few minutes, so I wasn't particularly concerned.

Moving the spatula around the greasy

pan, I turned over pink pieces of ground beef until all were the same shade of brown. As I poured the meat onto a plate lined with paper towels to drain the fat, another contraction came, followed by another. I turned the burner off, set the pan back on the stove, sat myself down at the kitchen table, and began timing them. The first few were six minutes apart, then five, then four.

Callie Mae had told me most first-time mothers had plenty of time once labor started before the baby came — hours, maybe even days. With this in mind, I remained surprisingly calm as I finished cleaning up, then packed my hospital bag with toiletries and a set of clothes for each of us to come home in. Lastly, I went into your nursery to make sure I was ready for you if you were indeed on your way.

The green paint didn't look so bad with the teddy bear border I'd put up and the white furniture I'd picked up at Goodwill. Thanks to Callie Mae and Fatimah, your changing table was stocked with plenty of diapers, wipes, and creams. My mother had sent a dozen newborn outfits, all but one in baby blue. When I turned the light off in your nursery, it finally struck me how dark it had gotten outside.

It was winter, so the sun set early, but not

before six thirty, which meant Trent was late . . . again.

Another contraction hit me as I stepped into the hallway. They were getting so close I barely had time to hold my breath between them. Your father had driven the car to work, so I had no way to get to the hospital, even if I wanted to. I considered calling an ambulance, but if it turned out to be a false alarm and Trent was left holding a several-hundred-dollar ambulance bill, I'd never hear the end of it.

Seven o'clock passed, then eight. The contractions grew further apart, but were still within the five-minute interval the doctor told me might mean that labor was imminent. Finally, I swallowed my pride and called Callie Mae. When she didn't pick up, I just assumed she was mad at me. Next I tried Fatimah's house, but it rang and rang.

Although I was afraid we might get charged for the call, I didn't feel like I had much of a choice, so I dialed the doctor's office and got a message directing me to the hospital's main number.

The operator paged the OB doctor on call. As I waited, the contractions continued. They must have made you angry because every time they let up, you kicked me like a cornered mule. I just wanted the pain to stop and your father to come home. Truth is, I was scared, Manny.

The phone rang and I snatched it up. "Hello?"

"It's a girl, Penny. She's had a girl!" Callie Mae exclaimed. "A nine-pounder. Can you believe that? Fati didn't look that big, did she? She's beautiful. Oh, she looks just like her. And tall! Oh, my word, the baby is twenty-three inches long. She's the biggest in the nursery. She's light skinned like her father, but has those bold features —"

"I thought she was going to deliver at home," I said.

Callie Mae laughed. "As soon as the first labor pain hit her, Edgard drove her stubborn rear to the hospital."

Grabbing my stomach, I groaned as another contraction hit.

"Penny, are you okay? Penny?"

The wave of pain passed and I caught my breath. "I'm sorry. I'm having some contractions."

Silence.

"Callie, are you there?"

"Yes. Yes, I was just surprised. It's too early. The maternity ward was bursting at the seams, and the nurses said that happens every time there's a full moon. Something to do with the gravitational pull or something. Maybe that's affecting you, too. Is Trent going to take you in?"

I couldn't bring myself to tell her he wasn't home yet. It was after nine now. "I'm waiting on the doctor to call me back."

"I need to get off your line, then. Call me once you talk to him. Let me know you're okay and what the plan is," she said.

I hung up and, figuring I'd missed the doctor's call, dialed the hospital operator again. Either I had bad luck or else there was only one lady on that night, because the same nasal voice answered. When I repeated the request to page the OB, she got snippy. "I've already given him your number. He just finished delivering a baby. He'll get to you as soon as he can."

Feeling as though I'd had my knuckles whapped with a ruler, I apologized and hung up. As I sat there rubbing my belly and breathing off the pain, I wondered if the doctor I was waiting on had delivered Fatimah's baby.

Picturing her infant was easy if she was as Callie Mae described, a lighter version of her mother. I hoped Fatimah would let me hold her. I missed her and Callie Mae's friendship more than I could have dreamed. They loved me and only wanted the best for me — and you. It was a far cry from whatever Trent and I were to each other.

A soft knock came at the door at the same time the phone rang. Looking at the door, then the phone, I wasn't sure which to answer first. I decided on the phone. "Hello?" I said hurriedly.

"This is Doctor Reynard. I understand you're having contractions?"

Another knock at the door.

I put my hand over the phone and called, "Just a minute!" Then, "Yes. They were really close together, and it's been going on all night."

"And now?"

"Further apart. Maybe five or six minutes."

"So they're not getting closer. They're getting further apart?"

Knock. Knock. Knock.

I tried to stretch the phone cord to the door, but it stopped short several feet away. "Sometimes, yes. Not always. I don't know."

"Have you been timing them?"

"I was, but then I stopped."

"Are you feeling the baby move?"

"Yes."

"A lot?"

"Yes."

When a face appeared in the window, I had to stifle a scream. It belonged to a gaunt, unkempt Norma. As my heart started beating again, I turned my back to her.

"Did you drink water?"

"Water, no. I mean, no more than I usually do. Why?" I asked.

I could hear something clicking outside, which told me Norma had found the doorbell but didn't realize it was broken.

"If it's false contractions, drinking two tall glasses of water and resting should make them go away. If they don't, then you need to come in. Or if you stop feeling the baby move. Try the water, and call me back in half an hour if it doesn't improve. Or if your water breaks — it hasn't, has it?"

"I don't think so."

Norma started knocking again, this time louder.

"I checked your chart. You're not due for a few more weeks, and this is your first, right?"

"Yes."

"Yeah, I think it's probably a false alarm, but do what I said and let's wait it out."

A tapping came from the window, which I ignored.

"Can I ask you one more question, Doctor?"

"Quickly. I just got paged to the OR."

"Did you deliver a baby for a Sudanese

couple?"

"I'm not allowed to say."

"She's my best friend."

"Drink two tall glasses of water, and call me back if the contractions don't subside."

I thanked him, hung up the phone, and went to the door. Before I could open it, tires crunched over gravel, which meant Trent was finally home. I put my ear to the door to listen. The car door slammed. Norma was "Hey, baby"ing him, but I couldn't hear his reply, if there was one. From what I could make out, she was asking for money. They both started yelling. Two pairs of footsteps climbed the stairs. More yelling. Then, something — or more likely, *someone* — slammed into the front door. She screamed. He yelled for her to shut the expletive up.

I turned off the lamp and peeked out the window. Holding her head as though she'd been hit, Norma tried to put her free arm around Trent's waist. He pushed her off. She was hysterical now — crying, screaming, and pleading. I almost felt sorry for her.

When Trent grabbed the doorknob, she yanked at his arm. Because he was facing me, I could see him snap before she could. In a blink, his hand was a fist and it met her on the side of her neck. Her arms flailed wildly as she fell backward off the porch and down the stairs. One of her spiked heels lay on the ground beside her.

She used her hands to shield her face from Trent, who was stomping toward her with both fists raised and ready.

I wanted to hide in the bedroom closet, cover my ears, and hope he didn't come for me next. As much as I despised her, my conscience wouldn't let me leave her to the fate awaiting her. I opened the front door, creating as much noise as I could in the process.

When Trent whipped around toward me, I saw murder in his eyes. Then, just as quickly, it was gone, as if my presence had scared the demon out of him. Knowing what I know now about the spiritual world, that might have been about right.

With Trent's back to her, Norma scrambled to her feet, faster than I'd ever seen her move, grabbed her shoe, and ran to her car. Trent screamed something I won't repeat as she burned rubber out of the driveway.

A moment later, he walked into the house as if nothing had happened. I could smell the whiskey on his breath as he kissed my cheek with his icy lips. Instead of an explanation or apology, I was met with, "What's for dinner?"

TWENTY-FIVE

"Just lie down, Penny." Trent handed me another glass of water.

I set the cup on the bedside table and turned away from the stench of smoke wafting off his sweatshirt every time he moved.

He pulled the quilt up, tucked it around my legs, and sat beside me on the bed. The mattress squealed and leaned under his weight. "I wish you'd let me take you to the hospital. 'I don't know nothing 'bout delivering no babies, Miss Scarlett.' " A fleck of tobacco clung to his chin stubble.

"Very funny," I said glumly, picking the debris from his face. If I'd been reasonably confident these contractions were the real thing, I would have taken him up on the offer to drive me to the hospital. But the more time that passed, and the more water I drank, the calmer you and my contractions became.

Trent timed them against his watch. A few

were five minutes apart, but then there would be one that was eight minutes, then two, and so forth. A clinic nurse had mentioned that false labor felt just like the real thing, except real contractions would get more painful and closer together. I was becoming convinced it was a false alarm after all, but Trent wasn't so sure.

When he put his cold hand on my round stomach, I jumped. "Sorry," he said, taking it away. He rubbed his hands together and blew on them. A set of fresh, catlike scratches ran over his knuckles and down his hand. I didn't have to wonder who gave him those.

"Where were you tonight?" I asked. "You can't just leave me here when I'm this far along without any way to contact you. What if it had been the real thing?"

The crease formed between his eyebrows. "I had to give Stu a ride home."

"And it took you four hours?" When he stared hard at me, I averted my gaze to the winged statue.

"Come on, One Cent. I just stopped off for a few. You won't let me smoke in the house, and you know I like a stogie when I drink. I'm getting ready to be a father — give me a break. Soon I'll be stuck here all the time changing diapers. Let me live a little while I still can."

The thought that he might really settle down after you came gave me hope. I patted the bed for him to lie beside me. I wasn't crazy about him referring to settling down as being stuck, but back then I was more than willing to take what I could get.

He looked down at my hand with those bloodshot eyes of his, and I could see his whole body sigh. "Sorry, babe. I just want to watch a little TV."

Why did it always have to be about him? I wished that just for once he could put aside what he wanted and give me what I needed. I turned on my side, placing my back to him, and fluffed the pillow under my head. Another contraction came, and I curled into a ball.

"Penny, you okay?"

I held a finger up indicating I couldn't answer right then. When the wave of pain passed, I kicked the mattress with my heel. "I wish this baby would either come on or leave me alone already."

Tracing circles on my back, he said, "I'm sorry, darlin'. I can't say I know what you're going through, but it don't look pleasant."

"It's more aggravating than anything." I shifted in the bed trying to get comfortable. "I'm just so tired of being pregnant." I looked down at the map of thin, blue veins sprawling across my bulging belly, then at the dark line splitting me in half from the navel down. "I feel fat. I have gas and heartburn all the time. I can't see my stupid toes, and the little bugger's always kicking me. It's starting to really hurt."

He chuckled. "That's my boy."

I moved away from his touch. "It's not funny." Staring at the yellowed wall, I wished he would go away, but then thinking of him doing just that made me want to bawl. I flipped back over to face him. He was looking down at me with that Cheshire grin of his.

Despite my trying to look mad, the corners of my mouth curled upward. "What?" I pulled the cover up over my belly. "Stop looking at me like that."

His expression grew stern. "I'll look at my wife any way I please." Softly, he ran his index finger over my cheek and down my neck. "You're just so beautiful, Penny. And you're having my baby. *My* baby."

I tucked in my lips and looked up at him. He was a few years older, a few pounds heavier, but he was still that swaggering cowboy I'd fallen in love with. I pulled back the cover, lifted my pajama top, and placed his cold, rough hand back on my stomach.

You kicked so hard right at that moment. I gritted my teeth as Trent's eyes filled with wonder.

"Did you feel that?" He sounded like a little boy.

"What do you think?" I said.

"I'll bet that does hurt."

"It does," I agreed.

He sighed and lay beside me, with his arms bent behind his head. "You think we'll be good parents?"

"I hope so."

"I'm sure going to try," he said.

You better, I thought. "You will," I said.

"I hope he has your laugh."

I leaned on my elbow and rested my head in my hand, studying his profile. "I hope he looks like you."

He turned his head and stared into my eyes for the longest time as if trying to read something there. Finally he said, "Penny, don't ever leave me."

A pang of longing squeezed my heart. "Where did that come from?"

"I know I can be a jerk sometimes, but you know I love you. And I love our baby. I don't want little Manny coming from a broken home like I did. I want him to have his mama and daddy. Every child should have that."

"They should," I agreed.

"You know, I never told you, but I was jealous of what you had with your folks." He looked up at the ceiling as if the water stain suddenly intrigued him.

"What do you mean?" I reached under his sweatshirt and twirled a tuft of chest hair.

"You had both your mom and your daddy. I know your father was tough and all, but at least he looked out for you. Mine did nothing but call me a worthless puke and tenderize my face. My mom was so busy shooting herself up with heroin, she didn't even know she had a son half the time."

He looked like he might cry for a minute, but then humor glinted in his eyes. "Man, do you remember your father's face when I was talking to you that day you were pinning up laundry?"

I smiled. "Like it was yesterday. If looks could kill —"

"— I'd have been laying in the bottom of the ocean with a bullet in my head and a knife in my back." He flipped over to his back again.

"Trent?" I laid my head on his chest. The familiar scent of his musky deodorant met me.

"Yeah?"

"Why did you do that to Norma?"

"She put her hands on me."

"You didn't have to punch her."

"She's on meth. She don't need to be hanging around my house and family begging for money."

"Is that all she wanted?"

"I ain't going to let no one mess with what I got."

"You could have just told her to leave, or called the poli—"

When he sat up, my head hit the mattress. He slid his legs over the side of the bed, then looked over his shoulder at me. "No one."

Soft light from the moon streamed in through the bedroom window and across my face. I rubbed the sleep from my eyes and stared up at the blurry halo. I pushed myself up and looked around. Beside me lay a rumpled pillow where Trent should have been.

As I slipped out of bed, I glanced over at the alarm clock. Three in the morning. Mama used to say if God woke you up at three, it meant you were supposed to pray for someone. I always thought she was a little superstitious, but just in case, I sent up a prayer for whoever might need it, then made my way to the living room to see if your father had fallen asleep in front of the television again.

The TV was off and the couch sat empty. I walked to the kitchen, but he wasn't there, either. Our house was small, so it took only a minute to make my way through it. Finally, I pulled back the curtain and checked the driveway.

Empty.

Staring out the window, I couldn't believe my eyes. How could he leave me there after what had just happened? How could he say he loved me but abandon me again in my condition? After a few minutes, I wiped my wet eyes across my pajama sleeve, but more tears just came to take their place.

I sat down on the carpet with my arms wrapped tight around my bent knees, feeling as sorry for myself as I ever had. Watching the shadows from the window move across the wall, I rocked myself back and forth, trying to keep from hyperventilating.

I didn't know I'd fallen asleep until the sound of a slamming car door woke me. I opened my eyes, confused to find myself on the living room floor. Outside, I could hear Trent coughing and mumbling obscenities like he sometimes did when he was in a foul mood and there was no one around to yell at.

Not wanting him to know I had been up, I hurried to the bedroom and crawled under the blankets. The front door opened and shut, then the refrigerator door. Footsteps sounded down the hallway and into the bathroom. A flush. The sink. More footsteps. Then, quietly, he tiptoed into our room and slowly pulled back the covers.

I pretended he woke me. "Trent?" I said faking grogginess.

He closed his eyes as though he were sound asleep.

"Where were you?" I asked.

He groaned like I'd just woken him.

"Where were you?" I repeated.

His eyes flashed open, and he gave me a foul look. "Watching TV. Where do you think?"

Blood rushed to my head as I sat up. "No, you weren't. You just came in."

He threw the blanket off his fully clothed legs. "I'm warning you, Penny."

Enough was enough. He left me not once, but twice without a car that night, and then he had the audacity to lie about it? Manny, I saw red. "Where — were — you?"

He jumped out of bed and jabbed his finger in my direction. "Don't start with me. I've had a rough night."

I yanked the covers off me, turned on the

bedside lamp, and got out of bed. "You've had a rough night? *You've* had a rough night?"

He stepped into a shadow. "I pay the bills around here. If I want to go out, I'll go out. I don't answer to you. I don't answer to nobody. You hear?"

My temples pounded with rage. "You don't pay the bills. I do. You don't do a thing but drink away what little money you bring home and make messes for me to clean up. And I've had enough." The temporary insanity that comes with anger gave me just enough amnesia to forget his fists. "I'm having your baby. I'm due any time now. You need to be in the house and in our bed."

"Is that right?" His voice became a whisper. Before I could step back, he grabbed my wrist, so tight it felt like a tourniquet. His fingernails dug deep into my flesh. I yelped and broke free. Courage left me as I backed against the wall.

He picked up a hand mirror from my dresser, and before I could react, whirled it at me. The handle just missed my head. Glass and plastic shattered against the wall. "You think you can control me? You're just like my mother."

The only other time he'd compared me to his mother was just before he broke my arm.

I was sorry now that I hadn't just let him be. All I could think of was that I needed to protect you at any cost. "What happened?" I asked, softer, trying to get him to calm down.

"Like you care," he hissed.

I rubbed at the indents he'd left on my arm. "Baby, I care. Tell me what happened."

"You don't care about nothing except that baby and those stupid friends of yours." He walked to my dresser and yanked up the statue Callie Mae had given me. He pointed it at me. The light from the hallway shone across his angry face. "They laugh at your stupid jokes and buy you a few presents so they think they own you."

"Please, Trent," I begged. "I'm sorry. We'll talk in the morning."

"Please, what?" he asked, in a mocking tone. He glared at me, then looked down at the statue. "What's this ugly thing supposed to be anyway? Some kind of human insect?"

I held my hand out to take it from him, but he pulled his arm back. Before I could lunge for it, he threw it at the head of the bed. I heard myself scream, then a crack. I thought for sure it was broken. I hurried over to it, examining the stained-glass wings. Miraculously, they were intact, except for a few hairline fractures.

Holding it behind my back, I put my hand on his arm. "Just come to bed. I shouldn't have said anything. I'm sorry."

He moved back into the shadows again. "I've got to get up in two hours."

"I know, so let's go to sleep."

He grunted and left the room, slamming the door behind him.

Twenty-Six

At five thirty in the afternoon, Trent crashed through the front door.

Knuckle deep in ground beef and spices, I hurriedly formed the meatloaf on the sheet pan and slid it into the oven, careful not to burn myself on the wire rack. As I washed the grime from my fingers, I felt his cold lips on my cheek and knew right away something was wrong.

He ran a hand down his chin, red from the cold, and looked everywhere but at me. "The cops might come to ask you about Norma."

I turned to give him a questioning look. "The cops? Did she file assault charges on you?" My first thought was he had it coming if she did. My second was dread over what the legal fees might add up to on a charge like that. We barely had enough money for a roof over our heads and a case of Trent's beer in the fridge, and that was before the added expense of diapers and pediatricians.

"No, they found her dead."

Stunned, I just stared at him.

He shook his head like he couldn't believe it. "On that farm that's for sale — you know, the one over on Gaston Road."

I had to catch myself on the counter. "She's *dead*?"

He walked to the back door and locked it. "She's dead, Penny. Dead. It's all over the news. She was beaten and strangled."

A bad case of heartburn had had me feeling sick to my stomach all day. The news Trent had just given me triggered what I had, until that moment, managed to avoid. I ran to the bathroom and vomited. As I rinsed out my mouth, I looked over to see that your father had followed and was staring at me with wild eyes. "They're going to finger me for this. You know they will." He started to pace. "People at work are already talking. I can't go to jail. You know what they do to men who look like me?"

Using the hand towel to wipe my mouth, I looked at him in the mirror. "Please tell me you didn't have something to do with this."

He flashed me an incensed look. "I can't believe you just said that."

Norma was choked — Trent had wrapped his fingers around my throat more than once. She was beaten — he had beaten me too many times to count. And he had disappeared last night.

I followed him to the living room. "Have they talked to you?"

"Who? The cops?"

I nodded.

He slid his flannel jacket off and threw it onto the couch. "They came by the shop, but they questioned all of us. You know she was fired."

I hadn't known, because he hadn't told me.

He rubbed his mouth and paced the carpet. "They were just asking questions like if we knew anyone that would want to hurt her. If she had any boyfriends. No one said anything about me specifically that I know of, but I was scared. They asked me when the last time I saw her was."

My mind began to fill with fog. "What did you say?"

"What could I? I tell them she was here and we argued, and I become their chief suspect. You watch those shows. You know how it works."

I moved his jacket over and sat down on the couch, feeling the full weight of you on my pelvis and Trent's predicament on my shoulders. As much as I wanted you to come, Manny, now I prayed you would hold off as long as possible. I couldn't imagine giving birth to you while worrying every second the cops would come to take your father away.

Trent ran both hands through his hair, making it stick up. "I know how your mind works. You want to do the right thing — so do I. But you can't tell them. If they come here, you have to back me up. If you don't, who's gonna take care of you and Manny?"

God, I wanted to say. *God will take care of us, and a whole lot better than you've been doing.* But the truth was I didn't really believe that — not the way I do now. "You were gone last night," I whispered. "Until almost four. What time was she — ?"

His eyebrows knit together. "I already told you where I was. And how am I supposed to know what time she was killed?" No, he hadn't told me where he'd been, but that didn't seem like the right time to call him on it.

Out of nervousness, I tried to cross my legs, but could no longer manage it with you in the way. "That's good. Then you have an alibi. Your buddies will tell them."

When he leaned against the front door

and closed his eyes, my heart dropped.

"You do have alibis right? I mean, you were at a bar, drinking. People had to see you."

Blotches of red formed on his neck. "I was at Zoe's until three. Norma showed up there, high as a kite, hanging on the drunks, trying to pimp herself out."

I stared at the tracks he was wearing in the carpet, trying to swallow the pill he just shoved down my throat. "She was at the bar with you?"

He let out a disgusted grunt. "Not *with* me. Ain't you listening? I said she showed up there, but then left with some dude."

Were you the dude? I wanted to ask, but didn't dare. "Did you know him?"

He stopped pacing and looked down at me. The irritation on his face melted. "Not really. I mean I've seen him a few times. A real scumbag."

A siren sounded in the distance. We both turned toward the window, holding our breath until it faded. "Did anyone else see him leave with her?"

He looked off to the side, like he was trying real hard to remember. "Maybe the bartender. The only other guy that would have seen me was in the can. What if they don't remember?"

My thoughts turned to how pathetic his story sounded, even to me. Maybe especially to me. He had just told me she was hanging on drunks, plural. Suddenly the only guy in the bar besides the bartender and the so-called john was in the bathroom? A prosecutor would eat him alive. "So, you saw her leave with him, and that was it?"

"I followed them out. She's my friend, so I was worried about her."

His friend that he had punched to the ground. "You followed them out. Then what happened?"

He buried his hands in his pockets and started pacing again. "I told her she needed to get help. She's got kids, and there she is hooking for drugs. It ain't right."

The strangest feeling of calm came over me, distancing me from the emotions I could no longer handle. "Are you sure you didn't fight some more?"

He raised his palms in explanation. "We had a few words and I might have pushed the man, but that was it."

I should have felt panic at hearing this; instead, I felt numb. "And then?"

"Then nothing. She told me unless I was willing to pay for it, I needed to bug off. So I did."

Willing to pay for it. Those words repeated

themselves in my mind. Had he been willing in the past? If not with money, then with booze or drugs? I didn't want to know. "So, you're not the last one with her. He was. He's the suspect, then."

He sat down and put his head in his hands. "Yeah, but I don't know the dude's name. I don't know anything about him, except he's a tattooed greaseball. If the cops can't find anyone to corroborate my story, that leaves me holding the bag."

"So you didn't tell them she was a regular over here, or that you fought?"

His nose flared. "Are you crazy or just plain stupid?"

Both, I wanted to say. "You can't ask me to lie if they question me." You'd have thought as much as I'd lied over the years to protect him, one more wouldn't be a big deal, but this was different. Lying would make me an accessory, and if I went to jail, what would happen to you?

The look he gave me was one of betrayal. "I should have known you'd throw me to the wolves first chance you got. Go ahead and put me behind bars so you and your friends can gallivant all over town. Why should you take care of your husband? I'd lay down my life for you, but you can't even tell a little white lie to save my life. Real nice, Penny."

"The only person who would lay their life down for me already has," I whispered. And then, the truth of that really hit me. What God had done for me, that was love. This? I had no idea what this was.

He jerked his head away like he couldn't stand the sight of me anymore. "Don't start that again. Not now."

"He laid his life down for you, too. It's never too late to —"

"Penny, I'm warning you. One more word and —"

"And what?" I stood. "You'll kill me, too?" As soon as the words left my mouth, I wanted to take them back. Here I was jumping to the worst possible conclusion. Trent was a lot of things, but a murderer? If the law considered him innocent until proven guilty, surely his own wife could extend him the same courtesy. "I'm sorry. I shouldn't have —"

"Save it." He looked like I'd slapped him. "It's clear what you think of me."

I stepped toward him, but he put his hands up, warning me not to come any closer. A pang of guilt gnawed at me as I saw the pain I'd caused.

Not knowing what else to do, I went back to the kitchen and rinsed off the potatoes

I'd peeled earlier. Trent leaned against the doorjamb watching me with a combination of hurt and accusation in his eyes. After what felt like forever, he finally said, "Despite you thinking your husband is a lowlife murderer, I need to know you won't say that to the cops."

I scooped the slimy peels from the drain and dropped them into the trash can. "What should I tell them?"

"Just back up my story."

I picked a knife out of the drawer and pressed it across the length of a potato. "I don't know."

"If *you* think I did this, what are *they* going to think?"

"I don't think you did this," I said, "but you do have a temper."

"There's a big difference between hitting someone and murdering them. I didn't want her dead. What would I have to gain?"

A switch flipped inside me. It's not a pleasant thought, but maybe it was just the shift in power. "I don't know. What did you have to gain by all the black eyes you've given *me* over the years?"

"I've changed. Dag, Penny, you see that I've changed. I'm trying so hard to be the man you deserve. Your husband, Manny's father. Can't I have just a little bit of credit for that? When I hit her, I was protecting our family from a freaked-out meth head. Protecting you like a good husband does."

Good husband. I chewed on that while he pleaded with his eyes.

"What will your son think if you sentence his father to the electric chair?" He walked over to me and put his hands on my waist. "Baby, think about it. You tell them what really happened last night, and it looks like I did her in. Sometimes the truth leads people to a lie. I didn't kill her. I swear it. We had a fight; that's it. That man she left with, he's the one who must have done it. You should have seen him. He looked like someone who would get off murdering women."

Once again, he had my head swimming and my mind unsure. He had a temper, there was no denying it, but . . . I just didn't know what to think.

He knelt and gave my belly a tender kiss, then looked up at me with those eyes of his. "Please, Penny. Our son's going to be here any day. If you won't do it for me, do it for him."

Why did I have to be so weak when it came to him? "They wouldn't really sentence you to death, would they?"

He stood and cupped my face. "Of course

they would. They don't care about nothing except the collar. Innocent people go to jail every day. Innocent people die on death row. Don't make the father of your son one of those people."

Twenty-Seven

Neither Trent nor I slept much that night. Every little noise put us on edge, as we waited for the police to come banging down the door and arrest him. The next morning, with bags the size of luggage beneath his eyes, he called in sick. Although I fixed him his favorite breakfast of pancakes with bacon, neither of us could eat more than a bite or two.

We tried to go about our day, me cleaning and cooking, him fixing everything in the house he could think of to keep him busy. We watched the morning news, but there was no mention of Norma. The afternoon version flashed a quick picture of her and a short mention that her body had been found, and where, but that was all. When the evening news came on with another even briefer mention, Trent's shoulders finally stopped pushing up into his ears, and his dark mood brightened.

As I vacuumed the nursery, he wrapped his arms around my waist, turned the machine off, and whispered that I had worked hard enough. It was time to relax. To my amazement, he led me by the hand to the bathroom, where a tub had already been drawn, complete with a frothy layer of bubbles. The two candles he had placed on the back of the toilet and sink lit the room. The scent of vanilla and cinnamon mingled with the clean smell of liquid soap.

Drooling at the tub, I said, "They told me I'm not supposed to take baths, remember?"

"Yes, I did remember." He smiled. "The doctor on call said it was okay as long as you weren't bleeding and your water hadn't broke." His eyebrows dipped. "It hasn't has it?"

I shook my head.

The candle on the sink reflected off the bathroom mirror, making the small room glow a warm red. I couldn't believe he'd actually done that for me. He kissed my lips, told me to enjoy, and closed the door.

The warmth of the bath felt like heaven, and it was a relief to have the extra thirty pounds of pregnancy temporarily lifted. I scooped up a handful of bubbles and blew them at the faucet. They floated to the shiny metal and slowly glided down, back into the water.

Slouching until suds enveloped my shoulders, I sighed in contentment. You were less active than usual, and though I missed watching you move around, I was thankful for the peace.

I soaked myself until my fingertips were wrinkled and the water lost its heat. It gave me plenty of time to pray for Norma's family, for the police to get the person who did that to her, and more than anything, that the person wouldn't turn out to be Trent.

When my skin broke out in gooseflesh, I figured I'd better call it quits. I stood, letting the cool water trickle down my legs as I wrung the bulk of it from my hair. I stepped onto the soft bath mat, wiggling my toes against the loops to dry them, and wrapped myself up in the robe Trent left for me draped over the sink. After I drained the tub and wrapped my hair in a towel, I stepped into the hall to the smell of cooking beef.

When I entered the kitchen, your father was wearing his old grilling apron with an obnoxious "Marinate this!" slogan printed across the front. I hadn't seen that stupid thing in so long I'd forgotten he even had it. He opened the oven and worked the turkey baster inside a roasting pan.

"What've you got there?" I asked.

He looked over his shoulder at me and winked. My word, he was so handsome. "Roast beef."

I did a mental checklist of the inventory we had in the freezer. We didn't have roast beef, and he hadn't left the house to go to the store. We did, however, have a pot roast. "It smells delicious."

He nodded in agreement. "You married one good cook, One Cent."

"So, all this time, you've been keeping that a secret."

He shrugged. "Guess so."

"We still have the mashed potatoes from last night," I said. "I could make some gravy to go with them."

He closed the oven and pulled the hand towel off the cabinet door. Holding an end with each hand, he began rolling it like he was getting ready to snap me with it. "You get your rump in on that couch and relax. There's a cup of that fruity tea you like beside the couch. I laid out a blanket and some extra pillows to prop your feet up on."

Suspicion replaced delight. "What's going on?"

"I'm treating my wife to an evening of leisure."

"An evening of leisure? Why?"

He gave me a look like he couldn't believe I was questioning his motives. "I look at *Cosmo* sometimes when I'm in line at the store. I know what you women like."

I had to laugh at that. "Is that right?"

"One Cent, I'm warning you. Get over to that couch and let me finish dinner or I am going to . . ."

When he paused, we both felt the discomfort of our conversation the night before. Why couldn't it be like this all the time? Or if not all the time, then at least sometime when he hadn't just beat the heck out of me or someone else.

He pulled the hand towel back in the firing position.

"I'm going," I said.

I lay on the couch like he directed and propped up my feet. They were so swollen it looked like I had no ankles. You still weren't moving much, but every time I got to worrying about it, I would feel you shift, so I figured all was well. I turned on the TV and started thumbing through the channels.

In the kitchen, drawers opened and closed, and pots clanged. I just knew Trent was making a mess in there, but I wasn't going to ruin the evening by worrying about it. Being taken care of was nice for a change, even if it didn't sit quite right with what had just happened to Norma. It's not like I could do anything to help her. I told myself the only thing within my power right then was to be the best wife I could be.

Trent called from the kitchen. "You've got a doctor's appointment tomorrow, don't you?"

"That's right," I called back. One of the talking baby commercials came on that always made me laugh. I set the remote down and picked up my tea. I blew a plume of steam from the top as the TV baby made funny faces over his father's portfolio. "He wants to see me once a week now that we're getting close," I said.

His head popped around the corner. "I think he's just got a thing for you. There ain't a man alive who wouldn't be turned on by you, pregnant or not."

I felt myself blush. "You're crazy."

"Crazy for you."

He disappeared back into the kitchen, and I returned to flipping through the channels. A red newsbreak banner scrolled across the bottom of the screen and I froze.

The anchorwoman showed a picture of Norma. "Trent!" I yelled.

He ran to the living room as I motioned to the television.

The pretty brunette in a charcoal suit said a suspect had been arrested in the murder of Norma Brentwood. Trent and I exchanged glances.

She stood in the middle of the Gaston farm field where Norma's body had been found, holding a microphone and brushing strands of windblown hair from her face. "Police today have arrested the husband of the twenty-nine-year-old Gaston woman found dead in this field off of I-81."

Trent sat on the cocktail table inches from the TV, mesmerized. When they showed a picture of Norma's husband, it hit me Trent hadn't done it after all. By the relief I felt then, I guessed I, in my heart of hearts, must have believed he had.

He silenced the TV. "He didn't do it," he whispered.

"What do you mean, he didn't do it?"

"He couldn't have. She left with that man I told you about. The john."

I sat up and set my tea down on the table. "Maybe he caught her with him and —"

"Maybe," he said, sounding unconvinced. "I don't see him doing this. He's a wuss. I mean, he came home to find me in the house with his wife, drinking. Instead of busting me in the chops, which is what *I* would have done, he smiles and puts out his hand for me to shake. That strike you as a killer?"

He'd never admitted to being alone with Norma in her house; in fact, he'd adamantly denied ever setting foot in her home, but I decided to let it go. It's not like I hadn't already known it. Now didn't seem the time to bother with a molehill when we were dealing with a mountain, anyway. "If you think they've got an innocent man locked up, you've got to say something."

He huffed and stood. "Yeah, great idea, Penny. That's real smart. Then they start looking at me, wondering how come I know so much. No way. Maybe he did do it. I only met him that once. He might be a lunatic for all I know."

They flashed a picture of Norma's husband at the bottom of the screen. He was a lanky man with a baby face and an apologetic smile. He looked the way Trent described him, easygoing, but I had learned long ago that a kind-looking man could still draw blood. Trent, after all, had an infectious smile, just not while he was beating me. "Did she talk about him like he was abusive?"

He shot me a dirty look. "Abusive don't equal murderer."

It was no surprise I'd touched a nerve

with that one. "I'm just asking if she mentioned him having a temper."

He studied his boots. "Yeah, maybe she did mention that, come to think of it."

Your father could be the best liar in the world, but he could be the worst, too. "Maybe you could send them an anonymous letter about the john and the bar."

"Let the police do their job. They don't need help from amateurs."

Oh sure, I was supposed to let them do their job now that it didn't involve him.

My wheels started turning, wondering if I could write a letter, maybe pretending to be a patron from the bar that night who didn't want to get involved. I could make up a fake return address, change my handwriting, sign it anonymously, and maybe just mention she had left with —

Trent gave me a hard look like he could read my mind. Sometimes, I almost believed he could. "And don't you dare stick your nose in this. If he didn't do it, they'll figure it out soon enough. Don't you get them sniffing on my trail. Leave well enough alone. Hear me?"

I looked at him like I had no clue what he was talking about. "I wasn't going to —"

"Don't act like I don't know you and how that feeble mind of yours works." He went back to the kitchen, and I lay down again on the couch.

After a few minutes, he came back out. "Hey, you mind finishing up dinner? I want to go rub it in Jimbo's face that he owes me twenty bucks."

I pulled the blanket up. "Twenty bucks for what?"

"He bet me the cops would have me behind bars before the night was over. Apparently he don't have no more faith in me than you do."

Before I could answer, he was tucking in his shirt and grabbing the car keys.

Twenty-Eight

As soon as Trent left for work the next morning, I called our church to ask if I could seek the pastor's counsel. His secretary put me on hold, forcing me to listen to Muzak so long I was about to start drooling. Eventually, "Do You Know the Way to San Jose" clicked off, and she returned to tell me Nathan would clear his schedule.

Having walked the two miles to the bus stop, I waited beside a woman with a rump the size of two of my pregnant bellies as a plume of exhaust wafted toward us from the back of the city bus. Holding my breath, I held the railing and stepped through the grimy doors behind her. While she took her sweet time inserting two dollars into the slot, I did my best to smooth the wrinkles out of my cash.

Before I could even find an empty seat, the driver hit the gas. Catching myself on the overhead bar, I barely managed to keep my balance. A young woman in a McDonald's uniform picked up her book bag and slid over so I could sit. I thanked her and took the empty seat. The smell of french fries reminded me I hadn't eaten breakfast.

According to my route schedule, we had five stops and two miles before we got to the shopping center that sat behind New Beginnings Church. It took twenty minutes to travel that short distance because apparently people would rather risk their lives and ours than allow a bus to get in front of them. Cars cut us off left and right, slowing us down so much we managed to catch every red light.

Thankfully, fry-girl got off two stops after I'd gotten on, so I had plenty of elbow room, or in my case, belly room. The ride over gave me plenty of time to think about how I would raise my suspicions about Trent to Pastor Harold, or Nathan, as he still insisted on being called.

Over the months, we'd gotten to know the man no better than the first day we set foot in New Beginnings. There had to be a real person, with ups and downs like the rest of us, hiding behind that giant smile of his, but as far as I could tell, he never took off the clergy mask long enough for anyone to see. Then again, what did I know? Maybe the real him was truly always that happy. It didn't much matter. If he was half the counselor he was preacher, I figured he could at least steer me in the right direction. All I needed was a little guidance.

I could have called Fatimah or Callie Mae, but I already knew what each of them would say — leave Trent. If I told Callie Mae what I feared, I strongly suspected she would feel a Christian obligation to go to the police. She was a trustworthy friend, but her first loyalty was to God.

The bus sputtered to a stop beside a covered bench in front of Food Lion. I thanked the driver, who looked at me from glasses so marred with fingerprints, I don't know how she saw through them.

It was less than a block to the church from where I'd been dropped off, but it felt like miles with the frigid wind kicking up the dusting of snow that had fallen the day before. My teeth chattered so hard, I hoped they wouldn't shatter, and my hands were ice cubes inside my jacket pockets.

Finally, I reached the church. Opening the glass door, I was at last shielded from the wind. My hands were red from the cold, and I rubbed them together as I entered the warmth of the church. I walked down the carpeted corridor leading to Pastor Harold's office and turned in. His secretary, Carrie or Cara or something, looked up from her computer screen and waved me in.

The office was exactly what I would expect a pastor's space to look like, with hardwood paneled walls, ornamental crosses, and scenic prints with Scripture verses scrolled across the bottom of them.

Suddenly I had a bad case of buyer's remorse. What if she or Pastor Harold told Trent I had been there?

"I'm sorry to bother you." I took a hesitant step in. It was too late to turn back now, I thought. I didn't have to tell everything, just whatever I felt comfortable with. I'd feel him out first and see if I could trust him before spilling my soul. Besides, weren't religious leaders sworn to secrecy the same way lawyers were? It seemed I heard something about that somewhere.

"Bother me?" she gave me a curious look beneath her overplucked eyebrows. "It's no bother. You're one of our sheep. You're always welcome. Go on in; Nathan's expecting you."

The door to the inner office opened, and Pastor Harold stood there in a gray warm-up suit, a pair of bright-white Nikes, and of course, that smile of his.

He held out his hand for me to shake.

"Mrs. Taylor, I am so glad to see you. Please come in." He turned to Carrie or Cara. "Carla, if you could please hold my calls for the next few minutes."

She gave a thumbs-up, bringing attention to her badly chipped manicure. The pastor's eyes seemed to linger disapprovingly on her hand. She blushed as she slipped her fingers from sight.

"Thanks, Carla," I said, mostly just so I'd remember her name. She went back to whatever she was working on, and I followed Pastor Harold into the office. He closed the door behind me, and invited me to have a seat.

The narrow chair was made of hardwood, with the thinnest of cushions, as though he didn't want anyone to get too comfortable. Shifting in my seat to find a position that didn't make you lie on my bladder or press into my spine, I glanced around. Three of the walls were veneered in white brick; the last had been painted a warm gold. In the middle of that wall hung a simple, framed poster of a man standing on a summit with both arms raised in triumph. Beneath him were the words, "Failure is but success delayed."

He sat on the corner of his antique desk and motioned toward the poster. "I have to look at that every day."

"You could take it down," I offered.

He laughed. "Let me reword that. I *get* to look at that every day."

I wondered what he thought he was failing at. His church was affluent and full every Sunday. He drove a nice car, wore nice clothes, had the all-American family.

He pulled the leather chair out from behind his desk and sat. "So, Penny, what brings you here?"

I set my purse on the rug by my feet. With its tassel border and intricately woven design, it reminded me of something that might adorn an ancient castle. "I hate to bother you with my problems."

"You're my spiritual daughter; please bother me."

Spiritual daughter? I would have liked time to chew on that, but he was looking at me expectantly. "I think I mentioned on the phone I was struggling with some things with Trent."

"Trent?"

"My husband." *The man you speak to every Sunday.*

He hit himself in the forehead like he should have had a V8. "Of course. Trent. How is he?"

I played with my jacket zipper, trying to

look anywhere but at that smile. “Well, he’s been better.”

“He’s got quite a testimony.”

I raised my eyebrows, unsure of what he meant.

“What a miracle the way God restored his eyesight.”

“Yes,” I said. “God works in mysterious ways.” I still hadn’t figured out if there had been any divinity behind the loss and restoration of Trent’s eyesight, but I figured even if I didn’t understand, God did, and that might have to be enough.

He straightened the blotter on his desk. “That he does. That he does. So, what’s going on?”

Although I’d rehearsed how I could work into the conversation a hypothetical question of what someone might do if they thought their spouse had information the police should have, words failed me under the blinding glare of those teeth.

“It’s okay, Penny. You can trust me.”

The only other person in my life who’d ever told me I could trust him was Trent. So I guess it was only natural for those words to put me on guard. “What if —” I rubbed the zipper-pull between my thumb and finger — “a wife thought her husband might have done something — ?”

"Hold up, Penny." His smile faded. "Whenever I do marriage counseling, I insist on having both the husband and wife present. There are two sides to every story."

I felt myself blush, though I didn't know why I should feel embarrassed. "Trent's working."

"I'm glad to hear that." He folded his hands on the desk and glanced up at the wall clock. "A good husband should be providing for his family if he's able."

"He's a good provider," I said.

This made the smile return. "That's good to hear. Do you think we should postpone this talk until he can be here?"

At that moment, I so wished I hadn't come. There was no way he wasn't going to mention I was there. Visions of him on Sunday morning asking Trent when we all could get together to resume marriage counseling reeled through my head like a horror flick. "I'm not here for marriage counseling." I slid my hands under my thighs to keep them still. "There's something Trent might have done, or might supposed to be doing —"

Tapping his thumbs together, he sighed. "Okay, I'm going to break my own rule and hear you out, but please understand that I'm his pastor too."

His standoffishness made me feel an unexpected twinge of rejection, but I liked what he said just the same. It meant he was fair-minded. That's just what I needed. "I know," I said. "That's why I'm here. I want to do the right thing. I want him to do the right thing."

He nodded, looking deep in thought. "Okay then. How are things between you?"

The question caught me off guard. I hadn't rehearsed the answer to that one. "Okay — good, for now."

"For now?"

"Yes, good."

He stopped tapping his thumbs as he glanced up at the wall behind me.

I turned around to find he was looking at the clock. "Do you have somewhere you need to be?" I asked.

His cheeks mottled. "Sorry, no. I'm supposed to make a phone call in a few minutes, but it can wait. Do you know the question I'm asked most often as a pastor?"

I shook my head.

"Why does God allow bad things to happen to good people? And that's a fair question, but I think a better one is, why do we?"

He went back to tapping his thumbs, looking at me as though expecting me to answer.

I had no earthly idea where he was going

with the conversation, and it made me more than a little nervous, like he might know more about my situation than he let on. "I don't understand what —"

"Tell me about how you two resolve conflict."

"Conflict?"

"You know, how do you fight?"

I didn't want to talk about that, but it would be an effective lead into the dilemma at hand. "He has a temper."

He nodded sympathetically. "Don't we all?"

"Not like his," I said.

"Do you love him?"

"Most of the time."

He frowned. "What would you say is the number one thing missing in your relationship?"

I chewed my bottom lip, considering the answer. "Friendship, but I'm not here to —"

He leaned back in his chair. "Penny, I counsel couples every day. The husband almost always complains his wife wants him to be more like a woman. The woman almost always complains her husband doesn't understand her." He paused and looked at me for the longest time without so much as blinking.

Finally, I looked away.

"My answer is always the same." He glanced up at the clock again, then back to me. "Why isn't grace enough?"

Enough for what? I wondered, but the expression on his face told me I ought to know.

I left his office no closer to an answer about what to do regarding Trent, and feeling worse than when I'd come. On the ride home, I kept playing his words over and over. It felt like a slap in the face, a pat answer to a problem he couldn't possibly know the depths of — not to mention a problem I hadn't even been there to discuss — yet I couldn't help but to ask myself the same question.

What was wrong with me? Why couldn't I leave well enough alone, like Trent wanted me to? Why couldn't I be satisfied being a wife to a man who had his problems, but kept a roof over my head and food in my stomach? Why did I have to constantly long for something I couldn't give a name to? Hadn't God given me the desire of my heart with the baby inside of me? Why didn't all of that fill me with contentment?

Why wasn't grace enough?

TWENTY-NINE

It was nearly eight p.m., and still there was no sign of Trent. I was having contractions again, but they were nowhere near the five minutes apart required to go to the hospital, so I busied myself cleaning, waiting to see if they would progress.

After I got home from meeting with Pastor Harold, I'd gotten a bee in my bonnet about turning our little house into the kind of home you'd be proud to live in, Manny. I scrubbed behind every piece of furniture, appliance, and anything else that wasn't nailed down. All that was left were the baseboards. On my hands and knees with a potful of hot water infused with Pine-Sol and an old ripped T-shirt of Trent's, I scrubbed away grime, removing almost as many paint chips as dust and smudges.

A thought came to me as I looked down at the peppering of white paint flecks on the floor — a thought that should have come much sooner than now. Our home was old, and old houses had lead paint. Early in my pregnancy I'd read in one of the brochures at the doctor's office that lead could cause brain damage, but hadn't thought much about it until now. Horror filled me as I pushed myself up off the floor.

What if I'd already hurt you, I wondered as I carried the pot of dirty water to the bathroom. Warm suds sloshed back and forth, trickling over the edge and onto my hands. I dumped the liquid into the toilet. As I stood to flush, the room began to spin.

It's just stress, I told myself. *You've gotten yourself worked up over what's probably nothing, and now you're panicking. Just breathe.* Slowly I inhaled, then exhaled. After a few seconds of doing this, the dizziness left. Replacing it was the feeling my skin was on fire.

Making my way to the hallway, I fanned myself furiously as I checked the thermostat. It read sixty-two degrees. *It must be broken,* I thought, until I remembered the hot flashes Fatimah forever complained about. Fighting the urge to rip all my clothes off, streak through the yard, and dive into the creek, I settled on some fresh air, fully clothed.

Outside, the winter breeze felt blissfully

cold through my cotton shirt. The moon above was little more than a sliver, and the street stood eerily quiet. Snowflakes fluttered down on me. Pausing along the walkway, I lifted my face appreciatively to them. The longer I stared up at them, the more I felt like I was traveling through space — white stars passing me by as I flew upward into the black universe. Cold and soft, these star-flakes tickled my skin as they melted.

Snapping out of my trance, I wiped the wetness away and made my way to the curb to pick up the mail I should have retrieved earlier in the day. As I closed the thin metal door, I glanced down at the Christmas catalog, full of pretty things we could never afford, and the oil bill, which we would have to.

Across the street, I noticed once again, our neighbors had strung holiday lights from their gutters, windows, and bushes. Next year we'd be among them, I resolved . . . just like I had every year since we'd moved here. But next Christmas wouldn't be like all the others. Next year we'd have you, Manny. Christmas lights or not, it would be the best one ever.

To my right, the neighbor's calico pawed at something I couldn't see under a leafless dogwood. When I whistled, he turned toward me. His eyes looked like embers burning in the night. For the hundredth time, I wished Trent were home.

I carried the mail back to the porch and sat on the top step. The concrete felt cold on my bottom, which did wonders to bring my body temperature back out of the triple digits. The breeze whistled through the treetops and set off a distant wind chime.

I set down the catalog and bill beside me and considered the dusting of snow covering our lawn. Images of a future you building a snowman with me for the first time flashed through my mind, and I couldn't help but be happy. So many good memories were ahead of us, Manny, and I couldn't wait to start making them with you.

Light streaming out from our living room window reflected off a rectangle of snow in front of the boxwoods, giving it the appearance of being covered in tiny, shimmering crystals. When a car turned down our road, I strained to listen for the familiar sound of Trent's engine, but it ran too smoothly to be his.

A contraction hit just then. Grabbing my belly, I groaned. Gone was the tolerable sensation of someone hugging my middle too tightly. I'd now graduated to the feeling of being disemboweled and kicked in the back at the same time.

When the pain passed, and my eyes stopped watering, I remembered the glider swing your father had picked up on the side of the road one fall, and I decided the swaying motion might calm you and me both. Trudging around the side of the house to the backyard, my tennis shoes kicked up snow, allowing glimpses of the brown grass below it.

Like everything else, the bench swing was covered in white, so I pulled down my sleeve and swept it clean. The vinyl cushion was soft and cold. Leaning back against it, I pushed off with my feet, sending myself gliding forward.

Back and forth I swung, relishing the cold wind lapping at my face and imagining I was a little girl at a playground. I thought of my parents and what they might be doing at that moment. Daddy would be perched in front of the television, flipping channels and complaining about the politics of the anchors he loved to hate. Mama would be in the kitchen, maybe cutting him a slice of her apple crumb pie and singing a hymn they'd sung in church that Sunday — still doing her best to win him without words.

Several strong contractions came on each other's heels, jolting me from my thoughts.

Pursing my lips, I breathed through the pain like the book Callie Mae gave me had taught me to do. For several minutes none came, so I went back to swinging and clinging to Trent's promise that Mama and Daddy could visit when you were born.

As the tip of my tennis shoes dragged gently across the snow, a twig snapped in the distance. My eyes flew open and I squinted into the darkness. "Trent?" I called. Could I have been so deep in thought I hadn't heard his car pull up?

A dark silhouette seemed to glide across the snow toward me. I screamed and planted my feet on the ground, ready to bolt. White teeth flashed in the darkness.

I squinted harder. "Fatimah?"

"Peeny?" she called, moving toward me. "What are you doing out here?"

I was so relieved, I laughed. "Hot flash."

"Ha-ha! See, I tell you they are from the devil!"

As she moved closer, I saw the fat bundle she held and the little, round face peeking through blankets. "I have brought a special guest to you."

I climbed off the swing to meet her halfway. The baby's eyes blinking up at me were so big. Puffs of breath from her tiny mouth turned to frost.

"Let's go inside," I said. "She'll freeze to death out here."

Fatimah followed me into the house. Now that I'd cooled down, the warmth of the living room felt far less oppressive.

I shut the door behind us and pulled the cover away from the baby's chin to have a better look. She was not at all the beauty Callie Mae described, though I smiled at her just the same. Instead of a nice round head, hers was shaped like a cone. Her skin was marred by what looked like dozens of purple ink dots, and the whole side of her face was bluish-gray. Even her lips looked ashen as they glistened with several tiny bubbles pooling at the corner of her mouth. When I touched her soft cheek, she turned toward my finger. "She's something," I said.

Fatimah beamed. "She is most beautiful baby in world!" She gave her a tender kiss.

"Is she bruised?" I asked.

She nodded. "It was most difficult birth. She is stubborn, like her father, and stayed too long in birth canoe."

It took me a second to figure out she meant *canal*. "What's her name?"

She smiled shyly, averting her eyes. "Peeny."

I made a face at her. "I'm serious, Fati, what's her name, really?"

Lines formed across her forehead as she frowned at me. "It is really Peeny. And what is wrong with that name?"

My eyebrows shot up in surprise. "You named her after me?"

She shrugged. "You are a good and beautiful woman, and my best friend."

It overwhelmed me she would name the most precious thing she had in this world after me, of all people. As I looked down at the baby who now shared my name, I was so touched I could have cried. "Still?"

She rubbed noses with the baby. "Yes, still."

I wanted to ask how she spelled the child's name, worried she might have done so phonetically, the way she pronounced it, but decided not to ask. If she'd gotten it wrong, she would only feel bad. "That's the nicest thing anyone's ever done for me." All it takes sometimes, Manny, is someone believing in you for you to begin to believe in yourself. "Can I hold her?"

She looked at her lovingly, as if preparing for a long goodbye, then laid her gently in my arms. Callie Mae described her as a moose, but she was surprisingly light. I leaned in and took in her warmth and baby smell, then planted a kiss on her round cheek. "Hi, Peeny," I said.

Fatimah scrunched her nose like she smelled something rancid. "Why do you say her name like that?"

I glanced over at her. "That's how you say it."

"Her name is like yours. You must say it right."

"Penny?" I offered.

"Peh-eeny," Fatimah said slowly, coming closer than I'd ever heard her to pronouncing it correctly.

My stomach began to tighten, and I pushed the baby into Fatimah's arms just in time. A tidal wave of pain crashed over me and I doubled over.

When it passed, I opened my eyes to see Fatimah looking at me with alarm. "You are in labor, true?"

I shook my head. "No, I don't think —" Another contraction stole my words.

Fatimah set the baby gently on the carpet and led me to the couch. "I think yes you are."

"The contractions are all over the place," I said as the pain subsided. "The doctor says the real thing will be regular, and get closer together."

She didn't look convinced. "Do you have water?"

"You want me to get you a drink?" I was

more than a little irritated that she couldn't do for herself, with me hurting the way I was.

"No. You have water from this baby?"

When I finally realized she was asking me if my water had broken, I shook my head.

She eyed me suspiciously, then picked up little Penny and sat in Trent's easy chair with the baby against her chest. "You give birth by tomorrow morning. Place a bet with me and I will be rich."

I twisted my mouth at her. "I don't know. I've been having these contractions for days, and I'm still early."

She shrugged. "By tomorrow. You make relations tonight, and Manny will come."

I smiled, imagining you wrapped in blankets like Fatimah's baby. "I'm not too keen about the relations part, but I sure would love to meet my son."

Right on cue, your father's car roared into the driveway, and my insides tightened. "Trent," I whispered.

Fatimah gave the door a dirty look.

I stood, intending to meet him outside to warn him she was there and beg him to behave, but before I could take two steps, liquid gushed from me. It was such an odd sensation that I gasped.

I tried to smile. "I think I've got water."

"There is blood," she said, looking down at the puddle beneath me.

Trent barged through the front door, so drunk he couldn't walk straight, and sneered at Fatimah. "What's loudmouth doing here?"

"Your wife is in trouble. I take her to hospital."

He stumbled backward. "What's — ?" he looked down at the floor and his eyes widened. "What is that?"

Fatimah held her baby tight against her chest as she stood. "Bring your wife to my car, now."

He stood as still as a wax exhibit.

"Now!" Fatimah yelled.

Snapping out of his trance, he slurred, "I'll take her."

Holding her baby with one arm, Fatimah grabbed my elbow with the other. "You will not. You will kill her, the baby, and yourself." She nudged me toward the door.

His eyes drooped into bloodshot slits. "Don't you tell me what to do in my own house."

I felt myself wanting to pass out, but was afraid of what would happen to you and Fatimah if I did. "Back off," I said to him. A constant stream of warm liquid trickled down my leg, and I was scared.

Not waiting for his reply, I followed Fatimah to the front door. As I stepped onto the porch on Fatimah's heels, Trent shoved me in the middle of my back. I fell into Fatimah. In horror, I watched her clutch her bundle as she stumbled down the steps. Her right shoulder bore the impact on the sidewalk as she screamed. Safe in her arms, the baby cried.

I looked back at him in disbelief. With a look of utter shock, he stared down at her. "I'm sorry," he stammered. "I didn't mean —"

He hurried down the steps to help her up, but she ripped her arm from him. Still on the ground, she examined the baby, then allowed me to hold her while she got to her feet. Without looking back, we hurried to the car and Fatimah clumsily strapped the baby into the car seat.

"You will go to jail for that," she yelled from the window as we peeled out of the driveway.

THIRTY

Fatimah's car screeched to a stop in front of the emergency room. Red from the neon sign shone through the windshield, making me wonder if the liquid drizzling out of me was as bright-red as it appeared, or if maybe it was just a trick of light. My ears rang so loudly I could barely hear what she was saying as I drifted in and out of consciousness.

I opened my eyes to commotion and determined faces, only to fade out again. When I came to, a female voice was screaming, "Don't push!"

But I couldn't help myself. The pressure was unbearable. I vaguely wondered if I was dying when someone swiped something cold across my arm, then shot a needle into it. Warmth rushed through my veins, and I drifted off again.

When I opened my eyes, the room was a blur of color, and the sounds surrounding me were as muffled as if I had wet cotton in my ears. I tried to lift my head, but the room began to sway and shift. Laying my head back down managed to calm the sudden wave of nausea.

It was disorienting to find myself lying in a hospital bed surrounded by pink-papered walls, and it took me a few seconds to remember where I was and why. The scent of flowers hung heavy in the air. When I turned my head, I learned why. A bouquet of roses sat on a square table at my right. I didn't have to read the card to know they weren't from Trent.

An IV jutted from my forearm, allowing a bag of liquid attached to a pump to drip into my vein. A brunette in white scrubs pressed buttons on the machine, making it beep with each adjustment.

I could breathe way too easily, which told me that you probably were no longer inside me. The thought both exhilarated and terrified me. I looked down at my hospital gown to verify it. My belly was still round, but only half the size it had been. My gaze ping-ponged around the room, but I saw no bassinet. What felt an awful lot like a contraction made me groan.

"After-pain," the nurse said sympathetically.

When I tried to sit up, my head throbbed. I laid it back down on the pillow. "Is my baby . . . ? Where is he?"

"He's in the nursery with the pediatrician," she said. "We can bring him out to you when the exam is done."

I realized then that I was shivering. "Is he okay?"

She put two fingers on my wrist, right above my thumb. Her mouth moved as she counted my pulse in her head. After a few seconds, she let my arm go and pulled up a second cover that had been draped over the end of my bed. "He seems to be just fine. Thank God you got here when you did. Most babies end up in the NICU with your condition, if they live at all. You don't know how lucky you are."

The words "if they live at all" filled me with dread.

She picked up the plastic water pitcher from the bedside table and held it up. "I'll go fill this. Are you hungry? If you want, I can get you some Jell-O."

My teeth chattered as I shook my head, wondering what Jell-O would do for me if I was hungry. Before I could ask her to turn up the heat, she was already on it.

I pulled the covers up around my neck. I was so cold. "What happened to me?" I barely recognized my own voice. It sounded as raspy as a longtime smoker's.

She looked over as she adjusted the thermostat. The sound and smell of forced heat poured from the vents. "You had a condition called abruption. A little longer, and you and your baby might both have died. You've lost a lot of blood. We had to give you three units."

Might both have died, I repeated in my head, feeling the weight of that horrible possibility.

"You should've been sectioned, but your baby came before we could cut you. Feisty little bugger."

I must have given her a disapproving look, because she quickly added, "But just as cute as he can be."

The relief I felt brought tears to my eyes. You were alive and well. "Can I go to the nursery to see him?"

She took off her glasses, rubbed them against the hem of her scrub top, and slid them back on. "No, sweetie. You've lost a lot of blood, and your pressure's still low. You'd probably pass out on us. Besides, they'll be done soon. Then I'll bring him out to you, all clean and polished. Promise." She left with my water pitcher, bringing it back a few minutes later. "Take it slow," she warned, pouring the first cupful.

As soon as she was out of sight, I refilled that plastic cup and slammed down one after another until the pitcher held only crushed ice. I set the cup on the bedside table and peeked at the card on the bouquet — *Congratulations, Mommy. Love, Callie Mae, Fatimah & Edgard.*

Of course they weren't from Trent — I'd known that before even looking — but still, disappointment filled me. After putting the card back in its envelope and setting it beside the flowers, I noticed a phone that resembled an old-school TV remote. I dialed my parents' number. A recorded message told me long-distance phone calls required a credit card.

Hanging up, I pushed the call bell for the nurse, but it was Callie Mae and Fatimah who walked through the door.

Static sounded from an overhead speaker, followed by, "Can I help you, Mrs. Taylor?"

"Never mind. Thank you," I said to the voice.

Fatimah and Callie Mae grinned at me. Callie Mae carried a blue gift bag with a giant teddy bear on the side. Fatimah, dressed in a colorful skirt and matching head wrap, held a covered dish.

"How's our girl?" Callie Mae asked. She

wore no makeup for a change, and her hair had been brushed back into a tight ponytail at the nape of her neck. She almost didn't look like herself. Fatimah could still pass for six months pregnant with her protruding belly and full face. Baby Penny wasn't with her.

"I've felt better," I said. "They're going to bring out Manny soon. I haven't even seen him yet."

Fatimah set down the casserole dish on my bedside table and lifted off the cover to show me some sort of tomato-based stew. "You eat this. It give you strength."

I couldn't make out a single ingredient in the casserole, other than the sauce, and didn't want to ask. It smelled a lot like stinky feet. The hospital food would have to be pretty bad for me to dig into whatever this was. Still, I appreciated the love behind it. "Thanks." I took her hand. Her knuckles were ashy from the dryness of winter. "For everything."

She shrugged. "It was nothing you would not do for me. You look white as a coarse."

"A *corpse,*" Callie Mae corrected. "And I'd have to agree, though I would have put it a little more delicately. I guess that's to be expected when you lose as much blood as Fati said you did."

"How's your arm?" I asked Fatimah, feeling the weight of Trent's guilt.

She clicked her tongue in disgust, then slid off her jacket and pulled down the shoulder of her blouse. I figured she was trying to show me a bruise, but her skin was too dark to really see it.

"I'm sorry," I said. "Alcoholism is a terrible disease."

She pulled her sleeve back up. "It is your husband that is terrible disease."

Callie Mae sighed. "Ladies, this is a happy occasion. Let's enjoy it and put that behind us for the time being, shall we?"

Call bells and phones sounded from the hallway, along with laughter and a parade of what I assumed were family members filing by to visit the newest members of their families.

"Callie, did you bring your phone?" I asked.

"Are you wanting to call Trent?" she asked hesitantly.

Fatimah sneered.

"No, he'll come when he's sobered. I want to call my parents."

Callie Mae dug in her oversize purse, and her hand emerged holding a flip phone. I thanked her and made the call I'd been dying to for months. As soon as I heard my mother's voice, though, a cart with a middle-aged nurse grinning behind it entered my room. "Oh, Mama, I'm sorry. They just brought in Manny, and I haven't even seen him yet. Please come when you can." I heard her squeal in delight as I handed the phone over to Callie Mae to fill Mama in on the details.

My eyes fixated on the blue crib card taped to the top of his clear plastic bassinet.

Baby Boy Taylor.
Five pounds, four ounces.
Nineteen inches long.

I pushed the arrow button on the side of my bed to bend my mattress forward a bit more so I could have a better look at you. They had swaddled you as tight as a burrito in a pink-and-blue-striped blanket. Your hair was hidden underneath a baby-blue cap, and your eyes lay closed. You didn't look all bruised and misshapen like Fatimah's baby. You were perfect and pink, with a dimple just like your grandpappy's in the center of your little chin.

"Look who's here," the nurse practically sang, wearing the type of silly grin normally reserved for young children. She parked you close enough that I could see your sweet, sleeping face, but not close enough for me to pick you up. She insisted on rattling off a bunch of instructions I would never remember, first, and showed me a blue gadget in your crib I was supposed to suction out your mouth with if you started choking.

Choking. The word sent panic through me. I hadn't even considered that possibility. She continued her spiel, droning on about poison-control numbers and car-seat safety facts.

Go away, I thought. *Leave us alone so I can hold my baby.* But she took her sweet old time. It's not that I didn't think the information was important — I just wanted so desperately to hold you.

Even in that dim room, I could see your nose had that same flare to it your father's did. You were the most beautiful thing I'd ever laid eyes on, Manny. I couldn't wait to see your eyes and hair.

When the nurse finally left, Fatimah handed you to me. You tried to open your eyes, but then gave up and closed them again before I had a chance to see their color. You weighed practically nothing and felt as fragile as a hollowed egg. When I laid you against me, you bent your knees up against your belly and put your little hands under your head. And I was in love.

As Callie Mae and Fatimah watched, I pulled back your hat, delighted to see you had a tiny tuft of blond in the center of your head. I then checked to make sure all your fingers and toes were there. They were so tiny, but definitely all present. You had one birthmark the shape of a kidney bean on your left heel, but that was the only marking I could find.

I nuzzled against your warm neck, inhaling your baby smell. "I can't wait for your daddy to meet you."

Fatimah grunted. "He does not deserve this baby."

I pleaded with my eyes for her to stop. Now wasn't the time. I was so emotional already. "He didn't mean it, Fati. He was just drunk."

She waved her hand. "He is just drunk every single day of his pitiful life. Drunk is not excuse. He could have hurt my baby, or killed your baby."

She was right, of course. There was no excuse for what he did, but I knew he really didn't intend to hurt her. "Forgive him, Fatimah. Please?"

She waved her hand again as if trying to shoo the conversation away. "I cannot stay and listen to this. He hurt me, tried to hurt you, and still you make excuses for him. He deserves to have his hands cut off. He is no man!"

I held you tighter, focusing on your sweet little face instead of her scowl. When she continued her rant, I closed my eyes and nuzzled you. When I opened them again, she had gone.

"You can't blame her," Callie Mae said as she sat in the vinyl chair next to my bed.

I kissed your warm cheek. "I don't."

She held out her arms for you. It was all I could do in my greediness to give you up. She rocked and kissed on you, but you just kept sleeping away.

After what seemed like no time at all, the nurse returned and asked to take you again, this time for blood work. I didn't say so, but I wondered why they couldn't have done everything while they'd had you in there the last time. Taking you away after I'd waited so long to get you seemed unnecessarily cruel. But if you needed it, you needed it.

While she rolled you away in the bassinet, Callie Mae walked over to the dish Fatimah left and lifted up the glass lid. She sniffed it and made a face. "What in the world do you suppose that is?"

I laughed. "No telling."

"Bless her heart, it smells like gym socks.

I'll bring you some fried chicken tomorrow if you want."

"You, Callie Mae Johnson, are a real-life angel," I said. The mention of chicken made my stomach grumble. "I'm starving. The nurse offered me Jell-O, but do you think they might let me have some real food?"

She shook her head. "Already asked. They said liquids tonight, but you can eat tomorrow."

I sighed. "What sense does that make?"

"Between you and me, I think medical people are secret sadists. You should hear what they did to me during my colonoscopy."

"No offense," I said, getting a visual I could have lived without, "but I'll pass."

She sat down in the chair beside my bed. "Well, I guess I should tell you."

"Tell me what?"

"Your old man's in jail for assault."

I blinked at her a few times trying to process the information.

"Norma?" I asked, unsure.

She gave me a funny look. "No, Fatimah. Who's Norma?"

I laid my head back on the pillow and stared up at the grates in the drop ceiling. "She pressed charges."

"Of course she pressed charges. He

pushed her down the stairs with a newborn baby in her hands, for crying out loud."

"He didn't push her. He pushed me."

"Oh, well, my mistake. He didn't assault a woman who just had a baby, he assaulted his wife who was about to have a baby. Much better."

We sat silent a moment, as I wondered how much his bail would be and how I'd go about getting the money. What he did was wrong — very wrong — but I so wanted him to meet you, Manny.

Callie Mae started arranging the flowers she and Fatimah had bought in a glass vase. "She probably saved his life, you know."

I turned my head to look at her as she went on. "He was flying high and trying to get behind the wheel when the cops picked him up. Come to think of it, she might have saved more lives than just his."

I stared at the ceiling, thinking of all the times he'd driven drunk and all the beatings speaking up against it had cost me. Maybe a DUI would finally get through to him. "I still can't believe she had him arrested."

She pulled a white rose from the side of the arrangement and placed it in the middle. "Bad behavior has consequences."

I leaned my head back on the pillow and

closed my eyes. "I've been praying so long for that man to change, Callie. But my prayers always seem to fall on deaf ears. Maybe God will listen to you. Do you think — ?"

She brushed off her hands. "I can pray. I have and will, Penny, but God's not a co-dependent."

"What's that supposed to mean?"

"It means he won't force Trent to change. He doesn't manipulate people into doing what they're not willing to do, no matter how much the rest of us beg him to. Trent has to want to change. *You* can only change *you.* That's what you should be praying about."

I thought then of Fatimah telling me the same thing, and it almost clicked.

She said nothing for a minute, then continued. "Your mother and father are coming as soon as they can. You should have heard her crying for joy. She sounds sweet as a sugar cube. She said your daddy was out of town helping his brother repair a roof or something to that effect, but would drive home the day after tomorrow. They'll be here the day after."

"Will I still be here?"

"They said you and Manny should be released that morning, so probably not."

"Did you give them my address?"

She locked eyes with me a moment. "No, I gave them mine. I think you and the baby should stay with me for a while."

"He didn't mean to hurt Fatimah," I repeated.

She sat in the chair again and leaned forward. "Listen, sweetheart, I'm going to use a little tough love here. How would you feel if he hurt or killed your son? Could you live with yourself if you allowed that to happen?"

The word *killed* made me think of Norma, and her husband who was behind bars, like Trent. Would they be in the same jail? "He wouldn't hurt our baby."

She bit her top lip and stared down at the flowers. "Why not? He didn't think twice about hurting Fatimah's."

"He didn't mean it," I said again.

"It doesn't matter what he means. The damage is just as bad as if he did mean it. Would you say that at Manny's eulogy — he didn't mean to kill his son? He's an abusive drunk. You can't predict what he will or won't do. Penny, this isn't just about you anymore. You've got a child to protect."

I glanced out the window at a distant baseball field, several stories below, blanketed in white. "He wouldn't let me go,

Callie. I'm his wife. This is his son. He'd be coming around, insisting we come home. It could get real ugly. I don't want you to . . ."

"To what?" She crossed her arms. "Go ahead and finish the sentence. You were going to say 'get hurt,' weren't you?" She smiled tightly. "He doesn't scare me. But he sure better scare you."

Thirty-One

I'd agreed to stay with Callie Mae, at least until Trent was out of jail. On the way home from the hospital, she brought us by the house so I could pick up some of the things we would need.

Thankfully, Trent had cleaned up the mess I'd left on the floor, but other than that, everything was as I'd left it. He hadn't called, so I didn't know how much his bail would be, or the jail time he might be facing. I couldn't wait for him to meet you, Manny, but I was glad for the chance to think things through without him around to make up my mind for me.

Callie Mae set you and me up in her guest bedroom. It couldn't have been prettier, with its canopy bed, cottage furniture, and sunny yellow paint. In the corner of the room sat an antique crib she said had been hers as a baby, and her mother's before her.

Atop a small dresser lay a stack of diapers,

wipes, and the baby clothes she had brought to the hospital in that teddy bear gift bag.

You and I had just dozed off for a nap when the doorbell rang. I heard Callie Mae's voice, then Mama's and Daddy's. With a knot in my stomach, I laid you down as gently as I could in the crib. Breathing a sigh of relief when you didn't wake, I tiptoed out of the room and softly shut the door.

Mama was thanking Callie Mae for the directions. When she saw me, her mouth dropped. I must have looked a sight with all the weight I'd gained from the pregnancy.

She looked just the same as I remembered, save a little more gray and a wrinkle or two. Daddy, however, had gained at least fifty pounds, and didn't look nearly as tall as I remembered him. I rushed into Mama's open arms. She held me for the longest time, then finally pulled back and put her soft hands on my cheeks, examining my face. Tears glinted in her eyes. "Oh, my word, Penny Elizabeth, you're a woman!"

Smiling, I put my finger to my lips to remind her of you.

Her hand flew to her mouth. "Sleeping?"

I nodded.

She took my hands in hers as she looked me over, head to toe. "Oh, look at my baby.

Beautiful as ever."

Now that I was a mother myself, it hit me just how much my mother must have loved me. "Thanks, Mama. You too." I glanced over at my father, who had his hands buried in his jeans pockets. He'd always looked uncomfortable anywhere but in the field. Time, apparently, hadn't changed that.

"Daddy," was all that would come out of my mouth. With my heart in my throat, I walked over and ventured a hug. He still smelled like that musky aftershave he'd always worn. After barely a second, he pulled back and cleared his throat. "So, where's this grandson I keep hearing about?"

With a proud smile, I waved them down the hallway. When we got to the room you were sleeping in, I put my hand on the doorknob and slowly turned it to the right, cringing as it clicked open. The last thing I wanted to do was set you off crying again.

Mama tiptoed over to the crib and peeked down at you. With a hand over her heart, she bent her head to the side and admired you. I could tell it was love at first sight for her, just as it had been for me. After a minute, she looked over her shoulder at your grandpappy and waved him over. They watched you sleep for what had to be a good five minutes. Finally, we joined Callie Mae in the kitchen, where she fixed them a pot of coffee, gave me a cup of tea, and set out store-bought cookies. "Y'all make yourselves at home," she said, buttoning up her jacket. "I've got to get on down to the food bank before we have a riot on our hands. The delivery's late, and the crowds are getting restless."

After we said our good-byes, Mama and Daddy sat across from me at the kitchen table. Daddy's eyes fixated on the now-yellow bruise around my wrist, while Mama's gaze darted around the kitchen. It was at least four times the size of hers. "This place is beautiful. Is it yours or Callie Mae's?"

It dawned on me then that Callie Mae might not have filled them in on more than just an address. "Oh, no," I said. "Our house isn't nearly this nice. Manny and I are just staying here until Trent comes home."

"Where is he?" Daddy's nostrils flared so slightly no one but Mama or me would have even noticed.

I looked down at my hands wrapped around my cup, wishing for the phone to ring or you to wake up.

When I glanced back up at Mama, she was giving him a look that begged for him to leave it alone.

She forced a smile. "So, how much does he weigh?"

I was so thankful for the change in subject I could have cried. "About one-ninety," I said with a smirk.

Mama slapped my hand playfully. This time her smile was real. "Oh! You know I meant the baby."

"Five pounds, four ounces."

Daddy took a sip of his coffee. His worn wedding band was so tight around his finger it made the hairy flesh above it bulge. "Exactly what you were."

Mama made a face. "Don't listen to him. You were not, neither. You were seven-four."

He shrugged. "Close enough."

She rolled her eyes. "Oh, phooey. That man, I swannee he's getting that old-timer's. This year he gave me a card on your birthday instead of mine."

I laughed. "That's not Alzheimer's, that's just him. Remember when he —"

"That's enough," he said without humor. "We didn't come here to talk about me." He set his cup down, then surprised me by reaching over and giving my fingers a squeeze. His hand wasn't half as hard and calloused as I remembered, and I found myself hoping his heart wasn't either. When

I squeezed back, he dropped my hand, looking embarrassed.

I turned to Mama. "I think Manny's got your smile."

"They don't smile that young, do they?" Daddy asked.

"Not really." I took a sip of tea and realized I must not have mixed the sugar off the bottom well enough.

Mama winked at me. "Just when they mess their pants."

"Or dream," I added. "He smiles sometimes when he's dreaming."

A strand of gray worked loose from her ponytail and she tucked it behind an ear. "You did that — smiled when you slept. Your Nanny used to say you were dreaming of angels."

"I miss her," I said, thinking of my four-foot-nothing Nanny with the tight white bun and hands always covered in flour. She was the best grandmother a girl could have hoped to have. Always baking pies, telling terrible jokes, and laughing — always laughing.

Mama reached across the table and put her hand on mine. "I miss *you.* You didn't have to stay away."

I opened my mouth, unsure of what to say.

"Yes, she did. Because of him." Daddy's jaw set. "She stayed away because of him. You never answered my question about where he was."

Before my conscience could catch up with my mouth, I blurted, "Away on business." It wasn't entirely untrue, I told myself. He was away, and he certainly had business to take care of.

Mama snatched her hand from mine. "Penny, tell the truth, now. He's in jail for assaulting a mother and baby, ain't he?"

Daddy shook his head at me in disgust, as if he were any better. "What kind of man does that?"

"It's not what you think."

"He give you that?" Daddy jabbed his thumb toward the bruise on my wrist.

"Don't believe everything you hear." I could have killed Callie Mae.

When I think of lying to them to protect your father, shame fills me, Manny. But that's what an abused wife does — she covers. Covers for her husband's drinking. Covers with his boss when he's too hung over to work, and even covers up his abuse of her with lies to friends and family — even when the lies are as obvious as the bruises. I wasn't the first woman to "walk into a door" to explain away a black eye, and unfortunately, I won't be the last.

Mama glanced up at me, then back down at her coffee that was more milk than anything. "So what happened, then?"

I managed to keep my tone light, but I could feel my hands sweating. "He was just nudging me to hurry up and get to the car so he could take me to the hospital. My water broke and there was blood." Mama still wasn't making eye contact, so I focused on your grandpappy, whose expression I couldn't read. "When he did, I tripped into Fatimah. She fell down the stairs. The baby wasn't hurt. It was an accident."

Mama frowned. "That's not at all how your friend made it sound. Why would they arrest him for that?"

"They wouldn't," Daddy mumbled.

I waved my hand like the whole thing was silly. "Fatimah and he don't get along, is all. She thinks he did it on purpose."

My parents exchanged an unsure glance between them.

Just to make it more convincing, I added, "She thinks everybody does everything on purpose. She's one of those conspiracy types."

"But she had him arrested," Mama said.

I dipped my spoon into my cup, stirred the bottom, and scooped out the teabag.

Glad to have something to look at besides my parents, I wrapped the string around the spoon and pressed the teabag against the inside of the cup. "Like I said, she thinks he meant to do it."

Daddy cleared his throat. "So, how've you been? You have everything you need?"

I set the used teabag on my saucer. "We've been getting along fine. There's been some tough times, especially when Trent lost his sight, but he's back to work now, so we're good."

When Mama gasped, I remembered they hadn't known about Trent's accident. After I filled them in on the story, they both seemed to soften toward him.

"Well, I don't wish that on no one," Daddy said. He studied the pot rack hanging from the ceiling as if those stainless steel pans were really something to behold. "I tell you, girl, leaving the way you did made your mother so sick I thought she would never be the same aga—"

"Don't," Mama blurted, giving him a stern look. "That's behind us. We're here now. That's all that matters."

Daddy pressed his lips tight, looking between her and me. "Well, somebody tell me what we *can* talk about, 'cause I am out of ideas."

"How about that grandbaby?" Mama said. "We can talk about that sweet thing all day long."

I pushed back my chair, maybe a little too eagerly. "You want me to wake him?"

"Only if you want us to get hold of him before we have to get on home," Daddy said.

My heart sank. "Home? I thought —"

"Penny, honey, we can't stay." Mama looked even sadder than I felt.

"Why?" My voice cracked.

"Your daddy's getting a tumor removed day after tomorrow."

My breath caught. As many issues as I had with my father, Manny, I sure wasn't ready to lose him. "Tumor?"

"I told you not to say anything," he grumbled halfheartedly.

The look she gave him could have frozen Niagara Falls, and I wondered if maybe she had done some changing in my absence. I hoped so. "I'm not going to have my daughter think we're dying to get away from her. Besides —" she turned back to me — "it's benign. He's been putting off the surgery, but it's going to start pushing against his heart. Doctor says it can't wait anymore."

I turned to Daddy. "Are you okay? Does it hurt?"

He twisted his mouth like the whole

conversation was nonsense. My father could have an ax in the side of his head and get mad if anyone tried to make a big deal about it. "Naw, I get tired easy, but doctor says once they remove that thing, I'll have the energy of an eighteen-year-old again."

Mama raised an eyebrow at him. "God forbid." She turned to me, her smile back. "Could you imagine?"

Daddy had always been the restless type, always working, always moving, and when you tried to make him sit still, his leg bobbed around like he had to use the bathroom.

I tried to return the smile, but couldn't. "It's definitely not cancer? They're sure?"

When she looked me square in the eye, I knew she was telling the truth. If there was one thing my mother was not, it was a liar. "Don't worry. They're positive. Doctor Whiting says he's going to die someday, but not from this."

We all sat silent, listening to the hum of the refrigerator and trying to think of something to say.

"I'm sorry I left that way," I finally said.

"It hurt me," Mama said softly. "Your father's right about that, but finally getting that call from you, and now seeing you. Heavens, and now a grandbaby. All's right with the world again. We're not sore, honey. Just so grateful to God to have you back in our lives."

I swallowed the lump in my throat and looked to my father for absolution.

He gave a half nod, which was twice as much as I'd expected.

As if you'd been patiently waiting for the conversation to be over, you started to cry.

"My baby, a mother," Mama said. "How in the world did this happen?"

"Please," Daddy said, "there's some things parents just don't want to know."

"Oh!" Mama blushed and slapped his arm.

Your cry grew to an impatient shriek and we all stood.

Mama made it to your crib before I could and scooped you out. You gave her the funniest look, like she was an alien or something.

She set her forehead against yours. "I'm your grandma, Manny."

This made you cry harder. Your face was as red as fire.

She pulled at the side of your diaper, then turned to me. "I think I might know what the problem is."

I looked over my shoulder at your grandpappy. "You remember how to change a diaper, don't you, Daddy?"

He put his hands up like he was under arrest. "You made your bed. You lie in it."

"Men," Mama said.

"Men," I agreed.

By the time your grandparents were getting ready to leave, Mama snapped her last cell phone picture and we were all in tears, including you. Mama and me must have hugged for half an hour. She didn't want to leave, and I didn't want her to either, but you were cranky and Daddy was clearly ready to get home. They promised to call and let me know they were home safe, and I promised to call Mama at least once a week and send more pictures as soon as I could.

After I nursed you and changed your bottom for what seemed like the hundredth time that day, you finally drifted back to sleep. Exhausted, I closed my eyes, intending to join you, but as luck would have it, the phone rang. Your eyes flashed open, and before you could cry, I did.

Thirty-Two

The phone call was Callie Mae letting me know she would stop by Bitha's Biscuits and pick us up dinner on her way home. When she heard you crying in the background, she asked if everything was okay. Of course, I didn't tell her that everything had been fine until she called and woke you.

You'd been back to sleep for fifteen minutes or so when a knock came at the front door. It was too soon for it to be her. Thinking maybe it was Trent, I hurried over and opened it. The rush of cold air that met me was nothing compared to the chill I felt looking into the eyes of the police officer standing there with his hand resting on the handle of a holstered pistol.

"Can I help you?" I rubbed my arms, wishing I'd looked before opening.

"Mrs. Taylor?" His face was still round from youth.

My eyes moved from the metal badge

pinned above one pocket of his blue shirt to the name tag pinned above the other. It read: *J. E. Harrison.* "Yes."

"Mrs. Trent Taylor?" White puffed from his mouth as he spoke.

I nodded.

"May we come in, ma'am? We have a few questions we need to ask you."

"We?" I scanned the porch and yard looking for someone else.

He turned around and waved in another officer sitting in the patrol car — a woman. At his prompting, she stepped out, closed the door, and tramped up the sidewalk. She was barely five feet tall, but there was a hardness about her that made me think she could probably put a whooping on most men.

I was thinking they'd finally heard about Trent's relationship with Norma. Hanging my head, I backed away from the entrance and let them in. The man's gaze scanned the living room, then the hallway, while the woman's was set on sizing me up.

"You mind if we have a seat?" she asked.

I tucked my hair behind my ear and motioned toward the couch. "I have a sleeping baby in the next room, so we'll need to keep it down."

"I understand," the man said, taking a seat

in the wingback chair, diagonal from the sectional. "Congratulations, by the way. We tried to give you a few days. Wish we could give you more, but —"

The woman sat on the opposite end of the couch from me. "But we have an assault to investigate."

Assault, not murder. I breathed a sigh of relief. This had to be about Fatimah, not Norma.

Both officers removed their hats and rested them on their thighs at the same time, as though they'd been taught the move in police academy. The woman's dark hair lay plastered against her head in a severe bun. "Did you witness the assault by your husband of Fatimah Wek and her infant daughter?"

I straightened a stack of *Ladies' Home Journals* resting on the end table. "I don't know that I'd call it an assault."

They continued to stare.

"I was in labor, and we were in a rush to get to the hospital. I think he meant to nudge me to hurry, but I tripped and fell into Fatimah, knocking her down the stairs."

If I'd have blinked, I would have missed the look that passed between them. "What's your relationship to the alleged victim?" the man asked.

"She's my friend." *Was* my friend. She'd never forgive me for this, but even so, I couldn't let Trent rot in jail when he hadn't really meant to hurt her.

The woman spoke next. "Are you and the suspect married or separated?"

The question gave me pause. "Married. I'm just staying here until he comes home." So that was it. The words entered the universe, telling me what I guess I already knew. I wasn't leaving him after all, as if there was really any question.

The woman put her foot out, revealing a black dress sock with tiny balls of pink lint stuck to one side. "Let me be blunt, ma'am. Mrs. Wek was hysterical when she spoke to us. Very, um . . ." she looked to the male officer to help her finish the sentence.

"Emotional," he offered. "With the heavy accent it was difficult to understand her, but from what we could make out, Mr. Taylor allegedly pushed her down a flight of stairs with a baby in her arms. Does that sound about right?"

I'd already told them it was an accident. Maybe they were trying to force me to repeat my story, hoping to catch me in a lie. They were always doing that in those police shows Trent liked to watch. "It was an accident, like I said. And it wasn't a flight of stairs; it was four or five. She might have thought he meant it, but he didn't. She just misinterpreted the situation. My husband had a little too much to drink, and with me in labor, it was just hectic."

The man ran a tongue over his teeth, making a bulge move under his closed mouth. "We have prior complaints. From you, I believe. Two domestic violence calls over the last five years, in fact."

My cheeks caught fire when I realized they had me. "I didn't press charges."

The woman leaned forward. "Why not, if you don't mind me asking?"

I did mind her asking, but didn't think it would go over too well if I said so. I looked back at the hallway, hoping I'd heard you stir. "We fight crazy sometimes, you know? He's very passionate, and I guess so am I. We just fuss now and then. He breaks a few things, you know, to let off steam, but then it's over."

The man pointed to my wrist. "You want to tell me about that bruise?"

Instinctively, my other hand wrapped around my wrist to hide it. "I fell off my bike." Why did I say bike? How clichéd could I get? I didn't even own a bike. I prayed he wouldn't ask to see it.

Suspicion glinted in his eyes. "You were

riding a bike nine months pregnant?"

I looked at the floor, chiding myself for being so stupid. "That's right."

"So your official statement is that what happened the other night was not assault but an accident? I just want to make absolutely sure that's really your story."

I swallowed and nodded.

He shook his head at the woman cop as if he had seen it a million times.

She squinted at me. "So your friend is lying?"

I rubbed the back of my neck. "Not lying. Just mistaken."

The man pinched the bridge of his nose. "What do you think, Lisa?"

"You know what I think."

They both stood and put their hats back on. The woman pulled a card out of her front pocket and handed it to me. "This is my number, just in case you decide it wasn't an accident after all." She reached into her other pocket and pulled out another card, looked down at it, then tried to hand that one to me too. "And this is a number for the women's shelter. They take babies, too."

I made no move for it.

She hesitated, then set it on the windowsill.

"Sorry to bother you, ma'am," the man said.

The woman cop stopped to look at the tiny blue blanket draped over the arm of the chair. "Take care of that baby." There was a warning implied in her tone. "Your husband will be out soon. If he puts another hand on you, call us."

I huffed. "He didn't —"

She put her hand up as if to say, "Save it."

Thirty-Three

The smell of fried chicken and biscuits filled the air, but food was the last thing on my mind.

Callie Mae slipped off the glasses she seldom wore and let them hang from a thin chain around her neck as she watched me. "I heard nursing mothers were ravenous. So why aren't you?"

I pulled a piece of breaded skin off and set it on my napkin. "I'm just not."

She scooped up a forkful of coleslaw. "What's the matter?"

Leaning my elbow on the table, I laid my head in my hand and continued picking at the chicken. "I don't know."

She held her painted fingertips in front of her lips to hide her full mouth. "You're probably just exhausted. One of the things I want to ask God when I get to heaven is why parents get the least amount of sleep when they need it the most. And what's up with breast milk not coming in for a week, anyway?"

Although I knew she was trying to cheer me up, I couldn't muster anything but a halfhearted shrug. The guilt of talking to the police was weighing on me heavily. "I've got a few questions for him myself."

She took a bite of biscuit, licking a crumb from her lip. "Are you remembering to sleep when the baby does? Exhaustion will get you every —"

"Sleep isn't the problem," I said.

"No?" She eyed me a moment. "Oh, I'll bet you have those baby blues. That's normal. I had a terrible case of those with Sara." A shadow passed over her and she shook her head as if to throw off the memory.

I wondered then if she ever blamed herself for her daughter's death. If she had done this or that, if maybe Sara would have made different choices. My own mother probably wondered the same thing about me. I wished I could tell Callie Mae it wasn't her fault. No one can make a grown person's choices for them. But I guess that's easy for me to say with you all tucked away safe in your bed, isn't it, Manny? I'll probably change my tune if you ever find yourself on the ugly end of a bully's fist. God save that child from me if you do.

My being with Trent had nothing to do with Mama, though. Or did it? She had rolled her eyes when Daddy would rant and rave, but she never called him out on it. If she had, would that have made a difference? I didn't think so. I'd just picked a guy with problems, that was all. She rolled the dice and got Daddy. Fatimah rolled the dice and got Edgard. And I rolled them and got snake eyes. I'd been too young to be gambling to begin with.

"I'm not depressed," I finally said.

"What then? Did Trent call?"

I tore off a piece of biscuit I had no intention of eating. "No, but he will."

She took another bite of slaw. "You're probably right, but hopefully not for a while. He could wind up serving a few months, you know."

I laid my napkin on top of my barely touched food and pushed the plate away. "He'll be out tonight."

She choked down her mouthful. "How do you know that?"

Tucking in my lips, I looked everywhere but at her.

She gave me a hard look. "Penny? What do you know?"

"They were here," I whispered.

"Who were here?"

"The police." Shame filled me. She wasn't going to forgive me any more than Fatimah would. I lost my job; now I was going to lose my friends. My life was going to go back to the same miserable existence it had been before I'd met them. Except I wasn't just going to have Trent to worry about. I had you to look after now.

I couldn't help but wonder if I should have told the police the whole truth — that Trent hadn't intended to hurt Fatimah, but he had intended on hurting me. Then what? I'd keep my friends but lose my husband and force you to grow up without a father? Why should you have to pay for my bad choices? You shouldn't, I told myself. "They asked if I saw what happened the other night."

She closed her eyes like she knew what was coming. "And?"

"And I told them he didn't mean to hurt her."

Her eyes flashed open. "You didn't."

"It's the truth," I said, swallowing back the tears that wanted to form.

"It's not the whole truth, though, is it?" Her eyes bored holes through me.

"What do you mean?" It was a stupid question. We both knew what she meant.

"You know exactly what I mean."

"He didn't mean to hurt *her.*"

"Did you tell them that? Did you tell them that he had actually meant to hurt you?"

I remained silent, watching the bubbles rising in my glass of Sprite and wishing I could float away with them.

"No, of course you didn't. So they're releasing him, and you're going right back home, aren't you?"

"No," I surprised myself by saying. "No, I'd like to stay with you awhile and let him think about things. If you'll have me, that is." What I really was thinking is that it would do him good to stew for a night or two. Maybe that would make him miss me enough to start treating me a little better. It's funny how I understood that Callie Mae wouldn't have been able to control her daughter's life, and Mama couldn't have stopped me from marrying Trent, but somehow I didn't get that I couldn't manipulate your father into changing. That dangling carrot would always be out of reach, but that didn't stop me from running after it.

Her eyebrows rose. "Really?"

"Can I?"

"Really?" she repeated.

I nodded. "I need to think things through, and so does he."

She picked up her knife and sliced a pat off the butter. "Of course you can stay here. I wouldn't have extended the invitation if I didn't mean it. Have you told him?"

I shook my head.

She spread the butter over half the biscuit, then looked at me. "He's going to get angry. They always get angry."

I gave a half nod as something that felt an awful lot like cement dropped into the pit of my stomach. "I imagine he will."

"You can get a restraining order."

"Only if he tries to hurt me agai—" I stopped myself just in time, but she knew very well what I was about to say. The only one I seemed to be fooling those days was myself. "They won't give it to me without proof."

She turned to look out the kitchen window. "Crazy justice system."

I leaned my head against the back of the chair. "I just don't know what's best. I can't think straight."

She squeezed my hand. "I know how that feels. You've got so much on your plate right now. Maybe that's why we came into each other's lives when we did. Sometimes we need to borrow a brain when ours gets all jumbled. When Sara died, I felt like someone had replaced my brain with spaghetti. I couldn't make a single decision for myself. Poor Fatimah. I leaned on her so much. It must have gotten wearisome. I was like a child in so many ways."

Knowing what I did of Callie Mae, I couldn't imagine a time when she didn't have all the answers. I'd never met anyone who had her stuff together as well as she did. Where did that kind of strength come from, I wondered. Were certain people just born with it? Maybe the adage of what doesn't kill us makes us stronger was true after all. Maybe at the end of all this, I'd find some of that strength. But I didn't see how.

I'd never been on my own. I went right from my daddy's arms to Trent's. Some people just weren't meant to stand on their own, or so I thought. I believed back then I was one of those people. I could lean on Callie Mae for a while, but sooner or later she'd get sick of me like Trent did. And unlike him, she was under no obligation to take care of me. At least in his own dysfunctional way, Trent needed me. Callie Mae needed no one.

She sighed. "But slowly that feeling passed, and one by one my brain cells started functioning again, and I found my feet. You'll find your feet too, Penny. You'll see. Things are going to come into focus if you give yourself a little time and distance from him. Life's going to be okay again. I promise."

I sipped my soda, wishing I could tell her she was wrong. Nothing would ever be right again if I left Trent. "Callie?"

She raised her eyebrows.

"Fatimah's going to be mad at me, isn't she?"

Her eyes filled with sympathy. "Yes."

"Are you?" I hated feeling so vulnerable, but there was no hiding it.

"Disappointed. Not mad."

I nodded. "He really didn't mean to hurt her."

She turned to stare out the kitchen window. She probably couldn't stand to look at me anymore. "I know what he meant to do. The police ought to too."

They do, I thought. *They know.*

Thirty-Four

I figured Trent would come calling that night, and I was right. Callie Mae answered through the chain lock, so we could see only an inch or two of his face. I sat in a chair, with my back to the door, trying to get you to nurse. You were crying so hard, frustrated by my lack of milk, I suppose. You just wouldn't calm down enough to latch on.

"She's my wife," he said. "I have a right to see her."

My stomach flip-flopped. Would he kick the door down to get to me?

The louder his voice grew, the softer Callie Mae's became. "Your wife or not, she has a right to tell you she doesn't want to see you."

It wasn't true, though, Manny. I did want to see him. I missed him so badly it made my heart ache, but I didn't have the courage to tell Callie Mae that to her face.

"What about my son? I haven't even met

my own son. I should at least be able to see him."

"You should have thought about that before shoving —"

"It was an accident," he pleaded. "Penny! Penny, are you in there? Tell her it was an accident. Let me see my son. Please, baby!"

"He's fine," I called. "You'll see him soon. I promise."

Callie Mae turned around and shot me a frigid look, then turned back toward the cracked door. "We'll arrange visitations in a few days, after you've calmed down."

"One Cent, please. Let me meet my son, for crying out loud. He's my son. I'm sorry about all of this. You know I didn't mean to hurt your friend. You don't know how worried I've been about you. I love you, Penny. She don't know how it is for us. Let me just see him, please?"

Teardrops rolled down my cheeks onto the top your head. I wanted to run to him. To show him you had his nose. That you were beautiful and perfect . . . and that I forgave him.

"Your wife almost died," Callie Mae said coldly. "She almost bled to death while you were stumbling around drunk. You don't need to see them right now, and they don't need to see you. What everyone needs is for you to get help."

"You don't own her," he hissed. "She's my wife, not yours, you old bat."

Callie Mae's voice dropped an octave, and she spoke so quietly I had to strain to hear her just a few feet away. "I don't own her, Trent. But believe it or not, neither do you. Being a husband isn't the same thing as being a slave owner."

"Unlatch this door and say that to my face."

"This conversation's over." With that, she slammed the door.

He banged on the window, then the door, then the window again, screaming for us to let him in.

After a few minutes, his car roared out of the driveway, and I relaxed.

Callie Mae sat beside us. "He'll be back."

"I know." I looked down at you and saw, for the first time, a dribble of milk slip down the corner of your mouth, and you were gulping. My milk had finally come in. Maybe I wouldn't starve you to death after all. Maybe everything really would be okay.

Callie Mae pulled the ponytail holder out of her hair, letting it spill to the top of her shoulders. "Penny, I need to know when I go to the food bank tomorrow that you'll be strong enough to not let him in."

I knew that the moment he knocked on the door, I was going back to him sooner rather than later, and I was so tired of lying, so I said nothing.

"Promise me you won't let him in. He could kill you this time. He could kill Manny."

I thought she was overstating it more than a little, but I knew I'd never convince her she was wrong. Her daughter had been murdered, so in her mind, I might be too. But she didn't know that Trent was always sorry after an incident like this. He would be on his best behavior for at least a few weeks. There would never be a time when I'd be safer around him. And you were his son. He had a God-given right to at least meet you. And what about your right to have a father?

"I promise I won't let him in," I said reluctantly. That didn't mean I couldn't visit with him on the porch. He could at least hold you a minute or two. He needed us now more than ever, and in my emotionally unstable state, I thought we needed him, too.

She gave me a look that made it clear she wasn't convinced, but my promise would have to be enough for her. I was a grown woman, after all. She had just told Trent he didn't own me, and neither did she.

While you finished up your meal, she turned on the TV. We watched a game show in silence. As the contestants were informed of their parting gifts, the phone rang. I knew it would be him.

Jumping up, Callie Mae rushed over to the phone as though she was afraid I might beat her to it. "Hello?"

She looked over her shoulder at me and mouthed, *It's him.* "I've already told you she isn't going to see you right now. Don't call us. We'll call you." She slammed the phone down. "If he keeps it up, I'm going to have to report him for harassment."

I looked down at you to see you'd fallen asleep. Your long eyelashes fluttered as if you were dreaming, and the side of your mouth twitched up. I carried you to your crib, kissed your nose, and laid you down. After I covered you, I tiptoed back out of the room and closed the door.

Callie Mae was staring at the TV, which was now just a black screen. "I have a gun," she said through tight lips.

My eyes widened. "A gun?"

She walked over to a small table resting in the corner of the room and opened the drawer. "I loaded it this morning." She pulled out a white-handled pistol. "Do you know how to use it?"

This was getting way out of hand. I wasn't about to shoot my own husband. What was she thinking?

"Just in case. Know it's there."

"I don't need a gun, Callie." I tried not to roll my eyes.

"Sara didn't think she needed a gun either."

I rubbed away the goose bumps that had broken out over my arms. "He just needs a little time to think about his temper. He doesn't need me to murder him."

"You just pull the hammer back, aim, and fire." She held the gun with both hands, pointed it at the door, and pretended to shoot it. The glazed-over look on her face wasn't one I'd seen before, and it scared me. Slowly, she lowered the gun and walked it back over to the table. "That's all there is to it." She set it beside a phone book and closed the drawer. "Not murder. Self-defense. If he breaks in here and tries to hurt you or take Manny, you have a right to protect yourself."

"He wouldn't take Manny."

"You don't know what he'll try to do. He's going to get desperate. The behavior you've seen so far is nothing compared to what he'll do if he thinks he's losing you."

He's not losing me, I thought. Did she think I was going to keep him away from his own son forever? That I was just going to live in her guest room for the rest of my life? This wasn't home. I missed my kitchen, my bed, and my husband. We were a family — Trent, you, and me. She was my friend — a good friend — but that was no substitution.

The next morning, as soon as Callie Mae left for the food bank, I called Trent before I could lose my nerve. I thought he would cuss me out for not letting him in the night before, but he was just so relieved to hear I still loved him. He begged me to come home and I agreed, with the understanding that if he ever touched me again, I would press charges. He said I wouldn't have to. He would do it himself. Once again, I chose to believe him.

I left a note on the table apologizing for the trouble I'd put Callie Mae through and a promise, which I hoped wasn't empty, that everything would be okay.

I had no ride and just enough money for the city bus, so I walked the half mile with you snuggled inside my coat, lugging my bag of things to the bus stop, knowing I'd have another two miles to walk after the bus dropped me off.

When I finally got home, my arms were burning and the house was a mess. But surprisingly, there were no empty cans or bottles lying around. I thought for sure he would have gone on a bender when Callie Mae refused to let him see us. In my convoluted mind, this was confirmation he really was changing. I set you in the swing I'd picked up at the thrift store weeks before, and you were just as content as could be swinging to and fro as a lullaby played.

By the time the house was picked up and dinner started, the phone was ringing off the hook. I knew at least some of the calls were Callie Mae, so I didn't dare answer. I couldn't face her. I didn't doubt for a second her motivation was love, but Trent was right — she didn't know how it was for us. I wasn't Sara, and Trent wasn't going to kill me or hurt you. I promised myself if he got himself all worked up again, I'd leave. If he put one finger on me, or so much as looked at you the wrong way, I'd call the police and file charges.

About five thirty his car pulled up. He rushed through the front door, scooped me up, and swung me around grinning and kissing my face. "Oh, baby, don't you ever do that to me again." He gave me one more kiss before setting me down. "I couldn't live without you, Penny. I'd rather be dead."

"Don't talk that way," I said as my heart fluttered. I was so glad to be home — to be a family again.

He wrapped his arms around my waist and squeezed me so hard I thought he might fracture one of my ribs. His lips were cold against my mouth, but as soft as they'd ever felt. He tried to pull me toward the bedroom, but I stopped him, digging my heels into the carpet. "Doctor says not for six weeks."

He frowned as he let me loose. "Six weeks might as well be forever. What if — ?"

"No means no, Trent." I braced myself for his fury. The front door was unlocked. The car keys were sitting on top of the TV, and your swing was right next to it. In a matter of seconds, I could grab you and the keys and be gone.

He wasn't mad, though. He kissed my hand. "I missed you. Oh, baby, you don't know how I missed you."

I did know because I missed him the same way. "Would you like to meet your son?"

He glanced at you. "In a minute." He ran his hand through my hair, staring into my eyes like we were in some romance novel. "The police told me you backed my story up. That's the nicest thing anyone's ever done for me."

Well, at least one person thought so. "I told them the truth. That you didn't mean to hurt Fatimah."

He nodded. "I knew I could count on you to have my back, babe."

"It was the truth," I repeated. *Just not all of it.*

The smell of meatloaf wafted past us, and I decided it had probably been in the oven long enough. I motioned toward the kitchen. "I need to check that."

"Penny, thank you. You saved my bacon." He brought my hand to his lips and kissed it.

I walked to the kitchen and pulled open the oven. Heat escaped, along with the smell of beef and onion. The ketchup on top of the loaf was browning, and the drippings were turning black around the edges of the meat. I closed the oven and turned it off.

His arms wrapped around the back of my waist. "This time it's going to be different. You'll see. You've shown me the meaning of true love. You're a loyal woman, and I'm going to be the most loyal husband and father in the entire world. This time I'm going to deserve you."

I swallowed down my fear and turned

around. We were nose to nose, and I could feel his hot breath on me. I wondered if I should put more distance between us before saying what I needed to. "You know, you can't be hitting me now that we have Manny in the house."

"I didn't mean to — You know I don't never really mean to hurt you. I just lose my temper sometimes. It's hard loving a woman as much as I love you. Sometimes it makes me crazy."

I left his arms to reach in the cabinet and pull out a box of instant potatoes. "Well, you can't get crazy anymore. I can't have my son living the way I've been living. I won't have it."

When the crease formed between his eyebrows, I was terrified. But this had to be said. "I mean it. If you put your hands on me again, it's over."

He walked over and pinned me against the cabinets with the full weight of his body. He put a hand behind my head and kissed me too forcefully to be pleasant. I tried to turn away from him, but he had a handful of my hair in his fist. He tried to give me that macho look of his that was meant to melt me. "It's never going to be over for us, Penny. You know that as well as I do. You belong to me. You always will."

"I belong to no one." I tore away from him, as hair pulled at my scalp.

He scowled. "So, this is how it is now? You do me a little favor and now you wear the pants?"

"No." I rubbed the back of my head, eyeing the back door — unlocked. "I'm just saying, as the mother of your child, I can't have you putting your hands on me anymore. Things are going to be different and not just because you say so. Because *I* say so."

The smile on his lips didn't match the malice in his eyes. "Of course they are, love. Before God, I swear I will never put a hand on you again as long as I live."

I didn't believe him, but I would give him the benefit of the doubt, one last time.

"Come on, girl. Show me Junior. I'll bet he's beautiful like his mama."

I smiled, sweeping the worries from my mind. If I was really going to give him a chance to prove his words, then I had to prove it myself first, by showing him I trusted him. "He is, Trent. He's so beautiful."

We walked over to your swing, which was no longer moving. You were awake, looking at the ceiling like something up there fascinated you. When I glanced up, all I saw was a thin crack snaking through plaster.

Trent melted as he looked down at you. I could see in his eyes that you had him. "He's so little."

I laughed. "Of course he's little. He's a baby."

"Can I hold him?"

Had my husband asked for my permission to hold his own son? Maybe things really were going to be different. Maybe itty-bitty you would soften him in a way I never could.

I reached down and picked you up. You were so warm. I cradled you in my arms so he could see how to do it, then handed you over.

There are moments in life that should be savored forever, and this was one of those. Your father held you against him, and suddenly nothing else existed in my world but the two of you. He walked over to the easy chair and sat down with you. For the next few minutes he cradled you and told you what it meant to be a man. He whispered in your ear you should always treat your mama right because you only got one in life. He told you that drugs were bad and you shouldn't spend so much time in bars like he did and that the world was going to be a kinder place for you than it had ever been for him. Things you couldn't possibly understand. Things I didn't know he did.

No matter what you grow up thinking about your father, Manny, I want you to know he really did want to be the kind of man we deserved. But dreams don't come true just because you want them to. Like my support group always says, you have to do the work.

THIRTY-FIVE

Saturday morning was the best time I could ever remember spending with your father. We lay in bed a good portion of the day with you nestled between us. Enveloped in the warmth of layers of quilts, we admired everything there was to admire about you — your eyes, your gurgles, your toes. We were a couple in love with our baby, and one another. I told myself then even if he beat me tomorrow, at least I had the memory of today — a sweet recollection I could share with you someday. Which, I guess, I'm doing now.

When Trent kissed your little toes, you sneezed. He scratched at his bare chest and gave me a concerned look. "Do you think he's got a cold? I bet I brought home something from the jail. There was a guy in there hacking up a lung."

I turned to my side, bent my elbow, and leaned on my hand. "He did that in the hospital. The nurse said it was normal."

He picked your other foot up and kissed the bottom of it. You kicked your legs as if trying to get away. "I know I was drunk, but was that kid of hers as ugly as I remember it?"

I gave his hand a gentle slap like my mother was always doing to my father. "Oh, stop. She had a rough birth. She'll cute up. I mean, look at her parents."

When he gave me a dirty look, I realized my mistake. "Why don't you just go marry him if you think he's so hot."

I reached across you and touched his arm. "Come on, baby, you know I didn't mean anything by it. They're just both attractive. Don't you think?"

"So, you *are* attracted to him. I knew it." He sat up, sulking at the wall.

I ran my hand over the freckles running the length of his shoulders. "Honey, I only love *you.* I just meant the baby is going to get cuter. That's all."

He glanced down at you, then back at me. "I bet you think you would have made a better-looking kid with him."

I thought the peaceful lull would have lasted longer than one day, and then it clicked that things weren't going to be different just because we had you now. Something had to change. I was still of the mindset that the something was him. Swinging my feet over the side of the bed, I said, "I'm going to fix some lunch." I bent down, scooped you off the bed, walked you over to the crib, and laid you down.

He started to laugh as he pointed at me. "Gotcha!"

Over my shoulder, I gave him a weary look. "What?"

"Dag, One Cent, what happened to your sense of humor? I was joshing."

I didn't say anything as I studied his expression, his body language. Given he'd just been released from jail for assault, why on earth would he think that was funny? "I guess you must have knocked it out of me last time you punched me."

I went to the kitchen, knowing he would follow. I realized then I was trying to provoke him, but I wasn't sure why. Maybe because deep down I thought I deserved to be beaten. Maybe I enjoyed being the martyr. Or I was just addicted to the making up that was sure to follow.

He stomped into the kitchen behind me, wearing a look that told me he was ticked. "Why are you starting with me? I'm trying to be a better man."

I poured a cup of coffee, trying my best to

ignore him, knowing it would only add fuel to the flames. *What is wrong with me?* I wondered. It finally occurred to me that maybe Fatimah and Callie Mae were right, and he wasn't the only one needing help.

"Answer me, Penny!"

I whipped around, full of a fury that caught me by surprise. I jabbed a finger in his direction. "Don't you dare make the baby cry."

His nose flared. "You better get off your high horse there, little princess. I'm the king of this castle, and I'll raise my voice if I want to raise my voice."

I walked to the fridge and opened it, just to look like I was uninterested. He reached over my shoulder and slammed it shut, nearly catching my nose. "You know what I think?" His hot breath puffed across the back of my ear. "I think you like making me mad. I think you want me to hit you so you can run crying to your loudmouth, holy-roller friends."

Was he right? I was definitely trying to set him off, but not for the reasons I assumed then. Eventually he was going to start hitting me again, and I think I wanted to get it over with, rather than live with the torture of waiting for it to happen. At least if I provoked it, I had some control over the when and why.

But as I turned around and looked into his eyes, a new fear overtook me. I didn't have Fatimah's support anymore. I most likely didn't have Callie Mae's, either. I had told him if he ever hit me again, I would leave him, but where would we go? Who would watch you while I worked to support us? Did I really want my baby being raised by strangers in day care? And that's if I could even afford day care. He wouldn't just let us go, anyway. Even if by some miracle he did let me go, he would fight for you. What if he filed for custody and won? I wouldn't be able to afford a lawyer. Was leaving him worth the possibility of losing you?

I swallowed my pride. "You're right."

"You're daggone right I'm right. . . . Wait, what?"

"I said you're probably right. Maybe I *was* trying to provoke you. I guess maybe it's the hormones. I'm sorry."

His face was still red, and he looked more than a little confused about how to proceed. It's not like I'd ever admitted trying to get hit before.

The phone rang and I excused myself to answer it. "Hello?"

"I do not believe you!" Fatimah screamed.

"Calm down. I can barely understand you."

"I will not calm. You lied against me to protect that pig of a man. Why? *Why?*"

Trent watched from the kitchen.

"They asked if he meant to push you and I said no."

"You are liar. I take you to the hospital when he is too drunk, and that box of garbage pushes me and my baby. You lie against my word? Against my honor?"

The sudden pain in my heart was worse than any Trent had ever inflicted. "He didn't mean to push you. He meant to push me."

"You are dead to me. Dead!" I heard a beep, followed by silence.

I stood there holding the receiver, stunned and yet relieved it was over. I'd lost a friend, but I had my husband back. I had my baby. So why did I feel like I had a knife lodged in my chest?

"Was that the loudmouth African?" Trent asked.

I nodded, feeling miserable. "She hates me."

"Let her," he said coming toward me.

Wrapping my arms around his waist, I let him hold me.

"We don't need her," he said. "You've got

me. I don't hate you."

Not today, I thought.

Thirty-Six

Sunday morning, I woke up with you in my arms, surprised to find you'd already helped yourself to breakfast. I actually felt rested for a change. You were already sleeping almost four hours at a time, which was pure heaven.

After changing your wet diaper, I carried you to the kitchen. Trent was awake, dressed, and making coffee. "Good morning, my beautiful wife and strapping young son."

I offered a groggy smile. "Hey, you're up early."

He poured water into the coffeemaker, slid the pot beneath it, and hit the on button. "Early, nothing. You've got fifteen minutes to get ready if we're going to make it to church on time."

The thought of going back and facing Pastor Harold was less than appealing, but I had the perfect excuse. "I'm not supposed to take Manny into crowds for a few weeks. The doctor said his immune system's immature and he could catch stuff."

Trent looked relieved. "Oh. I guess that makes sense. How did our little prince sleep?"

I kissed your warm forehead and you tilted up your chin, as if I was offering you something new to put in your mouth. "I only remember him waking up once to feed. This breastfeeding thing is a lot nicer than having to get up and mix a bottle."

He fake punched your tiny arm and made a crude remark.

I wished he wouldn't talk that way, but decided not to say so. I needed to pick my battles, and this one hardly seemed worth it. "How did you sleep?"

"Not too bad, considering I felt like I had to check him every other minute to make sure he was still breathing. I tell you, Penny, I know what people mean now about kids giving them gray hair."

He really did worry about you as much as I did. Knowing that was more comfort than a thousand promises he would change.

He rubbed his freshly shaven chin. "What's the plan for today?"

I kissed the top of your little head. "Plan? I just had a baby. I thought I might, you know, feed him, change him, fix us some breakfast."

He leaned against the counter as the coffeepot sputtered to life. "Why don't we go somewhere and do something?"

What in the world did he think we were going to do with a brand-new baby? I'd already told him you weren't supposed to be out in crowds, and it had to be twenty degrees outside. "How about if we go pick up a Christmas tree and decorate it? I'd love to have a real one this year."

His shoulders drooped forward. "Baby, I just spent three days in jail, and the whole day staying home with you yesterday. I'm going stir crazy."

Holding you was making my arms ache, so I switched positions, laying you against my chest. "What do you propose?"

"We could go down to Zoe's, have a couple of beers and some wings for lunch. Wouldn't that be fun?"

I leaned down and smelled your neck so he couldn't see me rolling my eyes. "And what will we do with the baby?"

He walked over and put his arms around us, making you the center of our sandwich. "Bring him."

I looked up. "You want to bring our baby to a bar?"

"It's not like we're going to put whiskey in his bottle, Penny. Dag."

I twisted out of his arms. "I'm not bringing my baby into a bar, and I just got done telling you he's not supposed to be in crowds."

"What crowds? That place ain't exactly going to be teeming with people on a Sunday morning."

"No means no," I said.

His face turned to stone. "Fine. Stay here then and be bored. I'm heading out."

I glanced up at the wall clock hanging beside the back door. "It's ten o'clock on a Sunday morning. You're going to go drinking now?"

He threw his hand up and stomped to the bedroom. With you in my arms, I followed. I patted your back as I watched him get dressed. He opened one of his dresser drawers and pulled out a sweatshirt, then held it to his nose. Apparently he didn't find any offensive odors because he slid it over his head.

"Trent, please don't go drinking. You know what happens."

He snatched his jeans off the floor. The belt was still looped through the pants from the last time he had worn them. The buckle clinked as he slid his foot through a leg hole.

"I told you that ain't going to happen no more."

"Yeah, you've told me that how many times over the years? And yet here's another contradiction." I held out my bruised wrist.

A burp escaped your mouth. I looked down to see a dribble of regurgitated milk on my sleeve. It was a sight I was already quite used to. "You don't know what you're doing when you're drunk." I pulled up your bib and wiped your mouth with it.

Trent pulled his pants up the rest of the way and buttoned them. "Don't get yourself all worked up. I'm only going to have a few."

"That's what you say every time. You never have just a few. You don't know how to have just a few."

He sat on the bed and began working his foot into a boot. As he tied it, he looked up at me. "Things are going to be different this time. You need to trust me. It can't work if you won't believe it will."

I thought of all the times over the years I had heard those same promises from him. *I'm sorry. It'll never happen again. This time will be different. I swear. I promise. Trust me.* And each time, I had. What had that ever gotten me? Bruised bones and a broken spirit.

"I want to," I said. My gaze fell on the top

of my dresser, where the statue Callie Mae had given me had been. It wasn't there. I surveyed the rest of the room, but didn't see it.

He worked his foot into the second boot. "What are you looking for?"

"My statue. It was right there."

He sucked at his teeth, looking guilty.

"What did you do?" I asked, feeling sick to my stomach.

He slid on his other boot. "Baby, I'm sorry."

"Sorry for what?"

He grimaced. "I threw it out."

I could feel the blood drain from my face. "You did what?"

"She made me so mad the other night. I couldn't stand looking at that thing."

That statue meant so much to Callie Mae. It was a tie to her daughter. Maybe the last tie. And it had come to represent something to me, too. Something I was so close to understanding.

The mattress squealed as he stood. "I wasn't in my right mind. I thought you were leaving me. It should still be in the garbage. Just go get it out."

I felt myself breathe again as I laid you in your crib. I hurried to the kitchen, yanked the garbage can out from under the sink, and began riffling through coffee grounds, balled-up napkins, and a sight that made my insides knot — shards of stained glass. Finally my hand touched something hard, and something sliced into my flesh. I pulled my fingers back. Droplets of red beaded over a small gash. I grabbed a napkin off the counter and wrapped it around my index finger, doubling it up when red seeped through the first layer of white. With my good hand, I reached and pulled out the statue.

The woman was in one piece, but her wings were destroyed. Only one jagged section of stained glass remained, dangling by a wire.

When I glanced up, Trent was standing over me looking contrite. "Baby, I'm sorry. I'll buy you a new one."

I shoved the can back under the sink and slammed the door before standing. I held the statue out to him to show what he had done as blood soaked through the napkin and dribbled down my finger. "Not everything is replaceable. She bought this for her daughter right before she was murdered."

He took a step toward me, then stopped, looking unsure. "I'm sorry. I didn't know. I'll fix it."

"Duct tape and superglue aren't going to

fix this." Without wings, she would never fly now.

I thought of Sara and how this statue was meant to somehow save her, but never got the chance to, and I began to cry. Trent tried to touch me, but I jerked away from him. He scowled. "Get it together. I mean it. If me not putting my hands on you is going to turn you into a shrew . . . I ain't going to take this."

He ate breakfast, even cleaned up his own dishes and swept up the pieces of stained glass littering the floor, before leaning down to kiss my lips on his way out. With you in my arms, I turned my head, giving him my cheek and the coldest shoulder I could muster.

I sat there holding you at the kitchen table for what seemed like hours, staring at a wall yellowed from years of Trent's cigarette smoking, trying to make sense of my life and yours. The numbness I felt did wonders to help me look at things more logically than I'd been able to up until then. If he was going to keep drinking, he was going to hit me again. That was the cold, hard truth. I didn't think he would stoop to hurting you, drunk or not. But I had to admit that I couldn't know for sure, and I was no longer willing to play Russian roulette with our lives.

The old me argued with the new, reminding me he had changed since his accident. Not nearly enough, but it was a start. Maybe his love for you would compel him to get help. Then images of you as a toddler, hiding in your bedroom with wide eyes as you listened to him berating and beating me, flashed through my mind. What would growing up like that do to you? I didn't want to find out.

I fixed some toast and poured myself a cup of coffee, neither of which I touched. All I could think about was the statue's broken wings that could never be mended and Trent, stumbling through that front door drunk.

The biggest case of buyer's remorse came over me then. I shouldn't have left Callie Mae's house. Coming home had been a huge mistake.

I thought of my mama then and how good it was to have her back in my life. Her and Daddy would take us in, I was sure of it. But it didn't feel fair to Trent or you to take you out of state. If the shoe was on the other foot, I know it would kill me. And the thought of living under my father's roof again was even less appealing than staying with Trent.

If only God would come down from heaven and show me what to do. If I could only get a glimpse of the future you would have if I stayed, and compare it to what your life would be like if I left, knowing what to do would be easy.

I thought of the statue's broken wings — and of Sara — and realized that was as close to a glimpse of the future as I was going to get.

Why hadn't I stipulated that Trent had to stop drinking before I would come home? I set you in your swing, strapped you in, and cranked the handle until it wouldn't turn any farther. "Rock-a-bye, Baby" played as I got on my knees and pressed my forehead to the rug. I prayed until your swing stopped swaying and the music died. Although a clear answer didn't present itself, I was left with the thought that it was now or never.

The last thing I wanted was for you to have a broken home, but no matter which choice I made, I knew we were all going to end up broken in one way or another. Unless, of course, your father got help. That was the one solution that would keep us whole. That was it. That was the answer I'd prayed for.

Could I convince him to quit drinking and

see someone about his anger? It had never worked in the past, but maybe he'd be willing if he knew he really would lose us otherwise. Maybe.

I left you in the living room and walked to the bedroom. I reached under the bed and grabbed the Bible Callie had given me on her first visit. Needing God to speak to me, now more than ever, I opened it at random and read, "For those who are married, I have a command that comes not from me, but from the Lord. A wife must not leave her husband. But if she does leave him, let her remain single or else be reconciled to him. And the husband must not leave his wife."

What were the chances I would open to that, of all verses? My heart sank. Was this really God's answer to me, or just dumb luck? I guess I'd wanted to hear that I was free to remarry, not just separate from Trent. But separation was its own mercy.

I thought of Callie Mae asking me what I would say to my daughter if she told me her husband was beating her. Would I tell her to stay with him? The answer had been clear when she had put it that way. God didn't create anyone to be another person's punching bag. And didn't God love me more than I loved my own son? He wouldn't want this for me. But then it was his own Son he allowed to die on the cross. He didn't spare him that, so why should I be spared?

Tears spilled down my face as a knock came at the front door. I wiped my eyes and pulled back the curtain. Callie Mae stood there with her hand resting on her purse and her gaze darting nervously around the yard.

I opened the door and practically fell into her arms. My shoulders heaved as I fought to catch my breath. She held me like a mother would, rubbing my back and telling me everything was going to be okay. There, in her arms, I could almost believe it.

After a minute, I pulled back, and tried to smile through tears. "He's out drinking," I managed.

"Come with me, Penny. Get Manny, and let's get out of here."

"I have a better idea," I said.

THIRTY-SEVEN

Callie Mae didn't think it would do much good, but by refusing to leave my side, she was participating just the same. I'd never been part of an intervention before, other than the pseudo one Fatimah and Callie Mae had for me, but I had seen enough of them on TV to understand the concept.

I finally got through to Pastor Harold after the morning service, and he thought the intervention was a great idea. He even offered to pay for two weeks of rehab, if Trent agreed, compliments of New Beginnings.

The offer was more than I'd hoped for, but it didn't stop there. Callie Mae told me I could have my job back and offered to babysit you during the day until your father came home from treatment. Now all we had to do was convince Trent he needed help.

As I, Callie Mae, Pastor Harold, and his wife, Lela, sat in the living room making small talk, praying, and drinking cup after cup of decaf, the anticipation of waiting for your father to come home and wondering how he would react grew. We had been waiting over an hour already, and I had no idea when he would come rolling through the door, or in what condition. He'd gotten such an early start I figured it couldn't be too much longer, but then I never really knew with him. There had been plenty of nights he never bothered coming home at all.

"Just so we're clear," Callie Mae said to me, "if he refuses treatment, you're coming with me tonight?"

When I hesitated, she pressed her fingertips to her temple. "For crying out loud. Nothing's ever going to change unless you change it. The problem's you as much as him."

I looked over at Lela, who nodded. "She's right, Mrs. Taylor. People will only treat you the way you allow them to."

Although I knew she was right, there was something about the way she said it that rubbed me the wrong way. I doubted either of them knew a single thing about being an abused wife. "I don't *let* him hit me. He just does. When I try to stop him, it only makes him swing harder."

Callie Mae leaned forward. "I'll tell you

one thing, sure as the ground beneath my feet — he wouldn't be hitting *me.*"

I set my coffee cup down on the end table and tucked my hair behind my ear. "You don't know either, Callie. You don't know what it's like. Just thank God you had a husband who loved you without backing up his words with his fists."

"Love has nothing to do with it," she said. "He might have hit me once, but mark my words, the first time would be the last."

I didn't argue with her. There was no sense in it. I was ashamed I'd taken so much for so long, but no one in that room had ever walked a mile in my shoes, or even an inch for that matter. What did they know of loving someone so much they lost themselves along the way? They had never seen the sorrow written all over Trent's face when he sobered up and saw what he'd done. They didn't know the first thing about people who were so broken by their own childhood that they had an uncontrollable need to break those around them.

Of course, now I know that she was exactly right. The problem really was me. No emotionally healthy woman would have put up with it, and no emotionally healthy girl would have married a stranger just because he said she should.

Lela wrapped her hands around her cup. "If he's beating you the way you say, then you're putting not only yourself but your son in danger."

"This isn't a call for divorce," Pastor Harold broke in, "but separation is sometimes necessary. You're doing the right thing. He needs help, and we'll do our best to get him to see that."

"He won't change." Callie Mae stared at the front door, almost defying it to open. "But if this is what you need to feel you've done everything in your power to make it work, then by all means, let's exhaust every avenue."

"You don't know that he won't change," Pastor Harold said coolly. "Thankfully, God doesn't take that mind-set with us or we would all be hell-bound. Trent is just a lost sheep. We need to —"

Callie Mae cut him off. "Have you ever lived in fear of your life, Nathan?"

He just blinked at her.

"I didn't think so."

"I've borne my crosses," the pastor said with a sigh. "Unfortunately, this one is Penny's. We have to trust God has a plan. That he'll use all things, even this, for her good."

Callie Mae laughed bitterly. "Do you

really think this is God's plan for her? To live a life of abuse and degradation?"

He leaned forward and rested his elbows on the knees of his pleated dress pants. "No, I don't think abuse was God's will for the Taylors' marriage, but then sin was never part of God's plan for us, was it?"

Her eyes narrowed. "You think God would really handcuff her for life to a man who cuts her down every chance he gets?"

He turned to me. "Penny, did you pray about marrying Trent before you did?"

I wrapped my arms around myself, wishing everyone would just shut up.

"What difference does that make now?" Callie Mae demanded.

"We make our beds without first seeking God's direction. Then we blame him when things turn out badly," he said.

She huffed. "No one's blaming God. The only person to blame here is Trent for abusing her and Penny for putting up with it."

Lela tilted her head, making her auburn hair swing over her shoulder. She looked maddeningly together. "We're all sinners, Callie. If God can forgive us our trespasses, surely we can forgive one another's."

Callie Mae stood. "Forgive, yes; allow ourselves to be further trampled on, no." She unzipped her oversize purse and pulled out the Bible she carried around. She flipped through the Old Testament, cleared her throat, and began to read. "Deuteronomy 24 says, 'Suppose a man marries a woman but she does not please him. Having discovered something wrong with her, he writes her a letter of divorce, hands it to her, and sends her away from his house. When she leaves his house, she is free to marry another man.' "

I hung on to every word. Was it true? It came from God's Word, so it had to be. I knew about the out for infidelity, but I never had absolute proof that Trent had been unfaithful, only strong suspicions. This was something different. Would God really permit me to remarry if Trent divorced me?

Pastor Harold sighed. "That's the Old Testament, Callie Mae. We're under a new covenant now."

She slammed her Bible shut. "A covenant not of law, but of grace and forgiveness."

When Pastor Harold hung his head, I caught a glimpse of pink scalp through a thin patch of brown. "God's Word clearly states that he hates divorce. This is mentioned both in the Old and New Testaments. You can try to twist God's Word any way you want, but —"

She gave him a look that was pure anger.

"Twist his Word? Are *you* telling *me I* twist God's Word?"

His long eyelashes fluttered as his jaw dropped. "I'm just saying —"

She pointed her Bible at me. "You're just saying this child of God is supposed to stand by her man no matter how he treats her? She isn't Jesus on the cross. No one benefits from her beatings. Her blood covers no sins. I don't believe the God I know wants that for her. And last time I read the Good Book, there was only one unforgivable sin — and divorce wasn't it."

Pastor Harold's neck mottled. "And the last time I checked, neither was spousal abuse."

Lela patted her husband's knee as if to placate him. "I have to agree, Callie. God doesn't want Penny or little Manny to be in danger, and enabling Trent's drinking and abuse isn't helping anyone, including him. But what seems right to man isn't always right to God." She locked eyes with her. "Can we at least agree on that much?"

Before she could answer, Trent's car screeched into the driveway. My heart found my throat, and judging by the wide eyes and white faces, so did everyone else's.

Thirty-Eight

Even before climbing the porch steps, Trent would know we had company. The Harolds' Lincoln took up half the driveway, and Callie Mae's sedan sat along the curb right outside the house. Trent's walk through the front door was more stride than stumble, which told me that while he might be drunk, he definitely wasn't plastered. I wasn't sure if that was in our favor or not. There was no telltale crease between his eyebrows though, no flare of his nostrils or balling of his fists to indicate anger. Of course, the night was still young.

As he scanned the room, his gaze fell on Pastor Harold and his wife, then on Callie Mae, before finally settling on me.

I couldn't shake the fear that maybe I'd jumped the gun with this whole intervention thing, but it was too late for regret now. All I could do was pray this would work when everything else had failed, and that you'd never have to know about that night or the man your father had once been.

His hair was windblown, and his cheeks and nose were red from the cold. He wore his flannel shirt — which doubled as a jacket — unbuttoned, and his shirttail was half tucked into the waist of his well-worn jeans. He put on a plastic smile. "Hey, we've got some visitors. Penny, darlin', you didn't tell me we were going to have company tonight."

With that giant grin of his, Pastor Harold stood and stabbed his hand out toward Trent. "Mr. Taylor, I wish we were here under better circumstances."

Trent gave his hand a weak pump, then gave me a questioning look. "All right. What's going on? Did someone die or something?"

Pastor Harold shook his head. "No, nothing like that. We're all here because we're concerned about you."

When Trent shot me a side glance, my heart nearly leaped from my chest.

"I want you to know," Pastor Harold continued, hugging his leather-bound Bible to his chest, "that no matter what happens tonight, we have your best interests at heart. We are all sinners. Every one of us in this room. As such, we aren't in a position to judge you. Just to encourage you to get help."

"Help?" Trent asked between clenched teeth.

Motioning to the empty chair with his Bible, Pastor Harold said, "Please have a seat."

Trent frowned as he sat in the chair across from the couch.

Pastor Harold retook his seat beside his wife and interwove his fingers through hers. "Shall we pray?"

I bowed my head, afraid to look at Trent.

"Lord, please give us the right words to say," Pastor Harold began. "Let us all remember to speak in love, not judgment. We realize we are indeed our brother's keeper, just as he is ours. Give us the means to help him help himself. In your Son's precious name, amen."

All of us, with the exception of Trent, added our amen to his. When I opened my eyes, he was glaring at me.

Everyone seemed to note the exchange, which made me feel vindicated. The Harolds had to see now I wasn't just making the whole thing up.

"I would like to read a passage to you, Trent. Would that be okay?" Pastor Harold asked.

Trent held his hands over his mouth and nose like he was trying to warm them. "Is this about us not coming to church yesterday? It's just because the baby's not supposed to be in crowds."

"This isn't about missing church, you moron," Callie Mae said. "This is what they call an intervention."

"Please, Callie," Nathan's wife said softly. "This is a safe place. We're not insulting one another here. Trent is our brother and we're here in love."

"He's not my brother," she mumbled.

Pastor Harold opened the Bible he'd been holding, pulled out a woven bookmark that reminded me of one of those Chinese finger traps, and handed it to his wife for safekeeping. " 'Don't be drunk with wine, because that will ruin your life. Instead, be filled with the Holy Spirit —' "

"I don't understand," Trent said. "If this is about my drinking, I admit I like a few beers now and again, but hey, even Jesus turned water into wine, right? What's the big deal?"

Pastor Harold looked up at him, then back down at his Bible. " 'For husbands, this means love your wives, just as Christ loved the church. He gave up his life for her to make her holy and clean, washed by the cleansing of God's Word. He did this to present her to himself as a glorious church without a spot or wrinkle or any other blemish. Instead, she will be holy and without fault. In the same way, husbands ought to love their wives as they love their own bodies. For a man who loves his wife actually shows love for himself. No one hates his own body but feeds and cares for it, just as Christ cares for the church.' "

Trent shifted in his chair. "Did Penny say I had a drinking problem? You know you can't really believe everything she says. She makes the Amish look like party animals." He gave me a look I'd seen enough to know it implied a warning. "C'mon, Penny. Tell them."

"This isn't just about your drinking." My voice sounded more child than woman. "This is about your temper."

His jaw set. "*That's* what this is about?" He jabbed a thumb toward me. "Oh, come on! I'll be the first to admit I put my hands on her in the past, but that's what it is — the past. Ancient history. I'll bet you didn't bother to mention that, did you, Penny?"

Pastor Harold clamped his hands together on top of the Bible resting across his legs, then looked at Trent. "I'm sure you must realize abusing Penny is not the way God would have you care for his precious daughter."

Trent sucked his teeth, making that awful sound that was part whistle, part slurp. "What I don't realize is why my wife saw the need to drag y'all out here just so she could air out our dirty laundry — laundry that's already been washed, folded, and put away."

"Penny," the pastor's wife, Lela, broke in, "why don't you tell your husband the reason you thought it was important for us all to be here?"

I hated being thrust into the spotlight, but knew, of course, it was necessary. Keeping quiet had never changed anything. Not for my mother and not for me. "You have done some changing lately, and I'm proud of you for that."

He pressed his lips together and tapped his boot impatiently against the floor. "*Some* changing?"

"But the rage is still there," I continued. "You're like a time bomb just waiting to go off. When you drink, it gets worse. You know it does. I'm afraid you're going to hurt me again. I'm afraid you're going to do it in front of Manny, or that he'll be caught in the crossfire one of these days."

He gave me a wounded look. "Do you

really think I would do that? Do you really think I would hurt my own son?"

"Why wouldn't you?" Callie Mae said. "You hurt your own wife."

His gaze slid off her, to me. "I told you I would change, but you haven't even given me the first chance to prove it."

I wrung my hands together, trying to focus anywhere but on him. "You've told me things were going to be different so many times."

He looked at me for the longest time, as silence fell thick as fog over the room. Finally, he stood and walked toward me. Everyone stood with him, preparing to protect me, I assumed.

His anger seemed to melt away as he knelt in front of me like he was getting ready to propose. When he took my hand, I found myself completely absorbed, as I had been so many times before, into the flecks of gray in his otherwise-blue eyes. Eyes that could so effortlessly reach into my soul and either sear or heal me . . . and once again, I ceased to be anything in my mind but the woman Trent Joseph Taylor loved enough to marry.

Your father looked so broken at that moment, Manny, and I couldn't help but feel as though I had betrayed him. But I hadn't, I reassured myself. This was as much for him as it was for you and me. "I love you, Trent," I said, breaking the spell. "I know you want to be different, and you're trying, but you can't do it by yourself. You need help."

His eyes filled with tears as he continued to look into mine. "I need help? Is that what you think of your old man? You used to believe in me."

"It's nothing to be ashamed of, Mr. Taylor," Pastor Harold said. "We all need to lean on our friends and family at different times in our lives. There's no shame in that. We've arranged for you to leave tonight for rehab. It's not far, just a few miles outside of town. All you have to do is agree to go."

Trent never took his eyes off me. "Is this what you want, One Cent? You want me to leave you and Manny and go away?"

I set my palms on his cold cheeks. The smell of booze on his breath reminded me what needed to be said. "You've been through so much in your life, and the anger that keeps surfacing has to be dealt with once and for all. We've ignored it for too long. I don't want Manny growing up seeing his mother getting beat. I don't want him growing up thinking that sort of thing is right. What do you think that will do to him? What do you think it's been doing to me?"

He wiped his eyes across the heel of his hand. "Okay. You're right. You deserve better than what I've given you, and I certainly don't want Manny growing up the way I did. I said I was going to be a better father than what I had, and I guess it's time to put my money where my mouth is." He kissed my lips, then looked over his shoulder at the Harolds. "Okay. If this is what everyone thinks I need, then I'll go."

When he stood back up, there wasn't a dry eye. Even Callie Mae held a tissue.

"I don't know how we can pay for this," he said, looking embarrassed. "We're just getting by as it is."

Pastor Harold flashed another mouthful of white. "It's all taken care of. This is why you have a church family. Let us bear this burden with you."

I was waiting for Trent to say the Taylors weren't no charity case, but he didn't. He just nodded. "I can't tell you how much that means to me. To us. So, how does this thing work, anyway?"

"They're expecting you tonight," Pastor Harold said. "We just pack what you'll need, and then I'll drive you there. Easy as that. You'll stay for two weeks while you detox from alcohol, deal with your anger, and try to figure out the reasons behind both."

Trent gave him a sheepish smile. "Something tells me this is going to be anything but easy."

Pastor Harold squeezed his shoulder. "I expect you're probably right. Easy or not, though, you're doing the right thing. This one decision is going to set the course for the rest of your life. Now don't you worry about a thing while you're there. We — Lela and I — will look after your wife and son. All you need to concentrate on is getting yourself better so you can come back to this beautiful family of yours."

"You know," Trent buried his hands in his pants pockets, "this feels right." He chewed the inside of his lip, looking as nervous as I'd ever seen him. "I'm going to make one request, though. You've all had time to think about this, I expect, but it's a little sudden for me, as you can imagine. I need tonight to say good-bye to my family and take care of a few things before I go."

Pastor Harold stopped smiling. "I don't think that's a good idea."

Trent turned to me. "Penny, I need a little time to say good-bye. Just tonight."

So relieved by his unexpected response, I would have agreed to about anything.

I wiped at my wet eyes, then looked at the Harolds. "I think that's a pretty reasonable request given that he's going to be gone for half a month. Tomorrow, I'll take him. First thing in the morning. Do you think you could call the treatment center and arrange that?"

Callie Mae's eyes turned into saucers. "No way. Either he leaves tonight, or you do."

"I know you're just trying to look out for me," I said. "But this isn't your decision."

She huffed and gave Lela a look that made it clear she didn't approve.

The mood was on the upswing when we all said our goodbyes for the night. Pastor Harold led us in a final prayer. Afterward, Lela waved us all into a group hug, which Callie Mae refused. She was the only person who didn't look at all pleased with the way the evening turned out. After the Harolds left, she stood in the doorway trying to tell me something with her eyes as Trent looked on.

When I leaned in to hug her, the furry collar of her jacket tickled my nose and I felt the stiffness of her body. "I'll be fine, Callie. I promise."

She held me close and tight, like it might be the last time she would ever see me. I guess if I'd been through what she had with

Sara, I'd probably be thinking the same thing. As she started down the sidewalk, I noticed her purse still sitting on the floor by the couch. It was so heavy when I picked it up, I half wondered if she had packed the thing with bricks. Knowing how she felt about Trent, it wouldn't have surprised me. As I rushed out the door with it, the brittle night air bit at my skin.

"Callie, wait!" I called as I ran to her, waving the purse over my head. She looked right at me but still sped off.

Thirty-Nine

I watched Callie Mae's taillights disappear down the road, then went inside. Even though Trent would be leaving first thing in the morning for rehab, I still thought it better to not have her purse lying around to tempt him. Not that he would steal, but when he'd been drinking, I'd learned anything was possible.

I took her bag to the bedroom. When I set it down on the floor beside my dresser, something clunked against wood. Kneeling beside the bag, I felt the bottom of the fabric. Sure enough, the shape of a pistol emerged. Now it made perfect sense why she'd driven off without it.

I shook my head at her lack of faith and slid the bag into the corner, farther out of sight. I couldn't wait to return it to her with the satisfaction of knowing she would never again feel the need to protect me from your father.

Peeking at you sleeping soundly in your crib, my heart nearly burst with joy. You were such a beautiful baby with your wisps of blond atop an otherwise-bald head, lying scrunched up on your side with your knees to your chest like you were still inside me. You had your pinky and ring fingers stuffed inside your heart-shaped mouth, sucking from time to time in your sleep as though you were dreaming of being fed. You were beautiful, Son — and life was perfect in that moment.

With all my heart I believed you were going to have a charmed life, with both a mommy and a daddy who adored you and each other. Trent was going to come home from rehab a changed man. He was going to be the father you deserved, the man I thought I'd married.

When I returned to the living room, he stood in front of the window as if expecting someone. I walked up behind him, wrapped my arms around his waist, and laid my head against the back of his shoulders. The flannel of his shirt felt soft against my skin. "Guess I'll drop off Callie's purse on the way to take you in the morning."

When he didn't reply, I figured his mind must be focused on the long road ahead of us.

I nuzzled my nose into the crook of his neck, taking in his warmth. "I know this is scary, baby, but it's going to be the best thing that's ever happened for us. You'll see."

Without warning, he jerked around and shoved me so hard that the back of my head hit the wall. Confused and hurting, I stumbled to find my balance. His thick eyebrows knit together over eyes so dilated they were more black than blue. He looked both through and past me as his lips receded above teeth bared like fangs. I knew at that moment that I'd made the biggest mistake of my life.

Veins bulged on both sides of his forehead, like horns trying to hatch through flesh. His fingers, curled like talons, reached for me. I had the fleeting thought that this was probably the last thing Norma had seen.

"I've never been so humiliated in my life." He grimaced, as if what he was about to do disgusted him.

Before I could react, his arm bent back and white knuckles met me, full throttle, in the middle of my jaw. I heard the crack of impact and felt an explosion of pain. Before I could plead with him to stop, he punched me again, this time in the gut. A gust of air whooshed out of me, along with the taste of blood and a pain as bad as any broken bone he'd ever given me.

When I tried to crawl away, his boot caught my side hard and fast. My scream must have woken you, because you shrieked like you were the one being attacked.

The sound of your cry stopped him cold. He shook his head like he was coming out of a daze. Slowly, he started up the hallway toward you.

"Don't," was all I could say.

He turned and sneered at me. "Don't what? You told everyone you were afraid for your son, like I'm some kind of baby beater. Well, maybe I am."

He turned again and tramped up the hallway while I struggled to my feet.

When I got to the bedroom, he was leaning into your crib as you screamed. "Shut up!" he yelled, snatching you up too hard.

I couldn't think, Manny. I couldn't even breathe. "Put him down," I whispered. "You put him down right now, or so help me . . ."

Still holding you by your armpits, he looked over his shoulder at me and called me a name he had used so much over the years I'd almost started answering to it.

Your scream grew more frantic. When I reached for you, he yanked you back so hard he almost slammed you into the side of the crib.

They say when a person's about to die, their life flashes before their eyes. At that moment, your life was the one flashing by — your first step into my outstretched arms. The school bus window you'd never wave at me from. The wedding you'd never have. The grandchildren you'd never give me . . . all because I'd risked your life by rolling the dice one last time.

If a sound can be a prayer, the groan that escaped me then surely was. In that split second, I promised God if he'd get us out of this, I'd never gamble again, not with you. I'd get help. I'd get out. Anything.

"Give him to me," I begged. I saw then that he was holding you so tightly your arms had started to turn purple. Even though I'd seen him lose control plenty of times, I've never been that afraid before or since. It was one thing for him to hurt me. I always healed. But you were so fragile. One blow could kill you.

This is what Callie Mae had tried to warn me about. Some part of me must have always known the truth. How could I have deceived myself so thoroughly?

Reaching beside the dresser, I scrambled to grab Callie Mae's purse off the floor. With your shrill scream echoing in my ears and Trent answering it with another demand for you to shut up before he gave you a reason to cry, I unzipped the bag, reached in, and felt cold, hard metal.

My hands shook so badly I couldn't hold the gun straight. Blood trickled into my mouth as I said, "Put him down."

He looked back at me, his eyes glinting with something that looked a lot like amusement. "What's that, a toy?"

He was still holding you over your crib. If I shot him below the waist, even my aim couldn't be bad enough to hit you. He would drop you to the safety of the mattress.

"It's no toy," I said.

He snorted like I disgusted him. "What are you going to do, kill me? Shoot me when I'm holding your son?"

"Put him down or I'm taking out your kneecap." I felt like I was watching a movie starring myself. It didn't feel real, but your cry and the pain in my jaw and side told me it was.

The humor left his eyes as he laid you back down. I decided then and there that would be the last time you cried because of him if I could help it. When he stepped away from your crib, I locked my elbows as I raised my aim from his legs to his chest. "Get out of my house. You can go to rehab, or you can go to the bar, but you can't stay here."

"*Your* house?" He crossed his arms defiantly. "You don't even know how to work that thing. Look at you."

I used my thumbs to cock back the hammer. It was harder than Callie Mae made it look. When it clicked the second time, I said, "Yeah, look at me."

His smirk died. "Don't be that way. You know you ain't got it in you to shoot me. Everyone gets one more chance, ain't that right, One Cent?"

"Don't ever call me that again," I said.

It was a hard thing to know he had always seen my forgiveness as just another flaw. Staring over the barrel of that gun, I realized that, indeed, it had been.

This realization made me want to shoot him, Manny, not to kill him, but to kill the old me. The me who thought she needed him. The me who believed she deserved the abuse he'd dished out all those years. But if I pulled the trigger, I knew I would have swung too far the other way and become just like him. There was a better way, and I promised myself if I made it out of this alive, I would find it.

"Walk to the living room," I said, "and dial 911."

He gave me a slow once-over with a look that would kill if it could. Dragging his feet, Trent trudged to the living room with his hands raised in surrender. He put a hand on the telephone receiver and cautiously turned around. "What am I supposed to tell them, that my wife is holding a gun to my head?"

"How about starting with telling them you murdered Norma?"

Panic flashed in his eyes. "You can't prove anything."

At that moment everything I'd been denying became as clear as your cries. "Why did you have to kill her?"

He looked toward the kitchen as if he heard something. "Why do I do anything? For you. Everything I do is for you, Penny. She was trying to blackmail me with lies. If I didn't shut her up, she was going to poison you against me. I told you when I married you I'd never let anything come between us." He got that look in his eyes he always did when he was trying to manipulate me into forgiving him. "Come on, baby, don't do this. No one's ever going to love you the way I do."

"That's right," I said, forcing my mind to remain clear. "No one's ever going to *love* me like that again." A million thoughts went through my mind right then, but I refused to entertain any of them. Not with you still in danger. "You've never done anything for *me.* Everything you've ever done has been for you and you alone." I wiped the line of sweat forming across my brow. "Pick up the phone and dial."

He put the receiver to his ear as his finger hovered above the nine button. "You know you can't testify against me. You're my wife."

"That's a lie," Callie Mae said as she emerged from the kitchen.

Startled, I jerked the gun in her direction.

"But even if she couldn't, I would. I heard everything." She forced a smile at me. "I forgot my purse. You left the back door unlocked, by the way."

I saw the terror in Callie Mae's eyes before I felt Trent's fingers wrap around my hand. I held onto that gun like my life depended on it, knowing it probably did. The struggle happened so fast, I didn't have time to consider the risk of three people fighting over a cocked pistol.

Manny, there are moments in your life you want so badly to remember, but can't. And then there are those that no matter how hard you try, you'll never be able to forget. Even now, when I close my eyes, I can still smell the acrid stench of sulfur filling the air. Can feel the unexpected force of that gun unloading in my hand, and hear the ringing in my ears that drowned out the screaming. And to this day, I can't get out of my head his blood spilling onto the floor like wine from an overturned glass, or the way he touched his shoulder, then looked at his bloody fingertips in horrified disbelief.

As he lay on the floor, writhing in pain, Callie Mae picked the gun off the floor and pointed it at him with one hand, while she dialed the police with the other. I ran to my dresser and pulled out the first thing my hands touched. I balled up the T-shirt and pressed it as hard as I could against the spurting wound, praying the whole time your father wouldn't die. I wish I could say that prayer was for noble Christian reasons — turn the other cheek, heap burning coals of kindness, and all of that. But the truth of it was I still didn't think I could live without him.

Forty

Sitting on a gurney in the emergency room, I wanted to cry as the policemen questioned me about the shooting, but the tears wouldn't come. I felt them trapped in my throat and in the pit of my stomach. My answers didn't reflect that emotion, though. I refused to let them. They sounded strangely detached, as if I were simply regurgitating the synopsis of a book I'd read.

Between their questions, I paused as though I was thinking, but I was really listening for Trent's voice. I knew he was there being treated as well. Was he okay? Would he get out and come after us? I heard only complaining patients, beeping machines, and hurried exchanges among the staff.

The place smelled like an old folks' home, and in my small curtain-room, I felt claustrophobic with the two men. I wondered if Callie Mae was being asked the same questions at the police station. I pictured her trying to fill them in on the frustratingly little bits and pieces she had managed to gather, and I felt bad she'd been dragged into this mess I'd made. It was the thought of her that reminded me of the person I wanted to be. Of the life I wanted to have and what I must do to get it.

"I'm very sorry that happened, ma'am," the older of the two cops said, though he couldn't be more than thirty. "He'll be charged with two counts of assault."

They told me Callie Mae and I would not be charged, and that surprised me. Not that we wouldn't be charged, but that we might have been. He stood, pulled the chair back from my bedside, and slid it against the wall. His partner was already standing.

"Is he going to be okay?" I heard myself ask.

"He'll live," the younger said.

I touched the crust of blood beneath my nose, not caring if it was broken. My only real concern was getting home to you. You were left in Fatimah's care instead of social service's, and for that I was grateful.

As the police gathered their papers, I stared at the gum wrapper sticking to the heel of the older man's shoe. "There's more," I said, before I could lose my nerve.

They turned and looked at me expectantly.

I told them about Trent's relationship with Norma. About his assault on her the night she was murdered, about his disappearing that night, and about the story he gave me when I questioned him about it.

They frowned and warned me of the penalty of lying, but I could see in their eyes they knew I wasn't.

The new information disturbed them, but they promised to look into it.

They left, and I lay there for what must have been hours waiting for a doctor to check me out. A nurse popped her head inside my curtain and apologized for the wait. "It's unusually busy," she said. "And we're shorthanded."

I asked how much longer. She grimaced and shrugged.

I signed myself out against medical advice, feeling the disapproving looks from the staff as I left. Using the courtesy phone in the lobby, I called Fatimah. My stomach cramped as I waited for her to pick up. The last thing she had said to me was that I was dead to her. But I had no one else to call.

"Hello?" Edgard said.

I exhaled in relief. "It's Penny."

"My friend!" he exclaimed. "I am so sorry

to hear of your terrible ordeal. Fatimah has much concern over you. I must ask if you are all right."

I hesitated, not knowing the answer to that question. "I think so."

"She is okay!" he yelled.

I listened for her reaction and your cry. I heard only Fatimah. "Tell her Manny does well but is hungry."

Before he could relay the message, I said, "I heard. I hate to ask, but can you pick me up from the ER?"

"She wants me to collect her from the hospital," he said, but didn't wait for Fatimah to reply. "I come now."

When Edgard opened the door to his apartment, I saw you and baby Penny lying side by side on an orange blanket on the floor. The two of you exchanged gurgling noises, and I breathed a prayer of thanks to God you were alive and well. It could have turned out differently. The thought threatened to bring me to my knees, but I had no time to collapse because Fatimah rushed at me with open arms.

Only when I saw her tears did the dam holding mine finally break. She held me, making a soft cooing sound. "You be okay, Peeny. You be okay."

I let her hold and rock me until my tears were spent; then I pulled back and wiped my eyes. She showed me to her bedroom, which was decorated in bright colors and smelled of incense. I fed you, listening to you gulping furiously. I thought of Trent and wondered if he was in pain, and if he'd retain full use of that arm. Then I reminded myself he wasn't my problem anymore. He made his bed, and he was the one who would have to lie in it. I would have to make a new bed for myself — and for you.

The thought felt good — freeing and right. *I'm on my own now,* I thought, but what used to terrify me brought me a small smile. "It's just you and me now, Manny," I said, just to hear it.

Your eyelids grew heavy as I fought to keep my own open.

Callie's voice jolted me awake.

I found her sitting on the bed beside me. Her eyes were red and free from makeup, her clothes wrinkled and disheveled. She placed a hand over her heart. "Thank God you're okay."

Confused, I squinted at her, then around Fatimah's room, and I remembered — the nightmare was no dream.

I pushed myself up to a sitting position

and rubbed the sleep from my eyes. "I should have listened to you."

"You should have," she agreed as she drew me into a motherly hug.

"You saved my life."

At that she pulled back, still holding my shoulders, and looked me square in the eye. "It's time for you to start saving your own life, Penny Taylor. Manny needs his mother."

At the sound of your name, I listened for your cry, but heard only the muffled sound of the television in the next room. "I was dreaming about the statue you gave me."

She looked at me intently.

"I dreamed I had stained-glass wings just like her. I kept flapping them with all my might, but my feet wouldn't leave the ground. I was about to give up when I noticed the vine wrapped around my ankle." At last the pieces of the puzzle were coming together. "But all I had to do was cut it, and I was free."

Callie Mae gave me a tired smile. "It's about time."

I felt myself blush. "I'm a little slow on the uptake, huh?"

She tried in vain to brush a wrinkle from her top. "No, you just had to know that you had done everything you could to make it work. I respect that. So many of us pick and choose what we want to believe from the Bible and leave the difficult stuff untouched. Right or wrong, you wrestled hard. Something tells me, to God, there's beauty in that battle."

A torrent of emotion moved through me, but I wasn't ready to let it pour out just yet. As I sat there looking at Callie Mae, I thought of all the things she and Fatimah had been trying so long and hard to tell me — that there are things even more important to God than the preservation of a marriage; namely, the people in that marriage. I found solace in understanding, for the first time, that remaining single, with healthy relationships, wouldn't feel half as lonely as I'd been.

"I'm proud of you," Callie said.

I tried to smile, but couldn't. "I'm proud of me too."

Forty-One

Trent Taylor slunk out of my life wearing an orange jumpsuit, a pair of handcuffs, and an attitude I couldn't wait to take my eyes off.

To this day, I'll never understand why he didn't just throw away that stupid slag hammer he used to kill her. Instead, he washed off the blood, leaving just enough DNA to convict him, and placed it back among his tools. While he was still in St. Joseph's recovering from the gunshot wound, he was charged with first-degree murder.

Neither I nor the jury would ever learn exactly how or why he had killed her, because he pleaded the fifth, declining to take the stand in his own defense. Whether this was his idea or his attorney's, I never learned.

Instead, we heard theories from the prosecution. His motive, they said, was nothing more than jealous rage. Norma was prostituting herself and he couldn't stand it. It took the jury less than two hours to deliberate.

In the courtroom, Callie Mae sat on one side of me, Fatimah on the other, as I watched the back of Trent's freshly shaven head. Even through the hushed chatter surrounding me, I could hear the tap of his heel against the floor. He leaned to the left and whispered something in his lawyer's ear. She nodded, while looking away from him toward the door, as if she couldn't wait to bolt.

I knew just how she felt.

Fatimah and Callie Mae each took one of my hands as Trent and his lawyer rose to hear the jury's verdict.

He was sentenced to twenty years for second-degree murder. As the deputy sheriff handcuffed him, he turned and glared at me in accusation. In defiance, I stared back, unblinking. There's enough blame assigned to me from my own actions. I refused to accept his, too.

As he was led away, I felt my heart both break and begin to mend. I was finally able to look ahead at our new reality, our wide-open future full of possibility and promise.

Fatimah pulled me against her, hugging me so tightly I could barely breathe. "I am so proud of you, Peeny. I did not think you would speak the truth, but you have. It is the bravest moment I witness for any woman. Your mother will be proud of you."

I knew she was right. My mother would be proud. I called her after the trial to tell her the outcome. Again, she asked me to come home. "This is home now," I said, "but when Daddy's finally ready to retire, maybe you two could do it here. I want Manny to know his grandparents."

"Now there's an idea," Mama said. "*I* couldn't get him off the farm, but that grandbaby just might. You would think that child walks on water by the way he talks about him."

My eyes still well because my father's love for you registers in my heart as love for me.

"Are you going to be okay?" she asked.

I glanced over at Callie Mae, blowing raspberries on your belly, and laughed. "Better than okay, Mama."

FORTY-TWO

It's afternoon, and I'm returning to Callie Mae's house to pack our belongings. She has been more than kind to let the two of us live with her for the past few months while we waited for the trial to take place, but it's time for us to go home now.

"You sure you don't want to stay a little longer?" she asks, bouncing you gently through the air.

"I've never stood on my own, Callie. I need to learn how."

"How will you get by?"

"With a little help from my friends," I say jokingly, but it's the truth. I need the community I've begun to build around myself. Callie Mae, Fatimah, Edgard, my new church family at Sheckle Baptist, and the Alanon support group that meets on Monday nights. I don't think, when God said it's not good for man to be alone, Manny, he just meant that we need a mate. I had a mate and was never more alone in my life. But I'm not lonely anymore, and I make a vow to never isolate myself again.

"You should turn that into a song," Callie Mae says. "You could make a lot of money."

I smile as she rubs noses with you. Squealing, you reach up and grab a hunk of her hair. With a grimace, she pries your hand loose, then gives you another Eskimo kiss. She lays you flat on the bed, lifts up your shirt and blows a raspberry on your tummy. Your arms and legs flail at the stimulation and you squeal again.

"I see you got another letter from Trent," she says, motioning with a nod of her head toward the opened envelope lying on the dresser.

"It's not just a letter this time. It's divorce papers."

Her eyes grew wide. "Let me get this straight. *He*'s divorcing *you*?"

It's a twist I didn't see coming either, but it is the out I've been praying for. No matter how logical Callie Mae's arguments sounded, I still couldn't find a way to divorce my husband and reconcile it with God's Word. "Apparently he's been corresponding with a pen pal and they're 'in love.' " The absurdity of it almost makes me laugh.

Callie Mae squints at me for a moment, then says sarcastically, "Lucky girl."

"I never thought I'd be divorced," I say, cringing at the word.

Callie Mae tries to look sad, but I know better. I try to look sad too, but I'm not.

"So, what's the plan?" she asks.

I pick up the glass of iced tea I had set on the dresser and take a sip. Like this moment, it is both bitter and sweet. "I'm not sure. It's like there's this menu in front of me with way too many choices."

She tilts her head and smiles. "It's exciting, don't you think?"

I put the glass down and open another drawer. She's right — it *is* exciting. Exciting and scary at the same time. *I can do this,* I tell myself. Your name, Emmanuel, reminds me that I won't have to do it alone. "You think I'm college material?" I ask, hopeful as I pick up a stack of onesies.

Her eyes move off you, onto me, and settle there a moment. "Penny, I think you're capable of moving whichever mountains you choose."

I think I might want to be a florist, but I don't say so. Not yet. I have more thinking and praying to do. The next time I roll the dice, I want to be as sure as I can be that the prize is worth the gamble.

■ ■ ■ ■

Anxiety fills me on the drive. I wonder if it will still feel like home, now that your father is gone. I pull up to where our little tar-papered house should be, but it isn't there. In its place stands a charming little cream-colored stucco home with white trim and matching flower boxes dripping with blooms.

All the odd little questions Callie Mae and Fatimah have asked me over the past weeks finally make sense. It's a good thing I actually gave some thought to my answers, or I might have ended up with purple siding. Fatimah's LeBaron is already in the freshly paved driveway, and Callie Mae, who has followed me over, parks along the curb. As I unstrap you from your car seat, you look up at me with those Tweety Bird eyes of yours, and as it does every time I look at you, my heart overflows with gratitude.

"We're home, Manny," I say. Your arms flutter happily.

I hold you facing outward so you can see.

"It is beautiful, true?" Fatimah calls from an open window. All I can see is the white of her smile.

"True!" I call back. I stop to show you the

magnolia tree in the front yard that wasn't there the last time we were here. Its huge white blooms are almost the size of your head. You grab hold of a leaf and try to stuff it in your mouth. I kiss your soft cheek as I pry it from your hand.

"Do you like the tree? You said magnolias were your favorite," Callie Mae asks from behind me.

I turn and try to thank her, but the boulder in my throat won't allow me to speak. I feel guilty for the gift. She's already done so much for us.

Callie Mae must have read my mind because she says, "It's the least I could do after all you've given me."

Her words confuse me. "I haven't given you anything except a lot of trouble."

Sunlight makes her blonde hair look like spun gold, and the fine lines she always refers to finally become apparent in the harsh light. But to me, she's never looked more beautiful. "You gave me the grandson Sara couldn't. You give me friendship. You give me hope."

"I don't deserve this," I say.

"You've been given a lot in this life you haven't deserved, Penny." At first I think she's speaking of Trent, but as I kiss the top of your head, I realize it's you.

I don't know what to say, so I just hug her. It's the best I have to offer.

Her smile tells me it is enough.

A NOTE FROM THE AUTHOR

If you know someone who is or has been in an abusive relationship but have never experienced it for yourself, you may wonder why someone would put up with it. The answer is often a mixture of fear, shame, love, and embarrassment — or not even realizing that abuse *isn't* normal.

It is so difficult to watch family members and friends go through degrees of what Penny suffered in this novel. Many of the tactics Trent used are typical of abusers, and Penny's justifications and faulty thinking are typical of an abuse victim. She lies to cover up her husband's bad behavior, gets defensive when her friends confront her with the truth, and believes him time and again when he says things will be different next time. Like many victims of abuse, Penny wanted to believe that her husband would change because she loved him. In their own way, I believe abusers often want to change. But wanting to change and changing are two different things.

The hardest lesson I've ever had to learn is that it isn't my job to change anyone but myself. Once I really began to understand that, everything else started to fall into place. I began educating myself about boundaries, codependency, and what a healthy relationship is supposed to look like. We have a tendency to think only abusers need help, but victims of abuse need help just as much.

If you or someone you care about faces a situation similar to the one depicted in this novel, please consider some of the following resources for more information about how to get help.

National Domestic Violence Hotline
1-800-799-SAFE (7233)
TTY 1-800-787-3224
www.thehotline.org

Boundaries: When to Say Yes, When to Say No, to Take Control of Your Life — **Henry Cloud & John Townsend**

Boundaries define who we are and who we are not. They impact all areas of our lives: *Physical boundaries* help us determine who may touch us and under what circumstances. *Mental boundaries* give us the freedom to have our own thoughts and opinions. *Emotional boundaries* help us deal with our own emotions and disengage from the harmful, manipulative emotions of others. *Spiritual boundaries* help us distinguish God's will from our own and give us renewed awe for our Creator. Having clear boundaries is essential to a healthy, balanced lifestyle. Questions addressed in this book include the following:

- Aren't boundaries selfish?
- Can I set limits and still be a loving person?
- Why do I feel guilty or afraid when I consider setting boundaries?
- What are legitimate boundaries?
- What if someone is upset or hurt by my boundaries?

The Verbally Abusive Relationship: How to Recognize It and How to Respond — **Patricia Evans**

In this bestselling classic, you'll learn how to recognize verbal abuse, respond to abusers safely and appropriately, and most important, lead a happier, healthier life.

Drawing from hundreds of real situations suffered by real people, Evans offers strategies, sample scripts, and action plans designed to help you deal with the abuse — and the abuser.

Safe People: How to Find Relationships That Are Good for You and Avoid Those That Aren't — **Henry Cloud & John Townsend**

Many people invest themselves in people who shipwreck their lives in return. If you're one who has chosen the wrong people to get involved with or makes the same mistakes about relationships over and over again, then this book offers you a remedy. *Safe People* gives you solid guidance that will help you

- Correct things within yourself that jeopardize your relational security
- Learn the twenty traits of "unsafe" people
- Recognize what makes people trustworthy
- Avoid unhealthy relationships
- Form positive relationships

Codependent No More: How to Stop Controlling Others and Start Caring for Yourself — **Melody Beattie**

Recovery has begun for millions of individuals with this straightforward guide. Through personal examples and exercises, the author shows how controlling others forces you to lose sight of your own needs and happiness.

DISCUSSION QUESTIONS

1. Penny gets angry and defensive when her friends try to confront her with the truth about Trent's behavior. Have you ever reacted that way when someone tried to tell you something you didn't want to hear? How can we learn to be open to friends who try to "speak the truth in love" to us?

2. Trent repeatedly says — and occasionally shows — that he wants to change. Was Penny right to believe him? Did you believe him? What more could he have done if he was sincere about wanting to become a different (healthier) person? What do you think the future holds for Trent?

3. Callie Mae, a loving and godly woman, struggles with the habit of smoking. And she accuses the woman who confronts her about it of gluttony. What are some other

habits or lifestyle choices we sometimes develop that are bad for our health — and may compromise our ability to reflect Christ to others? What are some ways we might work on overcoming them?

4. There are a few times when Penny actually seems to *want* Trent to hurt her. "I think I wanted him to beat me then. Feeling the physical pain was so much better than the anguish eating me up inside" (ch. 20). And "I realized then I was trying to provoke him, but I wasn't sure why. Maybe because deep down I thought I deserved to be beaten. Maybe I enjoyed being the martyr. Or I was just addicted to the making up that was sure to follow" (ch. 35). What could make a woman feel that way? What are some ways she could get help for whatever it is that's causing those feelings? What are some other self-destructive patterns you see in your life or the life of someone you love?

5. Fatimah and Callie both tell Penny that if she wants things to change, she herself must change. Do you agree with that statement? Why is making changes in our own lives and behavior often so difficult? What holds you back from making a posi-

tive change in your circumstances?

6. Callie Mae tells Penny, "You're addicted to an abusive man." Do you agree with Callie's assessment? Why or why not? What are some other things — besides alcohol or drugs — that a person can develop an unhealthy dependence on? What does it take to break the cycle?

7. For a long time, Penny says she doesn't want to leave Trent because being with him is better than being alone. Why are familiar, though unpleasant, circumstances often more attractive than the unfamiliar and the unknown? What relationships or circumstances are you clinging to, just because they're familiar, when you might be better off without them?

8. Callie Mae helps Penny reframe her situation by asking, "If you had a daughter, and she came to you and told you her husband was treating her the way Trent is treating you, would your advice be to stay with him?" (ch. 23). Why is it sometimes easier to see what's going on in a situation involving someone else than in our own situation? What's going on in your life right now that might benefit from some

reframing? Who has God placed in your life who can help you do that?

9. Pastor Harold asks Penny, "Why isn't grace enough?" and Penny herself wonders why it isn't. How would you answer that question for Penny? Is God's grace alone sufficient for all life's challenges, or does God's grace sometimes require a response or action from us? And if it does sometimes require a response, how can we tell if a given situation is one of those times?

10. Callie tells Penny that God will not manipulate someone into doing something the person doesn't want to do, even if other people are begging for his intervention. Have you ever pleaded with God to change a loved one? What was the outcome? Why do you think God allows people to have free will even when it means other people might get hurt?

11. With the support of a friend and her pastor, Penny stages an intervention with Trent. Do you think that was a good idea? Why or why not? What might Penny have done differently that could have led to a better outcome? Have you ever tried to confront a loved one about a serious

problem in this way? How did — or would — you go about it?

ABOUT THE AUTHOR

Bestselling author **Gina Holmes** is the founder of the influential literary site Novel Rocket, regularly named one of Writers Digest's best sites for writers. Her debut novel, *Crossing Oceans,* was a Christy and Christian Book Award finalist and winner of the Carol, INSPY, and RWA's Inspirational Reader's Choice Contest awards, as well as a CBA, ECPA, Amazon and *Publishers Weekly* Religion bestseller. She is also the author of *Dry As Rain,* a Christy Award finalist. Gina holds degrees in science and nursing and currently resides with her family in southern Virginia. She works too hard, laughs too loud, and longs to see others heal from their past and discover their God-given purpose. To learn more about her, visit www.ginaholmes.com.

The employees of Thorndike Press hope you have enjoyed this Large Print book. All our Thorndike, Wheeler, and Kennebec Large Print titles are designed for easy reading, and all our books are made to last. Other Thorndike Press Large Print books are available at your library, through selected bookstores, or directly from us.

For information about titles, please call:
(800) 223-1244

or visit our Web site at:
http://gale.cengage.com/thorndike

To share your comments, please write:

Publisher
Thorndike Press
10 Water St., Suite 310
Waterville, ME 04901